"GOLD!"

It could hardly be anything else.

"I knew by the weight of that rock," said Stone-That-Shines, "that it was so different from other stones. I knew by its flame in the sun also. So I made a medicine bag and put it in. I had hardly done that when a rabbit came and sat up in my path and waited for me to shoot it with my bow and arrow. For the spirit of the stone had charmed that rabbit. Yes, and in my very first battle that medicine gave me three scalps! And you yourselves and all of my people have seen today what it can do."

"Yes," said The Colonel, who could hardly contain himself, "but did you never ride back to the white mountain to see if there might not be bigger and better stones there?"

The young Indian smiled. "Does the spirit throw down magic in great heaps? No, it is put in single things only. But I *did* ride back to seek for the white mountain and can you guess what I found?"

"No," said The Colonel, breathless, "I cannot guess."

He moved the torch a little nearer, and we could both see that there was a vein of yellow almost as big as a man's finger running through that piece of stone. It made me jump, and it put a fire in the eye of The Colonel.

THE STONE
THAT SHINES

MAX BRAND

THE STONE THAT SHINES

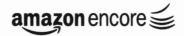

Copyright © 1997 by Jane Faust Easton and Adriana Faust Bianchi

Copyright © 1926 by Street & Smith Publications, Inc.
Copyright © renewed 1954 by Dorothy Faust. Acknowledgment
is made to Conde Nast Publications, Inc., for its cooperation.
Copyright © 1997 for restored material by Jane Faust Easton and
Adriana Faust Bianchi. All rights reserved. An earlier version of
this novel appeared in installments in Street & Smith's Western
Story Magazineunder the title "Trail of the Stone-That-Shines."

The name Max Brand™ is a registered trademark with the United
States Patent and Trademark Office and cannot be used for any
purpose without express written permission.

Published by AmazonEncore
P.O. Box 400818
Las Vegas, NV 89140

ISBN-13: 9781477838976
ISBN-10: 147783897X

This title was previously published by Dorchester Publishing; this version has been reproduced from the Dorchester book archive files.

∾

Chapter One

ONE OF THE DEEVERS

In that western country The Colonel was out of place. He should never have left Virginia, where he was born, where people knew his ways, and where he knew theirs. But even in Virginia he was a little too lordly for most folks. He acted a bit too much like Lord Somebody, instead of what he was — the second son of a rich planter, and not so rich as The Colonel would have had people believe at that!

My father came up from Georgia when I was only seven. He came up because he had lost all his money a couple of times over at the gambling table, and also because he had been in too many fights. If we had been a peg higher in the social scale, those fights would have been called duels in those days before the war. As it was, people simply said that the bad Deever blood had broken out again.

Before the war social station meant nearly everything south of the Mason and Dixon line. For instance, what were called little *amours* among the upper classes were ugly scandals among the lower. The South, before the Civil War, was the spot where what you did mattered least, but who you were and how you did it were everything.

Well, when the "bad Deever blood" had been driven out of Georgia, as I have said, my father skipped a couple of states and settleddown in Virginia. But he could never get on his feet again, and he reached a point in life where his worries became greater than his happinesses. He was a logical person, if nothing else, and so, when this point was reached, he simply wrote a little note of farewell to me, went out in the garden, and shot himself through the head with a dueling pistol.

That threw me adrift in the world, because I was all that remained of the family. During the next three years I wandered here and there, picking up wild ways among the poor whites and the Negroes. Among other things I learned how to ride horses, and that brought me to the attention of The Colonel.

Of course, you understand that, when I say I learned how to ride, I don't mean that I simply learned how to sit in the saddle without falling off. I mean to convey that I learned how to handle blooded English racehorses while I was still a child with not a quarter of a full man's strength. That was how I came to be noticed by The Colonel, who kept a little string of racers. Usually the exercising was done by Negro boys, because these youngsters developed a little faster than whites, and, while they were still midgets in weight, they had the nerves and the animal wits to stick on the back of a dancing two-year-old. However, I had the same knack in me that the others possessed. It is either born in one, or it is not — I mean the sense for a horse and the ability to think with a horse's thoughts.

The Colonel found me, liked the way that I rode, and took me in. I was ten at the time, and, when I saw The Colonel's boots with their fine golden spurs, I thought they were the most wonderful things in the world. So I sneaked into his room to steal the boots the first night of my coming. He heard a sound and picked me out of the darkness by the nape of the neck. I had an old sailor's dirk with me, and I tried to sink that into his body, but I only ran it through the thick of his arm. He carried me into the bathroom, where there was a light, and he picked that dirk out of his big arm with as much unconcern as though it were a needle pricking the skin. He washed the wound and made me tie it up.

"Now," he said, "what were you after?"

"The riding boots," I said.

"Go get them. They are yours. But the next time that you want something, don't try to murder me for it. Come and ask me first, Christy."

I give you my word that that was all he said to me. I went and looked down at the boots, and I was in an agony. Yet I think it was almost the first time in my life that I had been seriously bothered with remorse. Of course, I couldn't stay on the place, so I ran away down the river. But The Colonel sent hunting parties after me, and they found me three days later. They brought me back to The Colonel, and he said: "Christy, if you want to leave me, you're as free as the wind to go when you please. But if it's shame that's driving you away, I want you to stay on here with me. As for stealing a pair of boots, I give you my word that I have done much worse things myself!"

I stayed, and I began to worship The Colonel from that moment. About six months later he risked entering me in a race, because he had a weak filly that needed a vigorous ride even in a six-furlong sprint but that couldn't stand up under more than ninety pounds. I managed to lift that filly home first, by half a nose, and The Colonel cleaned up thousands of dollars, because the odds were terribly heavy against the little mare, and he had played her like the madman he was. That win made one of the gamblers so angry that the fellow took a shot at The Colonel one evening, grazing his head with a rifle bullet.

The Colonel accepted it calmly, as he did most things. But he decided that he would have to have a bodyguard and looked around him for someone to fit in with the post. There were plenty of men who were devoted to the family and who were good fighters with plenty of courage, but you could never guess which way The Colonel would jump. The bodyguard that he finally selected was I.

Yes, he took an eleven-year-old boy and made him into a body-guard! He brought me in and settled me in a room next to his, and he kept me with him night and day. I didn't want the job, and I told him he was foolish to put so much trust into my hands, because with all his jewels at the tips of my fingers the bad Deever blood might break out, and I might abscond with the valuables. The Colonel listened to this. Then he made me sit down in front of him, and he said: "What's all this about the bad Deever blood? Just what is your blood, my son?"

"Scotch and Irish," I replied.

"A noble strain," said The Colonel gravely. "Now, what was your father's business in life?"

"Gambling, fighting, and borrowing money that he never paid back."

"He gambled and fought and borrowed," said The Colonel. "I hope that I shall not be condemned for those crimes! Very well, who was your grandfather?"

"A sea captain in the slave trade."

"What would Virginia be without slaves?" asked The Colonel. "What would the whole glorious South be without black labor to maintain the plantations? Who was your great-grandfather?"

"He stabbed a man in Dublin, and he was sent over here when he was a boy as an indentured servant. He was a soldier in the Revolution."

"Excellent!" exclaimed The Colonel. "I see that you come from a fighting strain. Why, my lad, you speak as though you were ashamed of your blood, and what do I learn? That your great-grandfather was a hero who would not bear insults but killed his foes, and afterward he helped to liberate our land. And your grandfather was a steel-nerved sea captain, who roved across the ocean and took his chances where he found them. Your father was a worshiper of the goddess of chance, as your grandfather was of the goddess of the sea. Do not speak to me of bad blood. For my part, I look upon the Deever strain with the greatest respect. And for that reason, Christy, I am going to place my life in your hands."

I give you this as a sample of The Colonel's way of talking, because he always knew how to dress up the worst matters so as to make them have the best possible face. However, I took part of what he said to heart and stopped being ashamed of my name from that moment. Besides, there was a good deal of sense in this way of treating me. It made me try to live up to the reputation which he gave me, and, before that first week was up, I found a way of repaying The Colonel for some of his kindness and trust. A pair of thieves got into the house while he was away at a hunting meeting, but I gave them both barrels of one of The Colonel's pistols. One of them dropped with a slug in his leg, and the other made off as fast as he could.

The Colonel used this chance to justify his selection of me as a bodyguard. From that moment I received a good deal of attention from the rest of the household and even from the Rutherford field workers, while I was much lifted in my own estimation. Revolvers were being introduced at about this time, and The Colonel brought home one for me. I spent countless hours practicing with it and getting ready for the next brush with thieves, but there was no more trouble of that kind.

The next misfortune came in a different way. The Colonel had fallen more and more deeply in debt until finally he began to plunge on the race track. He got to such a point that he decided to venture everything that he could raise with mortgages on a final race in which his six-year-old brown stallion, Sir Turpin, was to run against Elliott Barnstaple's good mare, Lady Huntingdon. We ran three four-mile heats. I was only twelve, but Sir Turpin had a pull in the weights. The Colonel thought he would risk it.

I won the first heat handily, while the stallion was still full of running. The second was a very even thing, but the mare's jockey had more strength at the finish and got Sir Turpin by a head. For the last heat there was a great deal of excitement. I had a dram of brandy to brace me for the work, and we plugged along at a fine pace for three miles. However, in the last mile the mare began to leave us. I did everything that I knew, but I couldn't get Sir Turpin together.

11

The mare won by a dozen lengths, and The Colonel was a ruined man.

I was so sad after the race that I wanted to die, but The Colonel spent a whole hour sitting beside the bed where I was lying, weeping. He told me that he was tired of Virginia and had only been waiting to cut loose for the bigger and better country in the West. Now the knot had been cut for him; he was free, and he thanked me for it. It was like him to talk in this way, making matters easy for me, but I knew that a stronger rider would have won the second heat of that race, and the match would have been The Colonel's. However, that was the way things stood.

That night The Colonel sat up for hours, writing a letter of farewell to Martha Farnsworth, the girl he was engaged to marry. Prose wasn't enough for him. He wound it off with a poem, and I shall never forget how he lay back in the chair, staring at the plaster ornament in the center of the ceiling as though he expected inspiration to drop from it to him, and saying to me: "Wake up, Christy! Wake up, man! This is more important than horse races. Now, what the devil rhymes with 'evil'?"

"Weevil," I said.

"Bah," he said. "How can such a word fit into a pathetic poem of farewell? This is a sad poem, Christy. It will break her heart when she gets this."

It did seem pretty sad, too, because from time to time he would have to cover his eyes with his hand. All that he was losing and throwing away of his old life hadn't been able to sap the nerve of The Colonel. But, when he began to put the sorrow into a poem, it broke him up more than I like to say.

Now and then he would jump up and run across the room to a picture of her which he had painted with his own hands — because he was a fellow with more talents than you would have expected. A very fair likeness that was, too, though it always seemed to me that the hands were a bit crooked, and Martha Farnsworth would have been just as interesting if she hadn't been shown holding lilies and looking up to heaven like a martyr. However, The Colonel got a good deal of pleasure and inspiration out of looking at his painting, and he would go striding back and dash off a few more lines after every glance at it.

He should have sent that letter by the post, and everything would have been well. But he was so proud of the poem that he couldn't wait and had to send off the letter to her by a special messenger. In a matter as important as this, of course, I was the chosen messenger. I was dressed up in my best and sent away on Sir Turpin to carry the message to the girl.

Chapter Two

THE COLONEL'S DECISION

When I got to the old Farnsworth house, I was brought right up to Martha Farnsworth' s room. She said: "How does he bear up after the race?"

"Like iron," I said. "And he's sent you this."

She took that letter — it was a fat one — and weighed it in her hand. "Dick is about to do something silly," said Miss Farnsworth, opening the letter. She read a few lines and then she said: "Heavens! My poor Dick is in a poetic humor."

She went on, running her eye up and down the pages until she came to the poem. She had been a good deal worked up by the letter, and there was even a tear in her eye. But, when she came to the poem, she began to laugh.

"Did you help him write this?" she asked me at last, without looking up.

"Not a bit except on a couple of rhymes."

"Do you think it's a good poem?"

"Mighty good," I replied. "At least…the parts that I understood."

"So he read it to you?" snapped Miss Farnsworth every bit as quick as a whip flashing.

I saw that she had trapped me, but I didn't know what to say. However, she looked up to me in a minute and smiled and said: "Oh, I don't mind your knowing what a silly dear he is. You know already, Christy. In fact, I wish I knew him half as well as you do." She was serious, now, and she asked: "Will he really leave Virginia, Christy."

I said that I thought he would, and that I thought he had said so pretty definitely in the poem.

"The poem? Nonsense!" she said. "It's so mysterious and full of bad rhymes that *no* one could make head or tail out of it. I'm going right over to tell your master what I think of him. And don't you dare go before me to prepare him."

I saw that The Colonel was in for a sad time of it, but there was nothing that I could do. I had to ride along with Miss Farnsworth, as she commanded, and she put the whip to her pretty brown gelding nearly every other jump all the way to the house of The Colonel. When we got nearer, I raised a couple of whistles.

"What are you doing that for?" asked Miss Farnsworth.

"Trying to reach that hawk, yonder, with the whistle," I explained.

"Bah," she gasped as her horse jumped a ditch in the road. "You're whistling a warning of some kind to Dick."

I was, too. It was a signal which we had arranged between us long before to give a hint when something unpleasant was coming. But though The Colonel heard me, he didn't have a chance to settle on any plan before Martha Farnsworth's horse dashed up the winding driveway, and she threw herself down in front of the house. The Colonel barely had the strength to come to the door to meet her. I never saw a man look so sick and unhappy as he did.

"My dear, my dear," said The Colonel, "should you have come over here all alone with…?"

"Bah," broke in the lady. "Since when does a Farnsworth have to have an escort when calling on a Rutherford? And, also, I wish that you would stop talking like Father Time. How old are you, Dick?"

"I am…old enough to know what a mess I have made of everything," said The Colonel.

"Stuff and nonsense," she said. "You are young enough to start over again. You are barely twenty-five, and…."

"Martha," snapped The Colonel, "I am twenty-eight, and you know it."

15

I really hadn't dreamed that he was as young as this, what with his beard and his title and all. He looked thirty-five, at least. But he had got that military title in the militia, and he carried himself like a general of division, at least.

"And what is twenty-eight?" asked the girl. "Does that give you a right to talk like an exiled king…just because you've lost a silly horse race?"

"I wrote to you, my dear," said The Colonel, sad and solemn, "to try to make you understand."

"You wrote a poem which was like a silly book of quotations," said the girl. "I never saw so many familiar faces strung together with rhymes that didn't fit."

The Colonel got a white spot of anger in each cheek. "The language of a lady to a gentleman…," he began.

"Fiddlesticks," said Miss Farnsworth, looking too lovely for belief as she raged at him.

"If not a child to her elder…,"went on The Colonel.

"I am eighteen years old!" cried Martha Farnsworth. "And that's really older than you are…you tremendous baby, Dick."

"Really!" exclaimed The Colonel.

"You can't freeze me, either," she said. "I'm not the kind that can be frosted over and silenced. I'll tell you what you are doing. You are wrapping yourself in a mantle of gloom and trying to be poetic, but, as a matter of fact, you are simply silly. And it looks to me very much as though you are simply skulking away after a beating."

"Miss Farnsworth," said The Colonel, "I beg you to remember that you have a brother of an answerable age."

"And you would call him out, I suppose?" she said. "Why, Richard Rutherford, you're not fit to be out of a cradle, you're such a baby. I never saw a grown man, and a Virginian at that, who cried when he was spanked."

I thought that The Colonel would drop dead with shame and rage and astonishment.

16

"Besides," went on the girl, "you stagger me with your vast egotism. You men are all self-centered, but you're one of the worst of the lot. Here you are losing a horse race and a bit of money...."

"Martha," said The Colonel, "I wrote to you that I am ruined. I possess nothing but debts."

"Possess some more debts, then. Borrow money from Dad and marry me. Because I don't intend to be left here with a broken heart while you go West. Or, if it's pride that keeps you back, you foolish baby, I tell you that I'll ride a mule to the end of the world to be with you...but to be left behind...it's...it's just devilish of you, Dick. I hate you! I hate you!"

At this point she began to cry, and I turned my head away and rubbed the nose of Sir Turpin as hard and fast as I could, until he tried to snap my hand off. I watched the wildflowers dancing and quivering on the lawn, while I wondered with all my heart how The Colonel could make up his mind to leave behind him that beautiful girl. She was not such a tigress as her words may have made you think her.

She said enough to throw The Colonel into a fury, but it was pretty easy for people whom he loved to throw The Colonel into a rage. With an enemy he was the height of patient courtesy. With a stranger he made an exquisite study of everything that a gentleman should be. And for his chance acquaintances and friends he was simply a model of good-humored forbearance. But, when it came to those who were really dear to him, he was a devil and a tyrant. He loved them so much, in fact, that the least hint of a shadow on one of their faces threw him into an agony. That was the reason, I believe, that he left his home and set up an establishment of his own.

At any rate, there was Martha Farnsworth standing in the broad light of day on the Rutherford verandah, in the arms of her lover, and weeping some of her sorrows right out on his shoulder. Afterward she went back with him — she on the gelding and he on Sir Turpin, riding very slowly and very close together. But, though I was only twelve, and though I thought that she was the most perfect woman in the world and he was the most perfect man, still I had a very fixed idea that this marriage would never take place. A shadow of doom had fallen between them, I thought at the time.

However, back came my master in due course, with his head once more well in the air, his eye bright. "If I had only heard your whistle half a minute sooner, everything would have been well. But, as it was, she unnerved me. Good heavens, Christy, when I think of all that you know about me...." He broke off and shook his head and laughed a little. However, we were so close to one another that I could often tell pretty accurately what was passing in his mind. I knew on this day that, for all of his gaiety, he was really yearning to be back with his lady. Yet he wouldn't give way — not a single iota.

That same afternoon we were packed. He said he would take only the barest necessities because all the rest, even to his clothing, must be left for his creditors. And, when he had made his fortune in the West, he would return and pay them back the last penny that he owed to them — plus handsome interest. That was the way of The Colonel — always magnificent. But, if you asked him how he expected to make that fortune in the West, he would have had no answer. The reason that I got along with him so well was that I never asked embarrassing questions of him. Before the evening we were on our horses.

"We have had enough sorrow and gloom. Let us cheer up, Christy," said my master.

And we brought our horses into a canter.

Chapter Three

THE DEPARTURE

You will notice that we started on horseback though our destination was the Far West — not the Alleghenies, but the Rockies. And yet we started on horseback. Perhaps The Colonel really did not know how great the distance was. Although his education was complete and polished in some respects, in others he was as ignorant as a child. He could have told you that Virginia was the greatest state in the Union, the most glorious in history, the most distinguished for beauty of soil and gallantry of inhabitants. But he could not have told you what her products were, the amount of her exports, the number of her people, or the square mileage of that beloved territory. And I really think that he expected to remain on the backs of the same horses on which we started for the upper Missouri.

Yes, he was half man and half child, and one had a hard time deciding what part of his nature would show itself at any given time. For instance, when he selected the things which were "absolute necessities" for our trip, I thought he should take along reasonable things. He consulted me about everything that he did. We were in his room. The Colonel sat on the edge of an easy chair, wrapped in a brocaded dressing gown.

"What shall I take, Christy?' he asked.

"The things they need out yonder where the Indians are," I suggested, "are guns...and I suppose that there aren't many revolvers on the plains. Yes, you would need revolvers there. And some good rifles and as many clothes as there's room for."

"Clothes? Clothes?" repeated The Colonel. "I tell you, my boy, that a man can always buy clothes. But what about these things?"

He brought out an easel and a lot of tubes of paints and some canvas. Then he showed me a rack full of books. I saw enough there to load a horse, and I threw up my hands. "You can't have all these books, sir."

"The devil I can't," he said. "Not a thing that I could live without in that list. A man has to have his Bible and Shakespeare, of course. And then here's a bit of verse that one would have to take along" — he pointed to a dozen volumes — "and, besides that, who would be without his Rabelais and Montaigne? And *Gulliver's Travels* has got to go because it's the greatest book in the world, almost."

I looked these books over, and I said: "No, you can only take two."

"Curse it, Christy," he said, "what do you mean...two books? How could I live with only two books?"

"If you had only one canoe to move in, you won't have room for more."

"Why not two canoes?"

"Will you have money to hire men to paddle them?" I asked.

At this he broke into a storm and said with a groan: "You want me to live like a dog and not like a man out there, Christy, but I won't do it. A fellow has to have some comfort."

"You have to travel light," I declared. "Pick out two books and leave the rest behind you."

He took the Bible and Shakespeare, and then he closed his eyes to shut out the sight of the rest. "Send them to Martha," said The Colonel, "because they're a part of my flesh and blood."

They were, you could see that. And it cut the poor Colonel to the quick to leave them behind him. However, he couldn't be persuaded to leave the brushes and the paints and the canvas behind him. He said that it would be like cutting out his tongue and leaving *that* at home. I tried all I could to persuade him, but it wouldn't do. When he was silent and simply let me talk, I stopped. I knew to a hair's breadth how far I could go with him, and I never stepped over the mark.

It was a hard thing to leave that house in such quick order. And the dozen slaves on the place were pretty near heartbroken.

"I'd like to free them all," said The Colonel, "and I would, except that most of my money is owing to old Parnell, and he has no heart in him. He'd think that I was giving away his property if I freed them. Confound him, is he a man?"

I said that I thought that Mr. Parnell was a little sharp but probably a very honest businessman.

"He's human in form, I have to admit, but he's not really a man. He looks and walks and talks like a man. But he has a heart of flint. Yes, flint is closer to that Parnell than human flesh. He would never understand if I gave my boys their freedom, confound him. All I can do is to walk out and say good bye to them. Ah, well, I *shall* do something more. Take this ring to town and sell it for me."

It was a ring that had belonged to his mother, quite a fine emerald that he wore on his little finger. I knew that it was dear to him because it reminded him constantly of her. I wanted to argue with him, but I knew by the set expression on his face that this was one of the times when opposition would simply make him worse. So I went on to town with the ring.

It was just a little town with only one jeweler in it. When he looked at the ring, he thought that I must have stolen it, and he offered me twenty dollars for it. When I simply laughed at him, he called for a policeman. But the constable knew that my master entrusted all sorts of commissions to me, and so he refused to arrest me. Then the jeweler raised his offer to a hundred, two, three, and finally up to five hundred dollars. But there he stuck, declaring that that was the full value of the jewel.

I knew nothing about jewels, but I knew something about men. I picked the ring up and said that we would send it away to Richmond. He ran after me and stopped me at the door, finally giving me eight hundred dollars, which I presume was really a good deal more than half the value of the gem. Eight hundred was a lot of money before the war. I took the money back to The Colonel, and he told me to split it up into parts and to divide it all among his slaves.

With all my heart I begged him to keep that money, because we would need it so badly on the way West, but I couldn't budge him. So I divided the money into parts, with the biggest lot for old Ramsay, the white-headed old fellow who had taken charge of the horses for forty years in the Rutherford family. He had chosen to go with The Colonel when the latter left home, and now he was to be sold back to another family of strangers. However, I gave him a handsome allotment. On each other envelope I wrote down the name of the Negro to whom it was to go.

After that, The Colonel had all the boys called together, and, just before we were ready to start out, he stepped out onto the verandah and started to make a speech, walking up and down, frowning terribly and slashing at his riding boots with his whip. Old George, at the first word, burst into tears and nearly choked himself trying to keep from making a noise. But it was no use. The other boys began to break down, one by one, until finally The Colonel turned around and fairly ran into the house.

I found him in the drawing room with his face buried in his hands, groaning and swaying back and forth. "Take the money and give it to them, curse them," said The Colonel. "And then tell them to clear out, because I don't want to see one of their faces when I ride away!"

I went out and did as he had ordered. But I'll tell you a thing that may make you shake your heads — which is that not one of those men opened their envelopes. They just dropped them into their pockets in spite of the gold that clinked in them.

When The Colonel came out, there was not a Negro in sight. But, when he lifted his foot to the stirrup, there was a tremendous lot of blubbering from behind the trees and the corners of the house.

"Curse them," said The Colonel, "they ought to be whipped. I'm not going to leave today, Christy. I'm going to stay here and have them all whipped! I'm going to herd them all to town and have them flogged, I tell you. Christy, where's the gate? Open the confounded gate for me...the sun is in my eyes. Get me out of this."

He was so blind with tears that he couldn't see his way. I opened the gate, and we rode through and got down the avenue as fast as our horses could jump. Then we turned out onto the highway, and for five miles we burned up the road on the trail to the West. I didn't speak and neither did The Colonel, until a full hour had passed. After that, when he came out from under the cloud, he was as sunny as ever. That was his nature, indeed — to take everything suddenly to heart and to brush it away again. So he said that the rhythm of our traveling should be *andante* from now on, and we cantered merrily away. We found an inn by sundown, The Colonel in front with me lagging to the rear because, though my mount was almost as fast as that of The Colonel, I had the pack horse to lead, and he continually pulled back on the lead rope and would not make time.

I had an idea that, before we could cover three days of our journey, The Colonel would have enough of this slow business. But one could never tell how he would jump at a given moment. Like a half-trained horse sometimes the spurs made him race, and sometimes they merely made him smile. At the end of the third or fourth day he had a look at a map and saw that we had barely covered a hundred and fifty miles, though we had been working our horses hard. That hundred and fifty miles, compared with the enormous distance that lay ahead of us, looked really like nothing at all.

Just as I expected that he would break out into cursing and declare that we would have to sell our horses and go by train, he shook his head and vowed that he would be the first man to ride from Virginia to the upper Missouri on the same horse with which he started.

23

Chapter Four

THE JOURNEY

He was just as good as his word, too. I suppose that others had started on the same errand, but, so far as I know, we were the only lot to get through with the very same animals that we started on. The Colonel settled his mind to the business, and, after we had struck well into the journey, he reduced everything to a system. He said that we would consider ourselves an army, comprising five individuals. Three of those individuals happened to be horses. But the loss of one of the horses would amount to the same as twenty percent casualties. That, he said, was not to be thought of.

The eighth day out the pack horse, which had been having trouble with its right shoulder ever since the start, went dead lame. I thought that it was almost a hopeless case, and I suggested that we at least trade the brute with a bit of boot for a new horse. But The Colonel wouldn't listen. We had to go into camp and stay there for eleven mortal days, working over that animal for hours. There was never a shoulder so massaged and labored over. But on the twelfth day there was still a decided limp.

At that, The Colonel divided the pack between our two riding horses. We walked to lighten them somewhat for the new packs. The pack horse went on with nothing at all to carry. For three days we trudged on in this fashion. At the end of that time the pack horse was as sound as the day he was born, and so we could go on our way, as briskly as when we started.

I do not mean to infer that we rode all the way to our destination.

When we came to the Allegheny River, The Colonel bought a flatboat which would accommodate us and the three horses easily. We started the long trip to the Ohio, and then down the Ohio to the Mississippi.

That was one of the easiest and pleasantest times in my life. The Colonel was rarely in a hurry about anything that he did. When he was impatient, there was nothing that would hold him, but the incentive that started him westward was a deep-rooted thing that did not have to be performed in a rush. We idled down the two great rivers, usually drifting by day with the current, or, when the wind was favorable, we hoisted the clumsy square sail and that helped us down. When it grew dark, because then it was hard to mark snags and sand banks, we usually tied up at the bank. Those evenings were the pleasantest part of the trip.

We would start up a big fire on an open hearth which we had built on the deck of the boat, and, while the horses were pegged out on shore, grazing and exercising themselves as much as they could, we lay about and ate a hearty dinner. Then The Colonel, as a rule, read aloud. We had only the Bible and Shakespeare, but that was a new world to me. He read them both with equal enthusiasm. Whether or not he was a believer in immortality, I never could tell, but he certainly read the Holy Book like a priest.

It was a liberal education for me to be with such a man on such a journey — not only for the books he read and the way that he read them. The most interesting volume was his own heart and soul, which he got into the habit of opening to me with a perfect freedom. I think that it had hurt him a good deal to leave Martha Farnsworth, and it well might, because she was one of the finest girls that ever lived. But the long, quiet trip was a cure capable of destroying even a greater pain than this. Before we reached the yellow flood of the Mississippi, The Colonel had put everything behind him and was ready to face his new life with courage and enthusiasm.

I remember that on the way, when we reached the great Father of Waters, there was a stiff wind out of the east, and the sky was covered with an odd formation of clouds.

"Look," said The Colonel. "You can see for yourself, Christy, that good luck is behind us, and we'll have nothing but happiness on this trip. Because the wind is going to blow us straight across the big river."

It did, too. We were able even to steer up against the current a little, and, when we reached the farther side, The Colonel had the pleasure of selling his flatboat for a good deal more than he had paid for it to a merchant who was loading buffalo robes for New Orleans.

The Colonel now felt the hardest part of our journey was ended, but, as a matter of fact, we were only beginning the worst division. We went to the Missouri mouth, where it comes down in a brown flood out of the west, and we stood for a long time watching the seething mud in the current. That mud came from the land to which we wished to go. When we started up the Missouri shore, I felt that we were leaving the daylight world behind us and going back into some wild, early period. It was like traveling, not through mileage only, but through time also into some prehistoric epoch.

But there we were, logging up the Missouri patiently. We would have saved no end of time if we had taken a steamboat for at least the first part of the journey, but The Colonel wouldn't hear of that. He said that we must grow accustomed to the plains by degrees, and in a way I presume that he was right.

We reached the treeless regions where the land is frozen into solid waves of green or brown, according to the season of the year, and found the horizon pushed back around us into a circle so vast that men and the affairs of men seemed very small indeed. This went well enough for us until, one early evening, we saw straight before us in the northwest a single pale column of smoke rising. The Colonel made a halt and examined that column with care through his field glasses.

"It's a signal," he declared. "No one ever built a fire which made as much smoke as that, except on purpose. But what does the signal say, and to whom is it addressed, and may it not be talking about us, Christy?"

I was even more excited than The Colonel. For that matter, I don't think that I have ever seen anything more moving in its own way. I had seen fire smoke before. But this column rose through the windless air like a shaft of ghostly marble and lost its head in the sky above. It was like a warning. And if I had not been afraid of The Colonel, I should have started straight back for the mouth of the Missouri and more friendly regions beyond.

That one glimpse into the heart of the wilderness was enough to knock a great deal of the nonsense out of the mind of The Colonel. We camped that evening without a fire. With the earliest gray of the following dawn, The Colonel went through our packs and took out everything that was not an essential. These we buried in a shallow grave, because we didn't want to attract attention by making a fire. After that, we rebuilt the packs and settled the saddles with much care on the backs of the horses.

We did this work with as much haste as care, and we worked in silence with our mouths firm. In fact, we were beginning to feel that emotion which every dweller in the prairies grows accustomed to sooner or later — the sense that the plains have fixed a spying eye upon one, and that danger is creeping in closer and closer under the pale edge of the horizon.

That morning we started — with packs stripped pretty much down to essentials, except that The Colonel kept his painting materials. For a whole week we drove steadily along under that great sky where the sun burned white-hot each day, and the stars shone with unnatural brightness every night.

I don't think that we exchanged a hundred words during the whole time. In the day we attended to the horses grimly, and in the evening we cooked and ate our meals in the same long silence. We pushed our horses too hard, because it seemed that we were making no progress at all. During that week we did not see a living thing, not a beast, not a human being, not a sign or a track of one. And I know that, for my part, I felt that we *must* get more speed from the horses, or otherwise we would eat up the last of our provisions and die of want in this grassy desert.

On the eighth day we came suddenly against the wind over a swale of ground and found a dozen small deer beneath us, delicately beautiful creatures with broad white patches over their rumps. The instant they saw us, those white patches on the rumps flashed like so many tin pans in the sun, and they made off like jack rabbits. They seemed to me to be running faster than any creatures I had ever seen in my life, but The Colonel didn't seem to think they were so like lightning.

He shouted to me: "Antelope, Christy!"

With a dig of the spurs he got Sir Turpin underway at once. To lighten his racer, he unbuckled the heavy pack and let that fall, quite regardless of anything that might be broken in the crash. But that was the way of The Colonel. I agreed with him on this day. It was so long since we had seen anything living on these plains that I wanted to yell and sing — and, in fact, I *did* yell and sing while I watched The Colonel ride across the prairie.

It seemed at first that he was chasing so many flashes of lightning, but I soon noticed that, although the legs of the little deer flashed faster than the eye could well count, the long, easy strokes of the Thoroughbred first held the fugitives even and then began to overtake them. Mind you, it was a very even thing. But I have heard people declare solemnly that the antelope is the fastest creature that runs on four legs. I take this occasion to refute them — from the evidence of my own senses. I saw that good Virginia Thoroughbred, already pretty well tired from the march, far from the best of condition, with a heavy saddle and rider to pack, first hold the antelope even and then gradually overtake them. Then, in the distance, I saw the quick, bright flash of The Colonel's drawn revolver.

He actually got up to shoot two of them — one on either side. By the time that I came up with the pack horse and my own mount, on which I had strapped the things that The Colonel had discarded, Mr. Rutherford was already cutting up the kill.

Chapter Five

THE ACID TEST

He was like a very happy child. He shouted at me, his red knife waving as he talked: "This is the way to do it, Christy. Nothing like this, as an antidote for the prairie pain."

He was perfectly right. Having furnished us with more food than we knew what to do with, the prairie, which had seemed such an enemy before, was now almost a bosom friend. I set to work with much awkwardness, and The Colonel gave me a lesson in how to quarter venison — a lesson, he said, which had first been taught to the world by Sir Tristram.

"Who was Sir Tristram, Colonel?"

"Confound your ignorance," said The Colonel. "Sir Tristram was one of the first gentlemen in the world...if not the very first. Sir Tristram was the founder of all the sports of the chase."

I was much impressed and wanted to know when this great and good man had lived. The Colonel was stumped by this. He said: "Dates are of no importance. Forget dates, Christy. Banish that sense of dead time from your mind and make the past as much a part of your life as the present. In that way you will learn to look into the future, also, as a familiar. Do not push history away from you with dates, draw it close to you. See the face and hear the voices and let the devil take what is left in the way of hard, dry dates, and such things."

I made up my mind, for the hundredth time, that The Colonel was part wise man, part mystic, and part baby. As a matter of fact, he was all of these things and more. The composition of his nature was so varied that I could never understand him, really. Neither will you understand him, when I have finished my history of his life and his actions. But there he was, cutting up an antelope according to the directions of Sir Tristram, and lecturing a twelve-year-old boy on the inner science of history — and all this in the midst of the great American plains.

We camped on that spot for several days until we had sun-cured a good bit of the meat, and the horses had enjoyed the pasturage, recovering some most valuable weight in muscle and fat. Then we pushed on toward the north and the west, letting the windings of the great river determine our direction, again and again.

After that, I look into my mind and try to remember at what time certain events happened. I can only remember their order, and not the length of the intervals which existed between them. One day we came through some brush, and in a clearing before us a monster bear reared up with a clot of dirt still on its nose, where it had been rooting on the ground for grubs. I have heard people declare that all wild beasts, and particularly the grizzly, shuns the approach of man. I wish that those theorists, who live in countries where every "wilderness" is combed almost daily by bearers of high-powered rifles, could have been at hand to see that seven-hundred-pound monster roar at us and wave his thick fierce arms at us.

That bellow filled my ears. I turned and ran with all my might until I heard the bang of a rifle. Then I turned around and saw The Colonel, dropping his rifle and snatching revolver from his belt. His first bullet had stopped the bear and made the monster pitch up again on its hind legs with such a screech that the mere thought of it still scrapes the ends of my nerves. When bruin got the business settled in his mind and lurched toward The Colonel again, Mr. Rutherford met him with a stream of lead from the revolver.

The grizzly spun about in a grotesque *macabre* and finally slumped upon one side, dead. It was as fine a thing in the way of hunting as

I have ever seen, because The Colonel had about half a second in which to unlimber his rifle and get it to his shoulder. I think that the grizzly could not have been three strides away when the first stunning slug from The Colonel's rifle crashed into it. He finished the big creature with his revolver at what was hardly more than reaching distance.

I sneaked back to the spot with my head hanging, so terribly ashamed of myself that I did not know what to say, but The Colonel smoothed over that rough spot for me. He did not have a word to say about what I had done, or about his own actions. He talked all the while about the bear. He showed me the wonderfully constructed muscles in the forearm and shoulder of the grizzly with which it can crush the skull of a buffalo bull or tear out its ribs at a single stroke. He showed me the comparative smallness of the brain, and how it is well fortified with stout bony processes. But he showed me also just how vulnerable to a bullet the big bear was.

"As much as a chicken or a pig," said The Colonel. "But you have to shoot straight...you had better shoot *very* straight, Christy, before you stand up to game like that."

This was all he said at the time, but, of course, every word sank into my heart. I loved The Colonel for his forbearance, but I lived in an agony for days and days, hoping for the time when I should have a chance to prove that I possessed enough courage for one man's share.

That old bear was a great deal too tough and rank for chewing, it seemed to us. His pelt was too burly and bulky to be carried along, so that all we took were the fangs and the claws of the big fellow before we marched away.

This was a typical bear country through which we were passing. There was a succession of hills, covered with brush big enough to give shelter to a bear, containing billions of grubs and plants with succulent roots in the damper spots, furnishing also an abundance of little red haws that were bitter to our taste but that the bears seemed to relish greatly. Two or three times we came upon the sign of bears, but the cunning creatures kept out of our way. When we sighted the next one, it was totally unexpected and unwelcome.

It must have been a good many days after The Colonel had disposed of his bruin that the second adventure came. At least I have a recollection of having put much earnest practice with the rifle in between times. We were sitting around a very small fire one night, when The Colonel said quietly to me: "A grizzly is standing just behind you, Christy. I suppose that you will want to have your turn at this one."

Considering that I was only twelve, this was giving me the acid test with a vengeance, but The Colonel never treated me as though I were a boy. If anything, his tone was usually that of one who speaks to an experience older than his own.

He shoved the stock of his rifle toward me, and I scooped the gun up and turned around. I expected a monster, but not what was actually before me. At first glance that bear seemed much more vast than any elephant that ever battered down tall trees. It seemed to me that I was craning my neck and looking up to a prodigy whose head blotted out half the stars from the cold heavens.

"I am lost," I said to myself. "And even The Colonel cannot avenge me."

The bear, as I stood up and turned about, seemed to notice me for the first time. No doubt it was the fire that had filled his mind at first and brought him close, for a grizzly is by all odds the most inquisitive animal in the world, not barring the wonder of the poor, foolish antelope itself. However, now that the big fellow saw me, he intended business. He prepared to throw himself at me, and he only hesitated half a second to send his roar booming through the air.

As for me, I was too frightened to tremble. But the terror acted to numb my muscles, and I thought that I should never be able to get the stock of that gun to my shoulder. When it finally came to its position, I aimed at the beast and pulled the trigger. The recoil of the gun kicked me back just far enough to escape the swoop of the bear's right forepaw.

He did not strike again or swerve to cut at me with his paw or chop at me with his teeth. He kept right on falling, and, when he landed on the ground, his head was on our fire, blotting it out and almost casting us into a sudden darkness. It was a double darkness that lay before my eyes, because fear and shock and relief were working on me to such an extent that I simply leaned on the rifle and would have fallen, if it had not been for that support.

The Colonel reached me with a leap. "You're not hurt, Christy?" he cried, with a ring of fear in his voice.

I could not speak, but he seemed to understand. He turned away from me as fast as he could — so that he would apparently be taking no notice of the blue funk in which I stood — and began to talk about the bear. He kindled the fire again so that we could look at it, measuring the animal from tip to tail. Then he lifted a fore or a hind leg, guessing at the weight, and solemnly pointing out how much bigger this bear was than the one which he had brought down. By that time I was recovering my wits again and could feel the blood leaping in my body. The Colonel gravely pointed out that my bullet had struck exactly in the center of the vulnerable region of the chest. He said not a single word in actual praise of me. But when he looked at me, his eyes flashed with a wonderful fire, and his voice had a certain quality which had never been there before. For this was my baptism of fire, and, until I had passed through it successfully, he could not be sure that I was worthy to be treated like a brother.

Chapter Six

MYSTERY

Having been able to follow the example of such a leader as the big Colonel in this matter of bear hunting, I felt myself much expanded in importance, ready to lift up my head and call myself a man in any company. And The Colonel went out of his way to make me feel that what I had done was worthy of being remembered. I have said that something like this had to happen before he could accept me as a full brother in adventure. This is really the truth — from that moment forth, if my name had been Rutherford, I could not have been treated with more consideration by that strange and wonderful man. Indeed, I had never been treated as a servant by him.

He could not bear to make those who were around him feel anything lesser in their position. To hear The Colonel give an order to one of the slaves at his old home was like hearing a diplomat make a formal speech, almost. I have known him to eat a whole dish of a food which he loathed and call for more rather than hurt the feelings of the cook — even though this meant that the same dish would appear frequently on his table. But I had always lived in his house upon a footing even higher than that which he had established for the Negroes. I was his guard — at the age of eleven years. At the same time I was fighting his battles of chance on the track. Now there was a still further change. A door had been opened. There was freer communication between us and upon a higher level, if possible.

But I don't think that this made me love The Colonel more. It would have been impossible for me to do that. I lived, walked, rode, ate, and slept with my head always turned toward him. Partly I worshipped him, and partly I pitied and took care of him.

It was a matter of some days after the adventure of the second bear, while I was still carrying a rifle as though it were a scepter, that we came across the remains of a recent camp fire. In the mold among the brush, near that fire, I found the perfect print of a moccasined foot, hidden under some large dead leaves. I thought, at once, that it must be an Indian, but The Colonel was by no means sure.

He declared that the scouts and trappers often wore exactly the same garb as the Indians. He reminded me of the romantic appearance of some of the men whom we had seen while coming up the river. This was very true, but, for my part, I pointed to the smallness of the fire, the lack of any other sign, and therefore the pretty sound assumption that there was only one person concerned here. It was hardly likely that a single individual would venture his neck upon those dangerous plains unless it was an Indian of one of the neighboring tribes.

This seemed a reasonable logic to The Colonel, but he did not seem greatly interested thereafter. Yet, the second day after that, having fallen a little distance behind The Colonel, a queer, dumb panic came over me, and I found myself looking at the low hills around me as though each of them had the face of a charging grizzly. The very air that I breathed seemed to me to be filled with the tingling essence of danger. And I hurried my horse into a gallop, reaching The Colonel, breathless with excitement. When he asked me what I had seen, I hardly knew what to say.

I told him at last as well as I could. It was easy to speak of such a matter to him. The things which are unreal to the eye and the ear were almost of the greatest interest to him, and he heard me through with serious attention. Then he tried to make me remember if I had not seen something with the corner of my eye or heard something with the corner of my ear, so to speak.

36

"For," said The Colonel, "very often slight impressions come into our senses, and then usually they seem evil. For whatever is half known is dreaded. It may have been only that your eye half saw the bending of a treetop or a flicker of light on a stone, and that half-seen thing was translated into a menace in your mind. However, tell me what *you* think that the matter could be?"

"I've got just one idea," I told him. "But I can feel it right down to my toes. Colonel, there is an Indian following us, and there has been these last three or four days."

I believe that most men in The Colonel's position would have burst into a hearty laughter at this point, but that was the very last thing that The Colonel would do in any case where another person was speaking of a serious conviction.

"It may be simply fear," said The Colonel, "born into your mind because there *is* fear in this great, silent desert. Or again, it may be that the mysterious agency of the mind has thrown out invisible tentacles and drawn the truth out of the void."

That was the way that The Colonel often talked — as though the unreal were real, and as though the real were filmy stuff of ghosts! At any rate, he decided that from that moment we would begin to conduct ourselves as though I had seen an Indian brave, in full war paint, upon our trail — as though the maker of the fire, the leaver of the moccasin print which I had discovered, was the man who now tracked us across the plains.

As for the persistence with which he came behind us, we both felt that it might be because he was hoping to take us in such a fashion that he could claim both our scalps. The Colonel said: "We have one great advantage over this shadow, Christy. He will take us for one man...and a child. He will be apt to attack me and pay no attention to you. Therefore you must always be ready, for, while I may draw the enemy's fire, I think that you are the man who may have to finish him off."

After that, one of us was constantly on the watch every night. We alternated. He slept the first half of the night, and I slept the second half. Also, since this did not give me enough rest, we made another halt and had a rest in the middle of the day. We kept on in this fashion for what seemed to me a very long time. I believe that it may have been ten days. In all that time we had not the slightest indication of the presence of an enemy. Except for the fact that once, while lingering to the rear, I had been overcome with a panic, there was not the slightest grounds for our exceeding caution. Nevertheless the big Colonel would not abate a jot of his precautions, even when I, for my part, was certain that I had been wrong and that it was a mere whim of fancy that had attacked me.

"Give your soul a chance," said The Colonel, "and it will often take care of the body. But the body, Christy, can never take care of the soul. Pay heed to all these little premonitions. Cultivate them. Regard them as an extra self, above and beyond your mortal self. Regard that other self as a watchful hawk, at a great pitch, flying above your head."

So he insisted upon maintaining the strictest guard, and I thank heaven that he did. For one day, riding between two low swales of ground, with the grass yellow-green and as tall as a man's hips on either hill, there was a sudden glint of light in the grass to the right of me and behind me. I had the merest glimpse of it, and I did not have time so much as to speak. I merely cut at The Colonel's horse with my riding whip, because I suspected that he would be the first target in the case of a surprise attack. The big stallion bounded away so suddenly that it jerked The Colonel out of the saddle and tumbled him, swearing enormously on the ground. At the very same instant a rifle rang loud through the clear, quiet air of the plains. It was such a close affair that I could not really tell whether it was the bullet that had dropped The Colonel or the leap of the horse that had unseated him.

I had my own rifle at my shoulder by this time, but the spot where the wink of light had showed was perfectly tranquil. Somewhere in that long grass there was a human being, and I sent my horse scooting around the side of the hill just in time to see a man and a horse rise like veritable magic out of that tall grass. The rascal of an Indian had had a way of making his pony kneel down until it was hidden in the tall grass. It would have been a great deal better for the redskin if he had kept in hiding instead of taking to his heels. I took a shot at the highlight where the sun glistened upon the naked shoulders of the brave.

When I had my gun leveled, I felt a terrible shortness of breath and shakiness of hand with the knowledge that a human life lay in the pull of my trigger. I simply could not fire on the target, and, when I drew the trigger and the gun exploded, the bullet must have whistled rods and rods away from its goal. As far as I'm concerned, that would have been the end of the fight, but here there was a rushing through the grass, and The Colonel came storming up past me on Sir Turpin. He brought Sir Turpin up to a standing halt and pitched the rifle into the hollow of his shoulder.

He had a mark that was difficult enough. The Indian had thrown himself along the side of his horse farthest from the gun of The Colonel, and every jump of his scooting horse was taking him vital yards toward safety. All that The Colonel had by way of a human mark was the lower part of the redskin's leg. He didn't shoot at that target, as he confessed to me later. He took the whole horse in his sights, but, when he pulled the trigger, the pony raced on alone. The brave dropped to the ground with a great screech of rage and pain.

Chapter Seven

A GREAT IDEA

I had loaded my own rifle again by this time, but I didn't want to waste my effort punching holes in desert air while there was such a marksman as The Colonel along. I swung my gray mare, Kitty, alongside his horse and passed him my loaded gun, while I took his emptied one. He gave me a nod, and we drove in at that Indian from different sides.

The Indian was hurt by the bullet and more than half stunned by the fall from his horse. He had hardly done rolling head over heels when we were at him, and I suppose that his head must have been spinning like a top. But he wasn't ready to call quits. His rifle was lost in the grass, so he had pulled out a knife, and, staggering around on his hurt leg, he waved the knife and seemed ready to fight until he dropped.

If I had been The Colonel, I should have fired the loaded rifle into the rascal, but The Colonel's way was not mine. When he came up close to the Indian, he leveled his rifle. He waited until the redskin's head had cleared enough to understand what was happening. That required only a moment. Then the brave drew himself up to his height and resigned himself. It was plain that he expected to have the shot sent home through his heart or his brain.

"Plenty of nerve, eh?" said The Colonel.

"He shot at us from behind," I said. "And what wrong had we ever done him?"

"How do we know what other whites have done to him, however?"

asked The Colonel. "And these fellows put us all under one blanket, as I understand it. Make a sign to him to put down that knife and surrender."

I did it as clearly as I could, after which the redskin shook his head so that a ripple ran down through his long hair. By gesture he told us that, if he gave up his knife and surrendered, we would promptly cut his throat. At this, The Colonel tapped his rifle significantly, and the Indian nodded as much as to say: "I am at your mercy. I deserve nothing else. I expect nothing else."

"What am I to do with the fool?" asked The Colonel, greatly exasperated. "He won't surrender, and I can't butcher him like this!"

"Put a slug of lead through his head," I suggested. "That would be the best way for everybody, Colonel. It's what he has coming to him."

"I don't want to appear on the plains as a destroyer," said The Colonel. "Besides, what would we get out of this man? Nothing, Christy. Not even information, because we couldn't talk to him in his language."

"Very well, it looks as though he'll bleed to death."

The Colonel was a great deal moved. "Curse him," he said. "He'll stand there like a Roman and die. Won't trust himself to us and won't surrender. Christy, we can't go through with this. He's human under his red skin, after all. Open up the pack and get some bandages."

I did it, and The Colonel made me open a roll of cloth and show the brave how it would be used to wrap around his leg and stanch the crimson flow. Then Mr. Rutherford drew back, waved to the copper-faced man, and started off across the plains in our original direction. I was too staggered even to argue about the thing. All I could say was that he had now a double reason for wanting to trail us and kill us.

"If he were a wolf and not a man," said The Colonel, "he might do as you say, but they're human, these people. I have always found that a 'bad' dog has been made so by stupid treatment. And a 'bad' horse is generally owned by a brute or a fool. Give them half a chance and they turn out well. And so, Christy, we're going to give this Indian *his* chance."

"You're giving him *two* chances," I said, "and, I suppose he'll have both of them hanging at his belt before another day has gone by."

The Colonel laughed at this, but he wouldn't change his mind; and, as we jogged along through the wilderness, I began to wonder what would become of us — a boy of twelve and a madman like The Colonel, thrown out on the prairies together. He said to me a little later: "Now that we're getting well into the Indian country, we have to decide what we're going to do, Christy."

I admitted that this was true, and I said that I had been wondering for a long time just what his plans were. He took my breath by replying: "Plans? Not a plan in the world. I know what I have to do, but I haven't the slightest idea of how to go about it. You understand why I'm out here, Christy?"

"I know that you have to make enough money to go back and marry Miss Farnsworth."

"Exactly," responded The Colonel. "That's what I have to do. And I know that in a borderland like this, there is always a good chance for a fellow with a few wits and steady nerves. My wits aren't the best in the world, Christy, but my nerves are specially healthy. So here we are. Only I begin to wish that some money-making opportunities would show themselves. Martha can't wait for me forever."

I have written down these words, I believe, exactly as he uttered them, and I believe that this speech should be carved into stone, to stand as an imperishable monument of thoughtlessness. Idiots and madmen may have done such things, but I don't think that any other human with brains ever took a two-thousand-mile journey with no better idea of what he would do at the end of it. For my part, I would not walk across the street without a clearer purpose. However, The Colonel was The Colonel, though it strains even my credulity, when

I reflect on some of the things which he did and said.

He watched me with a good deal of anxiety, saying: "Christy, you don't seem to approve."

"I was only thinking it over, sir."

"But," he said, "you *must* approve, you know, because you are the practical head in this party. I would never have dreamed of starting out to make a fortune, Christy, without having you along to show me how to manage the thing. You *must* agree with me, Christy!"

Well, what could I do? Matter of fact, I wanted to cry like a nervous girl, but I simply said: "There's a lot of money out here. There isn't any doubt about that. Buffalo hides and such things. All we have to do is to get the hang of the business."

"Gold, too," said The Colonel, "billions in gold out here in the plains and the hills. Eh?"

"I suppose so."

"That's it. Rich land, too! Could make money farming this land, Christy. Take all we wanted to…enclose a hundred miles square …raise wheat. Confound it, this soil can grow such grass that it would have to do well with wheat. Get twenty bushels to the acre without any trouble…twenty bushels to the acre. Six hundred and forty acres to the square mile. Let's see, that's more than seven thousand…call it seven thousand bushels even, to the square mile. Say that we work only a hundred square miles. A hundred times seven thousand…seven hundred thousand bushels. Take in more land. Make it an even million bushels of first-rate wheat every year. Let's see…how much money would that bring in at present prices."

"A whopping big fortune, sir," I agreed. "You'd have to ship that crop out, though."

"Build rafts. Float it down the river. Right down the river, Christy. That's the thing. Wait a minute. Why not run up some flour mills along some of the fast streams? Yes, sir, that's it." He clapped his hands together and could hardly sit on his horse, he was so excited. "Think of that, Christy! Gad, but I'm glad that that idea popped into my mind. Plain inspiration! We'll run up the flour mills and grind our own wheat. Turn out the finest brand of flour that you ever saw. Old George knows all about milling flour, and what do you say that we send for him?"

I didn't laugh. No. I remembered that I was out on the prairies with this man — and I felt a long distance from laughing, I can tell you. "Well, sir," I said, "you'd have to fence in your ground first, before you sent for George."

"Why fences?" asked he. "The Indians can't be kept out by fences!"

"Maybe the buffaloes can't, either," I said. "But we'd have to try."

"Buffaloes, of course," he said. "Well, I'm glad that I have you along to remember the little things for me, Christy! But the fences are fixed. I'll build strong fences around the whole hundred square miles, eh? That's the thing for us!"

"We'll have to buy the posts and the boards some other place and ship them here. That would cost a good many thousands," I told him.

His face fell a good deal. "True. But we'd manage that. Can you think of anything else?"

"It would cost a good deal to bring men out here for farm work. You'd have to pay them for working on a farm and fighting Indians, and that sort of wages comes pretty high, you know. Then there'd be the cost of buying plows and harrows and seed wheat. After that, you can double the price for the cost of shipping it out here."

The Colonel looked so sad that I felt as though I had stabbed him in the back. "Money is the first necessity," he said at last. "One can see that. We'll have to rustle about and get us some money... through the gold mines...buffalo robes...or some such thing. When we've made a handsome stake, we'll turn it all into our land development project, eh? Would you agree to that, Christy?"

"Certainly, sir."

"Looks absolutely feasible to you?"

"Certainly, sir."

44

"Matter of fact, Christy, it's a great idea and you'll admit it."

"Certainly, sir."

"It came to me out of nothing at all. Plain inspiration," said The Colonel. "Write this day down in red, Christy, because it's the foundation of our fortune. Why, lad, we'll be so rich that you'll never regret the years of your life that I've stolen so selfishly."

"Stolen, sir?"

"Do you think that I'm not aware every moment," went on The Colonel, "that these are years when you ought to be in school? But here I keep you slaving for me. I am ashamed, Christy. Bitterly ashamed. But from the day that I took you by the neck, and you ran a knife into me...from that day, my dear lad, I knew that I would have to buckle you to me with hoops of steel. I knew that you had the stuff of which the poet spoke, if only I could bring it to light. And I *have* brought it to light, Christy...so much that I keep putting off the day when I must let you go."

Chapter Eight

IN EXCHANGE

At a time like this it was foolish to argue with him because, when he had fixed his mind on a subject, nothing would put him off. No one could explain matters or alter his ideas. I could not say that I hadn't the least wish to go to school — that I didn't have the money to go to school, unless he sent me — that simply to live with him was a grand education — that he had found me a little gutter rat and made me into a self-respecting youngster. I couldn't say any of those things, because he had his head firmly fixed among the clouds. So I made no attempt — and he went on working himself into a fine misery until evening, when we found a little creek and camped on the bank of it, building our fire down close to the water, where the blaze of it couldn't be seen at any distance.

After supper I sat at my watch and enjoyed the crispness of the pure prairie air and listened to the wind humming through the grasses on the plains, the water at my feet bubbling and singing. It was all *too* pleasant. I remember putting my head on my knees for a moment, to close my eyes and rest them a breathing space. When I looked up, the fire was almost out, and I was stiff from my cramped position. Besides, I was no longer sitting alone at that fire. There was a shadow on the farther side of it, and, now that my wits all rushed back upon me, I reached for the rifle with a gasp. For it was an Indian, hooded in a buffalo robe, and looking at me with a face of stone. Nothing stirred about him except the feathers in his hair, bending a little in the breeze.

I thought at first that his calm was caused by one of two things. Either a dozen other braves had surrounded us, and we were in their hands, or else this fellow had already cut the throat of The Colonel and made no account of a boy like me. Turning my head, I gave one swift glance at The Colonel. No, there he was with his fine face faintly lighted from the fire, sleeping with a smile like a child. When I looked back at the Indian, he raised a hand from beneath his robe and greeted me with a "How" — so soft that it could not possibly reach the ears of The Colonel and disturb his sleep.

I was badly shaken as to nerves. I managed to raise my own hand and whisper "How" in return — since that seemed to be the polite thing in the best Indian circles for the moment. Then I pushed a bit of brush toward the fire, and, as the flames leaped, I saw that this chap out of the night was none other than the very brave who had attempted to take our scalps that same day.

He saw that I was filled with wonder, and he smiled a little at me. Then he laid a finger on his lips and pointed to The Colonel, as much as to say that he would explain everything if he could, but not when his voice might awaken the white man. His smile had a strange effect upon me, because his features did not seem made for gentle expression.

But however much he did not wish to disturb The Colonel, I distinctly felt that this was a time when my companion should be alert. All seemed well, but there might be mischief which a boy's mind could not understand. So I spoke a word that brought Mr. Rutherford to his feet.

You will understand that The Colonel was generally so very well poised and at ease that one rarely saw him startled beyond control, and I hoped that the sight of the brave might shock him half as much as it had shocked me. Well, it was another disappointment for me. As he had said earlier in that same day, his nerves were fairly strong, and you would have thought that the warrior was an old friend whom he really expected to find beside his fire when he opened his eyes.

He stepped forward with his hand extended, saying: "Friend." A man from Mars could have understood that word from the gesture and the smile that went along with it. The brave took the hand of The Colonel with such energy that I could see the long muscles quiver and jump along his arm. And how his eyes flashed.

This red warrior was no ordinary man. For copper skin or white skin there are degrees of manhood, and this fellow was a hero among his kind and a person of importance, as anyone could tell with half an eye. He had a collar of grizzly-bear claws, and I had seen enough of those huge brutes to respect a fighter who decorated himself with such gear. His clothes were of the finest deerskin, fringed as fine as silk at the leg and arm seams, and the bead work on his moccasins alone must have cost the labor of a woman through a whole winter season. His horse, which was now in the background, was one of the usual dumpy, hairy beasts which the Indians rode, though it might have possessed extraordinary qualities, for all that we could tell. In addition, there was his rifle which was new and of a good make. What was more, it was well kept. This was an extraordinary feature with an Indian, as even such greenhorns as we could tell.

In spite of such dignity as this man possessed, it warmed my heart to see the way in which he conducted himself around The Colonel. In the first place he caught the word "Friend," and kept on repeating it over and over again, hitting a little bit closer to the correct pronunciation each time. When he managed that, all the while smiling and nodding at the big white man, he got busy in another way.

He went down the edge of the stream to the pony which he had been riding, and he came back, carrying the saddle which was an extraordinarily good one. Out of the saddle bags he brought a shirt which he had apparently taken along with him to make himself gaudy in case of a great occasion arriving while he was wandering across the prairie. He had some other trinkets, together with a hatchet with an edge as murderously sharp as a razor, an old-fashioned double-barreled pistol which had a rusted lock that could not possibly be fired, but which he handled with the greatest reverence and fear, and an excellent hunting knife.

All of this stuff he laid out before us, first throwing plenty of fresh brush on our fire, so that we could have sufficient light to know what he was doing. If he was a bit grandiloquent in this, he could be forgiven. For at the root of his nature every Indian is half a child. This was not all. When he had gathered everything he possessed, except for a little rope which was twisted around the head of his pony, he stripped himself of all of his finery. By this time he had reduced himself to the horse, the rope, and a little pouch-like affair made of the skin of a rabbit, and which we were too ignorant to know was his medicine bag.

Here he rested content, but not until he had made gestures to show that he would have given the horse to us also, except that he had a long distance to go to his home, and his leg was crippled with a wound. The rest went to The Colonel, with the blessings of the donor, so far as we could make out. I kept waiting for The Colonel to gather in this loot. It was a great thing to see him standing up there, the most magnificent man that ever walked this earth, as far as my eyes have ever seen. He had his arms folded and his big head thrown back a little. His face was quite impassive, except for a little glint at the corners of his eyes by which I knew that he was tremendously pleased. Well he might be, I thought, for here was almost enough stuff to open a museum. The Colonel could go back East and travel with lectures on this one batch, if he wanted to, and make a great deal more money than he was ever apt to gather by his visionary Western farm.

I was wrong again. He was a confounded man to decipher. Usually he jumped the way that I didn't expect. He waited until the brave was finished and was about to leave us. Then The Colonel picked up the saddle and carried it to the side of the pony. After that, he fetched the stuff that went into the saddle bags. Finally he pointed to the clothes of the red man and indicated that the night was cold.

More than that, he indicated the fire, the water flowing gleamingly by our little camp, the tall, romantic banks of the stream, the darkness of the night, and the glitter of the stars beyond. And having included the whole universe in his meaning, he took the hand of the redskin and repeated the word: "Friend." His gesture waved away the rest of creation and made it of infinitely less value.

I can feel in my old heart now an echo of the thrill of excitement that jumped in me at that moment. The Indian could barely contain himself; there were bright tears in his eyes. His whole body trembled, and his broad breast rose and fell as though he were in pain. So far as he was concerned, as the bowlers say, it was a ten-strike. He took back his goods, and he gave The Colonel his soul in exchange.

Chapter Nine

FRIEND!

You and I could have given back the Indian's loot just as well, but we could never have done it as The Colonel did. Before he ended, the material universe was simply banished and nothing but human relations remained to be worth a candle. After that, the warrior sat down by our fire, and we got his name out of him, which was Sanjakakokah — with a meaning which we were to learn later. The Colonel then introduced himself and me, and, when the poor Indian had tried to stagger through our appellations a few times and failed miserably, Mr. Rutherford suggested the title of Colonel for himself and Christy for me. He shortened the name of the brave to Sanja without perceptibly hurting his feelings.

We found out next that he was hungry — which we could have guessed by the flatness of his stomach, without the gestures by which he indicated that the sun had gone around the world twice since he had eaten. The Colonel put me to work cooking, and for his part he looked to the wound of our new friend. The red man had done a very poor job in bandaging, and the wound was very sore and inflamed, but The Colonel was a past master at first aid, and he fixed up the hurt as comfortable as you please in no time at all.

Then we sat back and watched Sanja eat, and, by the time he had finished, the sky was beginning to turn gray. That didn't bother Sanja, for, when his stomach was filled, he wrapped himself in his robe and was sound asleep before you could count ten.

I whispered to The Colonel and asked him what the upshot of

this would be. He hardly understood what I meant, but I told him that this man was certain to ask us to go along with him to his tribe, wherever that might be, and that then we must accompany him. The Colonel didn't like the idea. He declared that it would spoil everything to make use of Sanja, but that this little affair should remain simply a pleasant memory with no other material results.

That, of course, was what one could expect from The Colonel, but I pointed out that we had no better destination. If he wanted to make money out of the prairies, he would have to learn prairie ways and prairie people, and that this was a heaven-given opportunity for us. Finally he agreed with me, though I had a hard time of it convincing him. In the end he decided that we should surely accept the invitation, if we got one.

The sun was well up by this time, and Sanja suddenly stood up and stretched. The air was very cold, and the black water of the creek in the shadow looked just a bit icier, but that didn't deter Sanja. He stripped off his clothes, tied up his long black hair in a handy knot — ridiculously as a white woman might have done — and then dived into that stream, bandaged leg and all. He disappeared while we stood shivering, and he came up half way across the stream with a shout. Then he turned and came back toward us, frolicking like a child in that cold bath. When he had had enough of it, he climbed out, whipped the water from his body, and dressed for the ride. As for his wounded leg, you would have thought that he had never had any trouble with it in his life, and The Colonel had to force him to stop for a new bandage.

After that came the thing which I had foretold. He rode out a little in front of us and with many gestures persuaded us to ride, repeating: "Friend. Friend." He indicated a great number of people, as much as to say that he would take us to a place where everyone would be a friend to us.

"You are a rascally little prophet," The Colonel said to me with a smile, "and I suppose that we'll really have to go along to make this fine fellow happy."

So off we went, and there was a load off my mind. For I felt that now we were about to make a beginning of some sort, and with The Colonel's talents, if he wished to make money, he would soon succeed with half a chance to work his way on the prairies. We went along at a good clip. I think we were traveling for a matter of four or five days before we came in sight of the Indian town. The Colonel was much impressed. He pointed out to me that civilized men would not wander this distance from their homes through hostile country, equipped with only a rifle and a horse to make their living as they went along, and I presume that he was right. Here was Sanjakakokah, cruising about on the plains a hundred and fifty miles from his base of supplies, simply hungering for any sort of adventure, and most of all for scalps.

There couldn't have been a better way to learn the Indian language. Sanja was perfectly willing to try to speak our tongue, but we insisted on being pupils while he was the teacher. As a teacher, he was the best in the world. His gravity was so colossal that nothing could shake it for an instant, and our most ridiculous attempts to pronounce after him some of his gutturals and consonantal sounds never made him so much as smile. He was always encouraging us and telling us that we spoke so well he could not believe that this was the first time. In fact, he was a prime good fellow, this Sanja.

He was hungry to talk, and we were hungry to talk. He had a thousand things to say, and we had talked to no one except ourselves for weeks together. So we chattered away all day long as we crossed the prairie, while Sanja enlarged our vocabularies by leaps and bounds. I was never able, in after years, to make such progress with an Indian tongue. But then our minds were fresh. The first writing of the prairies was inscribed upon us by Sanja, as upon a slate, and we really made a remarkable bit of progress.

We learned that Sanja was a Mandan, that his nation had once

53

been great in war and in numbers, and that they were still as brave as any people on the plains. Their enemies — who were all the other neighboring tribes — were constantly pressing back the Mandans and thinning their ranks, until finally the Mandans were no longer of a sufficient strength to rove across the prairies with men, women, and children on the march. They could only send out small war parties, or single scouts like himself, to do what deeds came in their way.

In the meantime the rest of the nation was cooped up in a little city which they had built on the edge of a cliff beside the river, where the water and the rock covered two sides of their homes, and a strong wall guarded the rest. Here, constantly on their guard, like a cornered wolf which the dogs dare not close on, they kept the Sioux and the rest of the prairie dwellers at a safe distance. They planted corn — he showed us a handful of the dried seed, much smaller than any corn which I had seen before — and they gathered berries, sallying out to hunt buffalo when chance brought a herd within striking distance of their town. On the whole they lived very happily, though it was plain that San-jakakokah yearned to be out with his men, ranging across the plains as free as any Sioux chief to hunt down enemies and increase the number of scalps that hung in his teepee.

He talked to us about many other things too, and, as our vocabularies swelled, we could understand most of what he said, though in a fragmentary way. It seems that he had seen us a full three or four days before he had finally attacked us. And the second day of his trailing of us he had almost tried his hand in picking me off when I lagged behind, in the hope that, at the sound of the shot, the big white man might come hurrying back and be a victim to a second bullet. That was the day, indeed, when I had received the fright. We questioned him closely. He swore that I could not have seen him. Therefore, it must have been a pure matter of telepathy, though not a very strained one, I suppose.

54

We asked Sanja why he had planned to attack men who had done him no harm, and his answer was beautifully illuminating to people who were not yet accustomed to the Indian manner of thought. A long time before — how many years we could not find out, since Indians are apt to be a bit inexact in their chronology — five Mandans were paddling a big canoe down the river when a sudden burst of rifle fire from the bank filled the craft with dead and wounded. A party of whites — rascals, no doubt, of the blackest kind — had taken the Mandans by surprise. But one of the party, a cousin of Sanjakakokah's, had managed to dive overboard and swim to the farther shore in spite of a bullet through his body. He reached the Mandan town and gave an account of everything that had happened before he died. Therefore, as Sanja cheerfully told us, since that moment he had known that it was his duty to send to the happy hunting grounds every white man who fell into his hands. This he had done to the best of his ability, having accumulated two handsome scalps, as he assured us.

Before he had finished this narrative, I looked upon him as merely a cheerful murderer, but The Colonel seemed to have no such feeling toward him. He regarded Sanjakakokah with a calm smile and told him that he understood the exact feeling of the chief.

This was not all. Sanja went on to declare that he had hoped with all his heart to take both our scalps, and that he had followed us for many days full of this desire. He apologized for his lack of success, and he assured The Colonel that ordinarily he would not have delayed so long had it not been that the Great Spirit who governs all things had held back his hand against his own will. Of course, this was simply another way of saying that he had never been able to come upon an opportunity which exactly fitted his sense of safety. The Colonel seemed to swallow the entire yarn and rode on as full of friendship as ever until, in the distance, we made out the Mandan village on the bluff and saw that this stage of our wanderings had come almost to an end.

Chapter Ten

THE VILLAGE

When we stood there on the top of the rise from which we had our first view of the Mandan town, Sanjakakokah stopped his pony for a moment and laughed softly to himself.

"You are happy, brother," said The Colonel.

"How can I be anything other than happy?" said the Indian. "I see my city again. It is the most beautiful and wonderful city in the world. Other peoples build their dwellings with the skin of buffalo raised on poles, but our houses are so big and so strong that a hundred men could stand on the top of one of them, and yet the house will not fall down. The Mandans are not great in numbers, it is true, but they are great wits, and they are near to the spirits of the earth and the air."

I wanted to break out laughing at his silly speech, but The Colonel gave me a side glance that ripped down to the quick and sobered me thoroughly. He said: "Sanja, these things that you tell me come from the mouth of a man who speaks the truth. But I wish to know more. I have heard that the Lakotas and the Pawnees and the Cheyennes are very great nations."

I repeat the answer of Sanjakakokah as nearly as we could make it out from our imperfect knowledge of the language at that time. He said: "It is very true that the Lakotas, Pawnees, and Cheyennes are great peoples. And the Comanches in the south are wonderful with their horses. The Crows are a mighty people, also. Their beautiful hair hangs to the ground, and the tips of it trail when a chief walks out. All of these are brave and wise nations. They are no braver in battle than the Mandans. For the Mandans will not become slaves. We will not join one of the great tribes and become swallowed up in their numbers, because we are proud.

"I shall tell you the reason of our pride. When the first man was made, and the first woman, they were Mandans. All the other nations of the Indians came from that first Mandan. And he had a son who had a black skin. That son was the father of all the Negroes. He had another son with a pale skin, and that son was the father of all the white men in the world. Therefore, because we were the first people in the world, you will see that we could not let ourselves be taken into another tribe and lose our names. Because the Great Spirit would be angry with us."

The Colonel listened to all this nonsense with a face as grave as though he were hearing the Gospel preached. But he said at last: "I have heard that the Pawnees also say that they were the first people to be made, and the Lakotas say the same thing. Do they not claim it, Sanja?"

Sanja nodded and smiled with some contempt. "These peoples," he said, "because they have many braves on the warpath, and because they take many scalps, also flatter themselves with lies as you say. But I shall give you this proof that the Mandans are the first people in the world and the nearest to the spirits of the air and the earth and the underwater people also. This is my proof, which all men know.

"When the buffalo leave these hills and pass far away, we might starve for the lack of meat because we cannot go out and hunt at a great distance as the other nations do, for our enemies would come on us like rivers in the spring floods and wash us away. But, since we cannot chase the buffalo at a distance, we call them back to us with the buffalo dance. Sometimes it is very hard. We must make big medicine, and I have seen the dance last for fifty days and nights, but in the end the buffalo always come!" He said it with a childish smile of triumph.

"It is a great thing," said The Colonel. "I know of no other people

57

who could do such a thing."

"But we can do a greater thing than this," said the Mandan serenely. "There are times when it does not rain for many weeks. Then the ground becomes dry. See...it is dry now. And the roots of the corn may wither and die of thirst. Then one of our young men goes and stands on the top of a house and makes his medicine all day, and, if the rain does not come, then the next day another young man goes to the roof and makes his medicine. I have seen this work kept up for twenty days, but in the end the medicine of someone among the young braves is strong enough. We see a cloud blow in from the edge of the sky, and after that the rain falls, the corn drinks, and the harvest is saved. Since the ground is so dry, it will be strange if they are not making medicine to bring the rain to us even now."

There was a certain amount of very strong logic in all of this, even though I had to choke to keep from laughter. For if people could dance long enough, the buffalo were sure to return to the grass which they had left. And, if the young men of the village could make "medicine" long enough, one day it was sure to rain. However, even I could see that it would have been very foolish to attempt to point this out to the chief. He was perfectly satisfied with his reasoning and the reasoning of his tribe. As for The Colonel, he showed nothing but interest. He really looked as though he believed this stuff, and then we started on toward the town.

In the swale beneath the village we came to the corn fields. There were half a dozen Indian women and their daughters laboring, and every stroke of their hoes, made out of the broad shoulder bones of buffaloes, raised the dust. They were all white and powdered with the dust. When they saw us, they came as fast as they could run. It was a sight partly horrible and partly amusing to see one fat old squaw hobbling along as fast as our horses trotted, shouting questions at Sanja. He paid no more attention to those women and their girls than he might have paid to the blowing dust which they raised. He simply twitched his horse to a new course and brought it into a gallop.

While we were heading toward the village, I crowded Kitty close to Sir Turpin and called quietly to The Colonel: "Are we going right in with him now, sir? Wouldn't it be better to stay at a little distance and have a parley with the head chief before we go into what may be a trap?"

"Every man has to take a few chances," said The Colonel carelessly. "So we'll ride right in, Christy. Mind that Sanja doesn't see you talking to me like this, or he'll think that we don't trust him, and I wouldn't hurt his feelings for the world."

So we made our entrance into the town. We were sighted from the wall before we got near the gate, and there was already a fair-size crowd gathered as we rode in with Sanjakakokah. Women and girls and boys rattled questions at us like hail on a roof as we pushed our horses through the gang, but Sanja kept on, now and then raising his hand and hailing some friend among the warriors. They stood here and there, and each of them gave a start of curiosity when they saw the two whites. But they wouldn't demean themselves by babbling questions like children.

I was busy, taking stock of this village. Certainly Sanja had been right when he called their dwellings houses, and not teepees, because these were great round structures which might house a dozen families at a time. On one of them, just as Sanja had prophesied, there was a brave making his medicine to bring the rain. He had had quite a crowd around him, too, but they showed him their backs when we approached. However, this fellow had worked himself into such a lather that he did not seem to see us, even when Sanja stopped and hailed him as The Beaver and wished him good luck in his medicine-making.

The Beaver went right on. He was dressed in the white skins of mountain sheep, fringed with black scalp locks — a very flashy costume and a fiendishly hot one, I suppose, for a man standing on the roof of a house under such a broiling sun as this was. Heat couldn't stop him, however. He had a lance in one hand, and a shield, covered with gaudy daubs of color, was in the other. He kept brandishing one or the other of these at the sky and spouting out a speech of which we heard a cross section. I don't think that there was much else to it. He merely stood up there and repeated the same idea over and over again, all the long day. The only thing that he varied was his emphasis, which was screaming one moment and soft as a whisper the next, while the crowd stood about and drank this talk down like wine.

"Sun," he said, "I am The Beaver. I must have water to drink and water to swim in. Therefore, do not dry up the earth. Do not melt the clouds out of the sky. I know you, sun! You are trying to keep back the wind which is my friend. The kind wind has heard the voice of my medicine. It is trying to blow a good rain to us that will turn the ground to mud and make the river as yellow as paint. But you, sun, will not let it. You keep it back with your heat. You will see that the wind and my medicine are stronger than you today. The rain is coming! The rain is coming! I can taste it in my throat. I can smell the big drops hitting the dust. I hear the corn drinking. My medicine is not a liar. It is a true medicine, and the rain will come. Listen to The Beaver, sun. Listen to me, wind!"

Very silly stuff, but not so silly to me, as I sat my horse in the dust cloud of that street and watched the enthusiasm of that fellow on the roof. He was a grown man, a strapping big one, too. He had killed his enemies in battle — witness the scalp locks with which he decorated his very clothes. As I watched him broiling and shouting and groaning at the sun and the wind, I began to feel that perhaps we *had* come to a place where men could hold a convention with the elements. I didn't have long to watch this scene, for Sanja pressed ahead and was suddenly mobbed by three women and a couple of children.

Chapter Eleven

THE QUAIL

It was his family. The three women were his wives, and the two children — a boy and a girl — were his offspring. He had been away from them more than two months on his long hunt, and I know that he must have been wild to sit down and talk with them. However, that was exactly what he would not let himself do.

His son — eight or nine years old — came with a flying leap, boosted himself, using his father's foot, and sat laughing and shouting on the horse in front of him. It must have made the heart of Sanja jump. But he merely took the youngster by the hair of the head, held him squealing and dangling, and dropped him into the dust, almost under the hoofs of my mare. The mother scooped up her fallen boy with a scream of fear and shook her fist at me as I rode past. But that example was enough to hold the others back.

Sanja was asking someone if Ompah, the head chief, was then in the village. A middle-aged man with a good deal of dignity listened to this question, but, before he answered it, he ran his eyes over us. That glance lingered on me just the split part of a second — about as long, say, as it takes a hunting knife to drive to the handle. Then his eye wandered on to The Colonel and began to flame while he surveyed him. There wasn't any doubt about what he would do to us if he had the ghost of a chance. This gloomy chap answered our guide: "Do you know where the house of Harratta may be found? Go there. For Harratta has a daughter, The Quail. Harratta is gone on the warpath, and Ompah makes himself a fool and a woman, waiting for Harratta to come back, that he may ask the girl for his wife."

"Tell me, Rain-By-Night," said Sanja, "is it true that Ompah has at last decided to take a wife?"

"It is true," said Rain-By-Night, "that Ompah will be found making himself a thing that even the children in the city laugh at... *Waugh!*"

With a grunt of rage and disgust he threw an edge of his fine buffalo robe over his head, as though in mourning, and strode past us, with a sidewise thrust from his eyes that glided between my ribs to my heart once more. He was a gloomy fellow, this Rain-By-Night, and I was glad to be away from him. After he was gone, Sanjakakokah said: "This is a thing more wonderful than the absence of rain from the Mandans. You have heard what Rain-By-Night told me. Now I tell you that Ompah is a great chief. There was never a greater warrior among the Mandans than this Elk. He has never taken a wife. He would have nothing to do with women, and other men's wives and daughters cooked for him and made his clothes and his robes. But he never had much. He is a poor man except in horses, of which he has a great herd for himself. He could have bought the most beautiful girls in the village to have for his wives, but he would not take them. He wanted a life of peace when he was in the city, he would say, and he preferred doing his fighting from the back of a horse and against an enemy of the whole nation. However, now it seems that he has lost his heart. I am sorry for Ompah, but I am glad for the Mandans that we may have a son to such a great man."

It was doubly impressive to hear such talk about a chief from another leader of the tribe. As a rule an Indian prefers to talk about himself, and he can usually manage to expand his own exploits to a sufficient volume to fill the ears of every auditor that he can gather. But, when he talks about another man to praise him, it means that that other man is big medicine, you may be sure.

As we went on down the street, Sanjakakokah told us that The Quail was the daughter of a hardy old warrior — Harratta, The Wolf.

She was the prettiest woman that ever was seen on the prairies, and therefore it might be that Ompah had never taken a wife before because he had not been able to find one who filled his mind as a man's wife should.

Here we turned through a winding of the narrow alley, and we saw in front of us one of the queerest pictures that I ever hope to see in this world. In the entrance to a lodge sat an Indian girl who was, just as Sanja had said, the most beautiful thing that ever stepped upon the prairie. Just in front of her sat a middle-aged warrior, engaged in painting her face. His own face was made up in a wild combination of yellows and reds and grisly blues, so as to make himself attractive in the eyes of his lady love, I suppose. Now he was improving The Quail, as fast as he could.

This was the final touch in his work of decorating her. In the dust beside him lay three or four lengths of clothes of various colors which he had evidently tried on her but had not liked. The one which he had finally selected and gathered around her was yellow with a blue design and border, and rather a fetching thing, it seemed to me. He had put her in this. Then he had put half a dozen necklaces around her throat. He had wound pounds of gaudy beads around her arms, and he had woven quantities of the finest feathers into her hair.

When we came closer and he turned his face to us, I saw one of the harshest visages ever created. He could have posed for the central figure in a child's dream of an Indian raid. But this monster was so far lost in love that he actually did not see us. We were simply dim figures, moving through the mist that obsessed him. He turned his head back to the girl.

She, however, took more interest in us. A white man was a white man, after all, and I suppose that she had not happened to come across many whites like The Colonel. As a matter of fact, he was almost as much of an exception among white men as she was among Indians, but not quite. Because the daughter of The Wolf was not only an oddity among Indian women — she would have been an

63

oddity among any set of women in the world.

"Christy," said The Colonel, "what a wonderful golden girl she is …if she'd only wipe the old fool's paint off her face."

That was the word for her — golden! I never could find out just what blood was in her, because I never could learn any details about her mother. It may be that The Quail was not of the Mandan blood at all but carried off from some border town in a raid. It may be that her mother belonged to the tribe and had strange blood in her. It may be that she was simply a freak of nature, though of course I cannot help doubting this.

At any rate her hair and eyes were very dark, but they were not black. They were simply a dusky shade like the evening. Her skin was as far from copper as it was from white. Perhaps you've seen some of the Madonnas which the Italians painted when they were half mad with color? Well, this girl was like one of those golden-skinned Madonnas, except that her color was a bit more shadowy than anything an Italian would have put down on the canvas. Somewhere I've picked up the theory that the Indians may be descended from the Chinese, or an antetypal race from which both the Chinaman and the red man may have evolved. I never could take much stock in that theory, although it might do to explain the unusual complexion of this girl. She might have been a throwback of a type that was gone an unknown span of centuries ago.

These big, dusky, almond-shaped eyes looked at us with as calm a stare as any barbarian queen could have delivered from a throne. Then she deliberately wiped the streaks of paint from her face and gave us our first chance really to see her. For my part, I saw enough to understand why Ompah had lost his wits about her.

Sanja said: "Go into your house, Quail. I have to speak to Ompah."

"Speak to him, then," said this impertinent girl. "Or do I make Sanjakakokah dumb?"

There was a great deal about Indians and their ways that I did not know, but I *did* understand that Indian women do what they are told to do, and it chilled my blood a bit to hear the girl talk in this manner. Sanja was so enraged that he even lifted the whip in his hand as though he was about to strike her. But I suppose that the presence of the big chief stopped him. At any rate, the main thing was that the girl remained sitting there, staring at The Colonel.

The Colonel stared back at her. In the meantime Ompah pulled himself together a little and stood up, drawing his robe around him — a whale of a man he was when he stood up. But his eyes still had a dazed expression as he faced us. He asked what it was that Sanja wanted, and finally he seemed to make out what had happened. Sanja was talking four or five times faster than I could follow with my abbreviated understanding of the Mandan language at that time. But I understood enough single words and gestures to make out that the chief was telling the great war leader how he had trailed us and tried to lift our scalps, and how he had been followed, shot down, and then turned loose with a gift by this odd giant of a white man.

By degrees the big chief recovered from his trance and began to understand, and, when he understood and came wholly to himself, he did all that we could have asked of him. He came to The Colonel and shook hands with him. He said that Sanjakakokah was his brother, and that, having spared the life of Sanja, we had spared his own.

Then he led the way to his own lodge, pointed out that there was vacant room around its walls, and begged us to stay there with him. Sanja put in here to the effect that he could not allow us to go anywhere except to the house where he himself lived. Ompah could only wind up with offering us the freedom of the town and hoping that we would make them happy by forgetting to leave their nation. After that, he began picking up stuff to give us as a present, but The Colonel managed to extricate us, and we went off with Sanja sure of one thing at least, that with the protection of the war chief around us, no Mandan would dare to handle us lightly.

Chapter Twelve

THE MUSIC OF THE NIGHT

We found ourselves that night in a great hut of fifty feet in diameter, with a pair of beds assigned to us, and plenty of time to stare around at the strange furnishings of that house. There was a whole circle of these little bed chambers, each fenced in with elk and buffalo skins, and in the four- or five-foot space between the beds there stood a post on which the belongings of the warrior hung, his war club, his axe, his headdress, his spear, his quiver, bow, and arrows, his strong shield, his medicine bag, and, top of the post in every case, the head and horns of a buffalo with a pendant strip of skin and the tail sweeping the floor. Those buffalo masks stared at me with their hollow eyes that night like a circle of devils.

For half the night I could not dream of sleeping. It wasn't the strangeness of the place alone that kept me awake, but my ears were not yet accustomed to the noise of an Indian village. I had always imagined Indian towns as places of majestic silence in the midst of the prairies, but I was a thousand times wrong. If there had been nothing else than the dogs, the town of the Mandans would have made a good study for the noises of Hades. For in every family there seemed to be a score of wolfish, starving, skulking brutes, and every now and then a dog in a far corner of the town would discover something in the wind, or scratch up a buried bone, or get into a fight that would attract the attention of every other dog in the place. The whole canine population started with a yelp and tried to pile over to the center of attraction in two jumps. Then there was a grand turmoil of snarling, screeching, and howling, as twenty fights started. But, before those fights were settled, something was sure to happen in another corner of the camp, and the whole mob rushed in that direction.

The dogs were not alone as noise makers. Half a dozen young men felt inclined to have a concert that evening, and unluckily they selected the roof of the house next to ours for their show. It was a grand affair. Each of the young men took turns in singing the lead. The rest of them sat about, beating drums or rattling bones and moaning out a burden while the fellow who was elected to relieve his spirits for the time being screeched like a wild cat with a knot tied in its tail. When his throat began to show signs of wear—another pair of lungs of brass took up the good work where he left off.

I kept looking about our own house to see how long the grave and staid warriors would stand for this nonsense, but they paid no attention to it at all. Finally The Colonel said to Sanja: "The young men have strong voices, Sanja."

Sanja looked up and appeared to be hearing that vocal maelstrom for the first time, saying: "That is White Buffalo and some of his friends, and they are singing because they are to go on the warpath at the first favorable time of the moon. It is a pleasant thing to hear the brave young men of the Mandans telling how they will destroy their enemies and bring home scalps."

Even The Colonel was a bit staggered by this. It sent him off to his bed, and I retired to mine, as I've said before, only to lie, staring out through the entrance gap at the leap and glow of the fire which smoked or burned in the center of the house. I say smoked or burned advisedly. Sometimes the flames jumped up happily toward the big hole in the center of the roof which was supposed to serve as a chimney. Most of the time it *didn't* serve as a chimney at all; it wasn't even a partial excuse for one. When the wind puffed from a certain quarter, great white billows of that smoke rolled down and back and curled into the obscurest corners of the house — including my lungs,

67

as I lay there coughing and trying to breathe. It was not pleasant-smelling smoke, either, for anything that can be made to burn is good enough for a Man dan's fire. I only thank heaven that they had not discovered rubber up to that time.

After a while the sextet on the adjoining roof got a bit hoarse and went off to bed. But, just as I was beginning to give thanks, a young brave came walking into our own lodge, helped himself to a handful of buffalo meat from the pot that steamed night and day above the fire, and, when he had fortified himself with that, broke into a little impromptu dance, circling around the room, hooting and screeching in such a key that a pain settled in my brain and began to throb with every beat of my heart. This temporarily insane young man was merely telling how he had had a good evening gambling, and how he had won two horses and an old shirt from old Pipestem in the course of the night. He yelled himself out of the house at last and went off through the town, still whooping it up, leaving an echo and an ache in my mind. I actually prayed for the next dog chorus to begin and drown out the "song" of this young gambler.

Now matters quieted down to such an extent that I could hear the crying of the baby in our house. You may have noticed that a baby will usually make itself heard. Yes, time and patience may be required, but a baby has oceans of both qualifications, and a little noise-making art of its own. I have often looked with wonder at a baby. It is a standing proof of the old doctrine that only a poor workman casts blame upon his tools. For here is a mite of humanity whose lungs cannot possibly hold more than a handful of air, and yet which can handle that bit of air so deftly that it rivals the best and longest-winded piper that ever called down the eagles in a highland glen.

It is not mere volume; it is the way a baby does it, that counts. First it establishes a regular rhythm, and that rhythm of crying sinks in on your brain. You adjust yourself to the beat of the tune and get your nerves fortified and composed. But just as that happens, the baby shifts to an upper register and charges on your attention with an entirely new harmonic scheme of things. Take it all in all, a thunderstorm can be a considerable disturbance, but I would back any three-month baby against the most ripping thunder that ever deafened the mountains and shook loose the upper pinnacles of rock. A thunderstorm has a comparatively small register. Also it cannot help being rather grand and soul expanding. But the crying of a baby is simply mean and wicked and acid. It wears out the heart, like water dropping on a stone.

Well, as I said before, there was a crying baby in that lodge. I didn't think much of it while the sextet was performing on the roofs, or while the young gambler was telling the world about his good luck. But, after those disturbances died away and the camp reverted to the comparative silence of the dog fights, the snoring warriors, the talking women, the crackling fires, and the sneezing of smoke-irritated lungs, the baby began to assert itself. It had simply been getting in voice during the first part of the evening. Now it turned up in earnest, and in another ten minutes I was sitting up and gasping and wondering what could be done to keep the poor mite from choking to death. Or would it not be wiser to put a merciful end to its misery?

Just then the squaw shifted her position and brought herself into view of me. She was squatting by the fire with a year-old boy in her lap. That youngster was the one who was using his voice on the rest of the world. He gave his mother the full benefit of hands and feet. He kicked her, beat her, yanked her hair, and screamed most loudly when she dared to remove his grip from her nose, which the boy was extra fond of pulling. The manner in which the poor squaw absorbed this punishment and kept on dandling and stroking and cooing to the youngster was an amazing thing. I was twelve at that time, but I then made a surmise which I have repeated many times since — that a mother must be almost equal parts of fool and saint.

Presently a buffalo robe was thrust aside, and a tall brave appeared.

69

Now, I thought to myself, *the boy will get the first spanking of his young life. How I hope that the strong right arm of that warrior doesn't grow tired too soon.* But, no, I was entirely wrong. This fellow, who looked ugly enough to slaughter a sleeping city, merely squatted on his heels and looked at the little thing with much painful attention and affection. He seemed delighted when the boy stopped crying in order to get a good hold on his father's ear with one hand and whack him in the face with his other fist.

"You see," said this red-skinned idiot, "that, even before he can speak, my son knows his father, and this father knows his son. He is hungry. That is why he makes such noise."

He reached into the pot of buffalo meat and gave the baby a whole handful. The child had no sooner swallowed it than he piped up again a little louder than before. But there sat the pair of them — father and mother — dandling that devil-inspired youngster for another hour until he grew tired of pummeling them at last and fell asleep in the middle of a screech. The mother was asleep, too — poor tired thing — with her body sagged against one of the posts which supported the meat kettle. But even in her sleep she was smiling, as though to placate that yelling and wonderful son of hers.

After that I managed to get to sleep in my turn, and I dreamed that I was an Indian father with a whole flock of children. It was a rare bad one, even for a nightmare.

Chapter Thirteen

A DANDY

Perhaps I have allowed you to have the impression that this was an exceptional pair of Indian parents, but they were the ordinary thing among the Mandans and among all the other tribes, so far as I was ever able to learn. A child is considered to have its own privileges, and these are, first and foremost, the right to yell when it feels so inclined. An Indian would never dream of kicking a dog merely because it was yelling at the moon. Neither would he dream of punishing a child for crying.

In the morning I was a bit groggy, and even the magnificent nerves of The Colonel seemed to have been a bit strained by the ordeal of the night before — not that I intend to infer that the day was much quieter. The dogs were tireless. Day or night made no difference to them. Their lungs were simply equal to any and all demands that could be made upon them. The children were screeching all day long, too, and every now and then one of the braves would be inspired to break into a dance for no particular reason, prancing around in a circle, like a rooster courting a hen, and yelling or chanting at the top of his lungs. This comparison struck me that morning — that Indians are like schoolboys who are enjoying a recess, the difference being that the Indians never go to school and always are enjoying the recess.

Sanja was on hand as soon as we turned out. He showed us the best way down to the river, where we all had a swim, and The Colonel did his shaving in the cold water. That did not bother him, however, for small matters never weighted on his spirits.

We climbed back to the plain above in time to see an odd performance going on among the hills. All the boys, who were old enough to run at a decent clip and keep it up for any time, were drawn out of the town and split into two parties with a wise old warrior at the head of each band. They had play bows and rush arrows together with wooden knives in their belts, and each youngster had a little tuft of dried grass on top of his head to represent a scalp lock. After that, they were led through all manner of maneuvers. The two warriors got their bands into good, defensive positions among the hills, and then they started the two gangs for one another.

They went through all the work of sham attacks and feints and retreats, setting off the fine points of Indian tactics, and in the meantime giving those boys enough running to kill off most grown white men. Finally, the two lines closed — that is to say, they came to close range and began to shoot off their arrows. The moment that an arrow struck a vital place, the victim had to drop *dead,* while the lucky fellow who had shot the arrow ran up and *scalped* the dead boy with his wooden knife. The scalp tuft of dead grass was put into the belt of the victor, and then the youngster ran back to help his party as before.

I thought, altogether, that it was the most exhausting game that I could have imagined, and it made me ache to think of going through such maneuvers. Then, when the battle was ended, the whole party trooped back into the town, and we entered with them.

It was a great sight to see the boys carry on. They whooped it up for a while as though they had really done great things, and what amazed me was that the grown men stood around and seemed perfectly serious when they heard the boys boasting about what they had done.

The reason for that seriousness was partly to encourage the boys to fight and partly to encourage them to talk. For an Indian who cannot boast is not apt to be much considered. You must not think

72

that boasting and lying are practically synonymous among Indians, as they are among whites. When an Indian boasts, there is always a grain of truth at the bottom of what he has to say. The art of the speaker is in making that grain of truth color all his chatter. And the art of the listener is to be able to tell by the color of the boast the amount of real fact that is contained in it. So you would see the older braves listening to these screeching youngsters in turn and going from the windy ones to those who had actually done something. After all, this part of the celebration was only a preparation for what followed. The boys who had taken scalps then stepped forward and began a scalp dance that was fairly blood-curdling. For half an hour that dance had the city ringing. Then it subsided. The excitement vanished completely. But I could realize in what a manner the ferocity of these people was trained and encouraged from their infancy.

After the games of the boys had ended, The Colonel and I consulted about our next best moves, and we had a considerable talk on the subject. When he asked my advice, I admitted frankly that I had no idea how we could get into a prosperous business by the means of people like these. Neither had The Colonel a thought of how to commence. But I felt that this connection we had made with the Mandans was a foothold of some sort, and I suggested that we simply wait here in the town for a time — until we saw the Mandans a bit tired of our company, or until we had a chance to do something worthwhile for ourselves.

He agreed to this, but he seemed rather anxious. "I dreamed all night about Martha Farnsworth," said The Colonel. "Confound it, Christy, I haven't sent her a letter for a month or even for more than that. And it is a weight on my mind. Suppose that she gives me up for dead and picks up another man like Gilmore...that slick-faced young puppy. I worry about it. And we have to turn a trick of some sort. Have to get something out of this. Money or reputation, Christy. So look around you and see what there is ahead of us, will you?

73

Wake your wits, Christy. You're always able to find *something.* "

Sometimes it seemed to me a little unfair that The Colonel should put burdens of this nature and this weight on my mind. But I was fairly used to it. He always came to me when he was in a comer, and I was accustomed to thinking for the pair of us. Though how we were to make capital out of a lot of poor red-skinned beggars who had nothing worthwhile except runt horses and buffalo skins, I could not tell.

We went down the street together, and Sanja came along with us. He proposed that it would be a good idea to go listen to the medicine that was being made that day to bring the rain. He said that there was no doubt that the rain would come. The Mandan young men *always* made medicine which brought the storm clouds, but this time it seemed an extraordinarily hard job. They had used up a great many of their young men in a vain effort, but none had developed a medicine great enough to make any impression on the sky — strange to say.

Now he understood that a youthful brave named Stone-That-Shines had that day taken post on the roof of the medicine lodge, and he had heard that the brave was making a really heroic effort to bring down the rain. It might be worth our while to go listen to him and give him our good wishes — and what could be better than the good prayers of such a hero as The Colonel?

We went along with Sanja until our way was blocked by a young man who rode a horse very slowly before us, and who seemed to me the most beautiful picture of an Indian that I had ever seen or even dreamed of. It was a piebald horse and a perfect beauty, with its colors rubbed up and set off to perfection. The rider sat on a saddle of beautiful white mountain sheepskins. Saddle and bridle were a mass of jingling little brass bells, all burnished until they shone as brightly as they tinkled. He had an elaborate headdress of feathers, and his clothes consisted of a tightly fitted suit of shining white skins, all covered with beautiful beadwork. His long black hair hung down beneath his stirrups, and, as he rode along, he cooled himself by waving a fan of feathers.

"What great man is this?" asked The Colonel softly of Sanja.

"Great man? Great man?" said Sanjakakokah, his lips curling with disgust. "Ah, my friend, this is no great man, but a shadow and a disgrace to the Mandan people. His father was a worthy man and my friend. If he were living now, he would first use his knife to stab that rascal in the heart and let the crows eat his flesh. There is no greatness about him. You see that he has fine clothes and a pretty appearance. But that is his whole work. He does not ride to battle with the Mandans. He does not work to gather game for the meat pots. All that he performs is to make himself beautiful and to whisper lies to the women as they are working, so that they may make beadwork for him and give him food when he comes begging like the coward and the villain that he is."

"A dandy," said The Colonel to me with a smile. "Nothing to do but to make himself fine. Oh, Christy, how I wish that some of the dressy young men in Virginia could be on hand here to listen to what Sanjakakokah can say of dandies and dandyism. It did me good to hear him. But there is another dandy on the roof of the medicine lodge."

It looked like another beau, as a matter of fact. But, when we came a little closer and mingled with the crew which was listening to the shouting of this youth, we could see that there was a difference. For instance, the burnished necktie which he wore was made of the narrow, deadly claws of a mountain lion, which this brave must have killed in battle. His shield was beautifully whitened, to be sure, but it was so ponderously made of the thickest hide of the buffalo's back, joined together in layers, that it looked capable of turning a rifle bullet. At the end of his lance streamed the scalps of three enemies. This was very apparently a young man, but it was certain that he was an important man already, in spite of his youth.

75

Chapter Fourteen

THE MEDICINE BAG

This warrior on the roof of the medicine lodge was capering and dancing and shouting and crooning a good deal as the man of yesterday had done. Yet there was a difference which struck even inexpert eyes like those of The Colonel and myself. This brave had made himself fine because he was going to stand the eye of his nation and of his god. Furthermore, he knew that the corn was dying in the fields and that a famine might follow. He was not only excited; he was desperate; and religion seemed to give him a drunken enthusiasm.

He said: "Hear me, wind of the southeast. Hear me, clouds of mist which are filled with cold water in rivers. I demand that you hear me, and I am worthy of being heard. Because I stand here to make a sacrifice. Others have offered you their best buffalo robes. Others have killed for your sake their favorite dog or even their fastest horse. But I shall do something more than this. Hear me, wind and cloud, and all my dear people...unless the rain falls on our city this day, I shall sacrifice myself! And this is how the thing shall be done. Unless the rain falls this day, I shall take off this shield. I shall throw away my medicine bag. I shall throw down my rifle and my spear and my knife. I shall creep away and never raise my head where the warriors boast again. I shall burn my three scalps in honor of the Great Father. And I shall live among the women and the dogs! This I shall do unless I draw down the rain. But I shall draw it down. I feel the coolness of the shadow of the clouds coming upon my heart.

Do not fear, women who hoe the dust of the corn field. I shall bring down the cold showers of the rain this day. Or else I shall be a sacrifice!"

This was his speech, repeated over and over with a very few variations, throughout the entire day. His audience didn't mind repetition. They listened with silent enthusiasm and awe, for the thing which the young Stone-That-Shines was offering to do was a good deal more than a threat to commit suicide. He declared that he would condemn himself to a life among the women and the dogs, giving up his standing as a warrior, if he failed to bring the rain this day. The danger in which he stood, from the Indian's point of view, was that of a sort of living death.

It impressed the Mandans terribly. They grew positively pale when they heard of this dreadful sacrifice which the youngster was offering to make. Sanja could not look on the picture after a single glance, but he turned away, saying that it made him sick and weak to think of such a thing — and such a useful warrior lost to the not over-thick ranks of the Mandan fighters.

Here there was a general murmur of applause, for young Stone-That-Shines, in the midst of a frantic capering across the roof, suddenly opened his medicine bag and took out its contents. Now, a medicine bag is a sort of a secondary soul to an Indian. He first goes out, when he is on the verge of manhood, and, sleeping in the midst of the prairie or on some dangerous buffalo trail, he dreams of an animal which is then sacred to him. It may be a mouse or a beaver or a toad or a rabbit. When he wakes up from his dream, he kills the first specimen that he can find of the creature which had appeared to him in his sleep, and with its cured skin he makes his medicine bag. Sometimes it is a huge affair and great inconvenience for a warrior to carry about with him. Sometimes it is a tiny skin of a young frog which can be tucked away out of sight and never noticed, except in the most careful search of the person of a fallen warrior.

77

Such searches are always made when a warrior drops a foe. If he can come out of battle carrying his own and his enemy's medicine bags, it is not only a curiously interesting battle trophy but also a double-soul equipment. It doubles a man's importance on earth, and it doubles his importance in the shadowy life hereafter.

Once a medicine bag is lost or stolen or taken in battle, it can never be replaced. The greatest chief in the whole tribe would not dare to fabricate a new medicine bag to take the place of one which had been disposed of. But, if he can lay hands upon the medicine bag of an enemy, then he is saved again, and he is able to lift his head without shame among his fellows.

I have enlarged on the theme of the medicine bag so much and so long because I want it to be understood that an Indian fighter would almost as soon open his heart as open his medicine bag before the eyes of the world. Usually the bag is stuffed with dead, dried moss or some other stuff which is very light but *givess* the bag a living shape. In addition, it holds some mysterious element of the spirit world. That is its great importance.

Stone-That-Shines opened his medicine bag before the entire crowd and, with a groan of wonder at his daring courage and recklessness, passed it over the host that watched him. Then he extended above his head in one hand what looked to me like a ball of living yellow fire. It appeared to be a segment of the blazing sun itself, which now poured down from the center of the sky. I looked at The Colonel, and I saw in his eyes a faint reflection of that same yellow fire which blazed in the hand of the warrior. It was perfectly easy to understand how the brave had acquired his name. He had actually found a stone that shone. But my thought was The Colonel's thought, and The Colonel's thought was mine. Who could tell if the Indian might not have discovered some wonderful outcropping of diamonds on the prairies or among the hills that bordered it?

We crowded as close as we could and strained our eyes, but the instant that Stone-That-Shines had finished prancing in his first direction along the roof of the medicine lodge and had turned back toward his first position, the blazing fire died out of the stone which he held, and all that was bright in it was a few glittering, dazzling eyes of fire. Whatever it might be, it was certain that it was no jewel — no diamond at least.

The Colonel, having stared his fill at it, suddenly turned around and drew me out of the crowd, asking: "Christy, what can the thing be?"

"Wouldn't I give my eyeteeth to get a look at it?" I said. "But I can't tell what it is any more than you can. It looked very much like fire to me at first."

"Christy," he said, "you may doubt I know, but I tell you that we have had the first sight of the treasure which I'm trying to find to take back to Virginia with me, where I'll marry Martha Farnsworth and send you away to school."

He was beginning to have this dream right out in the middle of the day, which wouldn't do. It didn't seem healthy at all. I said: "Colonel, that's no diamond. Looked to me like a big chunk of glass …and that's all."

"What?" cried The Colonel. "There was something that glittered in that glass, though."

"Yes, some sort of coloring. They used to make balls of glass with sparkling stuff in it when I was back in Virginia. You've seen them, too. And what that brave has in his hand is simply a chunk of one of those broken balls, I think."

This took down The Colonel a good deal. He complained: "How could a grown man be such a fool over a piece of broken glass, Christy? Will you tell me that?"

"Why," I said, "the Indians never go by the price of a thing. Beads are just as good to them as emeralds and rubies. It's just the first flash of a thing that counts with them. So this Stone-That-Shines has turned a little broken glass into big medicine."

"And now," growled The Colonel, "he stands on the roof like a perfect fool and tells the sun to notice the part of himself which he is holding in his hand. And he is pointing out to the rest of the tribe that the bit of sun which he holds does not burn him, although it is hot enough to shine. What rot, Christy. If there's nothing in the thing, why don't the Mandans make a laughing-stock of him?"

"Because partly they're too polite," I said, "and partly they really like to believe in wonderful things."

I think that The Colonel's feelings were really badly hurt because I refused to allow him to make anything wonderful out of this glittering handful which Stone-That-Shines had in his medicine bag.

It was about time for eating, we thought, so we stepped into the first lodge that we came to and helped ourselves from the pot of buffalo meat. That was the rule for a stranger. It didn't make much difference whether he was a guest of one man or of another. As long as he was a friend of the tribe's, he could go to any man's food supply and take what he wanted — and welcome, too. The squaws didn't scowl at us for invading their larder. They came up, grinning and nodding, and a wrinkled old hag reached into the meat pot almost elbow deep until she found a sizable and tender chunk, which she handed out to me.

I couldn't refuse. I think that I would have, if it hadn't been for The Colonel's eye, fixed steadily on me with a good deal of danger in it. I had to take that meat, thank the old squaw, and eat it in front of her eyes. Otherwise she would have been insulted, which would have meant an insult to the lodge, which would have been an insult to every warrior living in that lodge. Which gives you an idea of how Indian courtesy worked forward and backward, from high to low, and big to little.

We were getting out of that lodge when a bit of misfortune came my way in the shape of a brave who was just balancing between boyishness and manliness, with nothing much to give either way.

Chapter Fifteen

AN AFFAIR WITH A KNIFE

The disturbing Indian was about a month or so short of fifteen, but he had managed to take the scalp of an enemy, and there it was, hanging at his belt. It was a rather smallish scalp, to be sure, but that didn't make any difference to the Indians. A scalp was a scalp. Having taken the trophy, this youngster was a full-fledged warrior. He was a big chap, with a frame that promised to fill out heavily with muscle. Just now he was in the awkward stage, in spite of his new dignities. I was on the edge of thirteen, so that he was a good deal bigger than I was as well as close to two years older. Just the same, he was more of a boy than he was a man.

Yet I took him fairly seriously because of the knife at his belt and the bow and arrows at his back. I stepped aside as he came into the lodge to give him room to enter. When I turned to step back again, thinking he had passed, a foot was inserted between my feet, and I was tripped up as neatly as you please. I came down on my face with a whack, and, when I sat up, a little stunned, I heard The Colonel saying rather sternly: "Pick yourself up and don't make any trouble, Christy. You ought to watch yourself better than that!"

I got to my feet, rubbing my nose, which had been badly banged. This was too much for the Indian. He had been standing by, fairly bursting with pleasure because of his little performance, and now he couldn't stand it any longer. He rocked back and forth, from his heels to his toes, roaring with laughter and delight. I think that I could have stood for the laughter of that young buck, but over in a corner of the lodge there was an old man working away on a war bow's decorations. He had stopped his fumbling, old hands and was gaping with laughter at me, showing his toothless gums.

That was a bit too much. It looked as though the audience was siding with Two Big Buffalo — that was the name of the young brave. In spite of the warning of The Colonel, I couldn't help going for him. I stepped up and tried to flick him across the face with the back of my hand. I missed. He appeared to be blind and reeling with laughter, but all the time half of that mirth was a mask, and he was watching me sharply enough to dodge my blow and leap in at me. I was a fairly good wrestler, and I had had enough practice at rough and tumble to hold my own with boys my own age or even a little more. But this fellow had weight and age on me. Besides, he was stronger in the arms than most Indians are. Also, he had the advantage of taking me with a surprise attack. I slapped at his face, cut the air, and the next instant found myself sprawling on my back.

Two Big Buffalo kneeled on my middle, whipped out his knife, and slid the back of it neatly across my throat to show that, if this had been a real battle, he could have cut my throat and taken his second scalp as easily as nothing at all. By the nasty look in his eyes I knew that he wished it *were* a real battle.

I managed to give myself a twist that put me face down, and he commenced to work on me frantically to flatten me out once more. However, he didn't understand how to go about it. Indians are fair wrestlers, but only fair. They aim to throw a man down, but they don't understand the fine points of mastering the other fellow and making him helpless *after* he has hit the ground.

We scuffled there for about five minutes, until we rolled out of the door of the lodge, and a big crowd gathered around to watch the fun. Two Big Buffalo tried to laugh and tell the surrounding specta- tors that this white boy was no trouble at all for him — but, just the same, Two Big Buffalo was not a third of the size that he had been when this little ruction began. He had tired himself out, dragging and heaving at me, and presently I managed to roll away and get to my feet.

He came lunging in with a snarl and got something which was not in his books. The whack of my fist in his face was sweet music to me, I'll tell you, and Two Big Buffalo went down on his back like one small calf. He didn't like that business at all, and, when he got up again, he had his knife out, ready to skin me. However, his head wasn't quite clear. I managed to knock him down again before he could see just what to do. Then I sat on top of him, telling him that, if he dared to stir, I would cut out his gizzard and feed it to the first hungry buzzard that came along. He didn't stir, either, so I stood up and told him that I would keep his knife to remember him by — and to scalp him with it if he ever bothered me again.

I thought that Two Big Buffalo would curl up and die with shame and rage. It was plain by the look on his face that he would have thrown his own life away with a smile — if that would have guaranteed the destruction of mine at the same moment. But there was nothing for him to do but sneak away through the crowd, with his battered face muffled in the corner of his buffalo robe.

The Mandans tried not to show any partisan feeling, but it was plain that they were not pleased. Everything had been delightful while their fellow was on top, but, after he had been whanged on the nose and sprawled on his back a couple of times, their faces turned to stone. The point which troubled them seemed to be simply that a smaller and younger man, no matter what his color, had been able to down one of their braves — no matter how young that brave might have been.

The Colonel was terribly troubled. "You should have let the whole thing go," he said. "Now, you walk into that lodge and tell them that you are sorry that you forgot yourself and started to fight in the house where you had just eaten the food of friends. You are sorry for what you have done, and you wish to leave the knife of Two Big Buffalo, who you hope may be a good friend to you hereafter. And say that as though you mean it, Christy!"

I went into the lodge, therefore, just as I had been ordered. One of the mature warriors of that house was now present, smoking a pipe near the central fire. I went up to him and made him my speech, repeating everything that The Colonel had told me to say.

That villain didn't say a word in answer to me. He let me talk away in a blue streak. All the while his eyes looked through me and past me, as though I had turned into a thin mist. At the end of my little speech he picked up the knife, which I dropped in front of him, and threw it away with a backhand flip. It struck the edge of the beams at the side of the big room and stuck there, humming like a wicked hornet. With a chill working up and down my back, I got out of that place a good deal faster than I went into it.

"What's wrong?" asked The Colonel, when he saw my face as I came out. I told him what had happened, and he brooded over it, very much discontented. "You've done wrong to get into a fight in this fashion. Just the same, that brave in there is old enough to know better than to talk to you the way he has done. A gentleman is a gentleman, no matter what his color or what language he speaks. I'll talk to Sanja about this. Something has to be done to patch things up."

Sanja had heard that there was trouble in the air, and he found us just as we started looking for him. He was a good deal cut up by the account of what had happened. When he heard how the brave had thrown the knife across the room, he was very angry, saying that it was an insult not to me, because I was only a boy and not expected to understand such things, but to The Colonel and to Sanja, through The Colonel.

Sanja declared that he would smooth this matter out or else make them pay dearly, but The Colonel begged him not to. I have never forgotten the little speech that Dick Rutherford made on that occasion. He said: "Big troubles grow out of little ones, and big wrongs out of little wrongs, as you know, Sanja. Now, Two Big Buffalo acted like a child, and not like a warrior, when he tripped up Christy. He acted like a child, again, when he sat on top of Christy and drew the back of his knife across his throat. Even so, Two Big Buffalo was not as much to blame as Christy was. Two Big Buffalo started to play a game...even if it were the very rough game of tripping people up. But it was Christy who tried to strike the first blow, and that was what caused all of the bad feeling. As for us, we are men, Sanja. We are above losing our tempers over little things like this. Christy was much to blame. And you can tell the braves that I have said so, and that I'll see that he behaves better hereafter. You may tell them also that, if anyone bigger and older than Christy dares to put a hand on him again, I'll break the rascal in bits!"

That was not a very pacific way of concluding his peace talk. But The Colonel had a habit of losing control of himself for just half of a breathing space, now and again. When he did, it was like seeing the red lightning run amuck through the sky. It made people wish to dodge, and even a hardy old scoundrel like Sanja fairly blinked when he listened to the end of this talk.

Then he went off to find the knife thrower.

Chapter Sixteen

RAIN

When Sanja left us, he gave me an ugly look in passing. He did not like me. He had never liked me, and the other Indians were of one mind with him. As a matter of fact, people are not usually pleased by the dark and ugly Deever looks or by the gloomy Deever way of speaking and acting. A white man will make some allowances. He likes a smiling face almost as much as an Indian does, but a white man will wait for a gloomy man to show whether or not he may not have good cheer in his heart of hearts. If he has, the gloomy face is willingly forgotten. The Indian is not that way; he takes things at their face value.

So they never liked me. As long as I knew them, their hearts never went out to me as they went out, for example, to The Colonel. No matter how much I studied good Indian behavior, I could not please them. I got on with them as a whole well enough, but that was because I finally managed to command their respect. It was never because I won their love.

This present squabble was brought to no good end. Rapid Water, who was the brave who had thrown the knife across the cabin when I had asked him to give it to Two Big Buffalo, turned out to be a warrior of a great deal of importance. He would have been a war chief and a very considerable one, had it not been that he was too impulsive. Charging straight through the enemy's line was his favorite form of exercise, when he got into the war parties. His body was pock-marked with bullet wounds and covered with the slashes of arrow or knife. Consequently, such a man, with such a repute, could be expected to take a little leeway in his manners. And he refused to send any courteous speeches back to The Colonel — to say nothing of me.

I had seen The Colonel angry before, but never much angrier than he was on this occasion. He wanted to go right back to that lodge and wring the neck of Rapid Water. I almost wished that he would do it, because I wanted these Indians who loved battle so much to see a real warrior in action. The Colonel was a warrior after the heart of the god of battles. However, he controlled himself, and we strolled over to see what progress Stone-That-Shines was making in the course of his prediction of big medicine. We found nearly half the Mandan population standing about, watching the show with a breathless interest, for the sun was rapidly declining toward the horizon, and there was never a clearer sky since the world began. If that sun fairly got down beneath the western horizon before a cloud appeared, it was the finish of the day's work for poor Stone-That-Shines.

It meant that he entered a living death, as I've said before, and the dreadful prospect enchanted even the sternest warriors in the tribe. Man, woman, and child, they stood about in a solemn conclave, looking first at the sinking sun and then at the staggering, exhausted form of the young brave. The hardiest of these Mandans shuddered when they watched.

It was a shuddering matter, and it was plainly to be seen that that poor, deluded young brave on the top of the medicine lodge was putting his last strength into his work and hoping to kill himself with the effort at making rain, if he failed to do it by the setting of the sun. The sun sank lower and lower, and it was hardly half an hour above the horizon's verge, having turned to a brilliant orange color, when the wind, which had been in the northeast the entire day and the days preceding, now swung sharply about to the southeast and began to blow with a force that knocked up scores of little dust

87

fountains throughout the village.

This change took place almost instantaneously, and the Mandans grew prodigiously excited. There was not a man or woman or child in the little city who attributed the change to anything under heaven except the work and the medicine which Stone-That-Shines was executing on the top of the medicine lodge. It happened that when the wind changed, Stone-That-Shines, exhausted of body and sore of throat from his vocal efforts, had been standing with the stone raised above his head — silent and motionless. Therefore it was plain, of course, that the change of wind had been the work of the stone alone. If it had been considered big medicine before, it now became translated into almost the greatest medicine in the world.

Every housetop in the city now held its excited spectators, and in another moment or two there were wild screams of excitement, for up from the southeastern horizon came the drifting shadows of a herd of clouds. It was a miracle! It did not matter that every Mandan knew that the wind from that quarter was nearly always rich with clouds. What was important was that the magic stone had changed the wind and loaded it with clouds. As the first ecstasy of the Mandans on the roofs rang out through the air and then sank to silence, while they watched the clouds rolling toward them on the storm wind, the voices of the working women came far and faint from the corn fields.

I understood prayer then as I had never understood it before. Now the clouds were a third of the way across the sky, and it was certain that Stone-That-Shines had triumphed. Even if not a drop of moisture fell, still he had brought such a host of clouds that his fame was fixed and established upon a granite foundation. You may be sure that he did not overlook this opportunity. He stood there with the blessed bright stone raised and bathed in the redness of the dying sun, flashing like a dark eye of flame.

Very strange glass, it seemed to me. And very strange it seemed to the good Colonel also. He stood beside me, staring and staring, with his heart in his eyes, and I knew that he would have given a great deal to see that stone in his own hand and to learn from what place it came.

But there was really not a great opportunity to think about our own affairs. The coming of that sweep of clouds occupied our minds. Now, beneath the coming clouds, we could see a great shadow trailing across the face of the earth, very like a garment of rain. And rain it seemed that it must surely be.

Stone-That-Shines was in ecstasy. He danced about on the roof, brandishing his spear at the skies and shouting: "Speak to me, wind! You hear the voice that calls to you. You know the strength of the medicine which has brought you up from the edge of the world. Speak to me, now, and let the people hear that the voice of Stone-That-Shines is known where the...."

Here his eyes were startled by a flash of lightning that ripped through the center of the clouds. Immediately afterward there was a thick boom of thunder that rolled across the awed and delighted town of the Mandans.

What a shout was raised. Instantly the crowd was quiet again, for fear lest they should miss any of the words of Stone-That-Shines. He had words for them, too. He was commanding the lightning to fall and the rain to descend. He was ordering the earth to be made as wet as a blanket dipped in the river. He was announcing to the corn in the field that it might drink until its roots were lost in the mud. He was telling the nation that he would have the rain descend until they came to him and bade him stop the storm. For these things were easy for him, and he would not fail to direct that storm exactly as though it were a horse, with his bit and bridle on its head. He was in such a frenzy that those Mandans did not dream of disbelieving him, and with the storm approaching we could not help but half believe him, also.

The sun was almost down now, but, before its upper rim dipped out of sight, the first rattling volley of big raindrops came down on the town and raised the sharp, alkaline scent of moistened dust. It was the final triumph for the young warrior who had been chanting and shouting and dancing all day on the top of the roof of the medicine lodge. He stood there now with triumph on his face, dropping everything except the magic stone, while he held up his hands and welcomed the coming of the rain. It was a grand moment for him, the grandest that could come to an Indian, I suppose.

From this time on he was medicine of the very biggest and most useful order, and it was specially noteworthy that he would never have to make rain again. That task would be left to other young men of the nation who wanted to make a reputation for themselves. The great point with Stone-That-Shines was that he had apparently been so sure of his medicine that he had been willing to venture himself as a sacrifice, in case his magic did not work.

The sky was dark with black clouds, cracked in a hundred places with lightning strokes. The rain came sluicing down in torrents. Stone-That-Shines let it fall on him. He laughed, still holding up his hands, thanked the rain, called it his friend, and blessed it. When he finally came down from his high post, his head was in the sky, and he had the air of a man who had really been talking with the gods.

The beautiful part of it was that he was the last person in the town to think that he had been working a hoax. He was so elated that his head hardly knew where his feet went, but, if he were a little proud, the rest of the Mandans were perfectly willing to excuse him — particularly the women who could go out to work on their blessed corn fields the next day without raising mere choking dust with their hoes.

Chapter Seventeen

THE RESCUE

That storm was a real one. On the prairies, where the wind has a chance to get a running start over several thousand miles of open going, it gets to be a tyrant. I have seen the wind blow on the plains until we had to lie flat on our faces. I have seen it blow so hard that I wondered how the brush could stand up against it, and I have actually seen shrubs torn up by the roots.

It was one of those storms that came smashing and crashing about the Mandans. Every gust of wind carried a burst of lightning to show it the way, and a few tons of rain or hail by way of ammunition. The houses were drenched; the narrow alleys were turned into deep trenches of mud; and then the water began to rise in them. Here and there were obstacles and little obstructions which dammed up the flow of the rain water and raised its surface above the level of the entrances of the houses. The muddy flow began to wash in over the floors.

It should have been a very simple thing to open the streets and clear out the obstacles, or to block up the doorway and keep out the flood. But the Mandans didn't look on the matter in this light. They felt that this thundering out of the sky had a meaning. Someone was extremely angry with the Mandans, and he was talking about what he intended to do to them. While his thunderous conversation continued, a wise Mandan should cover his head with a blanket and pay strict attention to the welfare of his spirit — which might be about to start on a long journey for the Happy Hunting Grounds. As a matter of fact, the great boobies in our lodge sat about with stricken faces, and Sanjakakokah, who was the greatest man in the house and who should have set an example of *sang froid* for the rest, turned as yellow as an apple and sat in a far corner, hooded in his robe. He was more like a scared girl than like a celebrated warrior.

The Colonel and I looked these Indians over, and I was apt to smile at them, but The Colonel warned me not to. He said that a frightened man will seem to pay no attention to mockery during the period of his fear, but afterward you learn that every jibe has gone down to the bottom of his soul.

So I mastered myself as well as I could, but it was certainly a ridiculous sight. Most of the braves in our lodge had crept into their own little bedrooms with their families, but, every time the wind reached down its hand and shook our solid lodge, you could hear a chorus of moans. An extra hard blast was sure to bring two or three out from their places of refuge, for fear lest the house was about to fall down on them. Then a broad sword of lightning would be brandished over the smoke vent, and I saw even as great a chief as Sanja yelp like a kicked dog and jump back into his bedroom again. The only Indians in the lodge who showed the slightest nerve were the boys. These came creeping out from time to time, seasick with fear, and shoved some wood on the fire to keep it going. Then they scampered back to cover once more.

In the meantime the water began to flood in over the floor of the lodge. The Colonel and I went out into the alley, where we found that a big bank of dirt, which some of the little playing children had made the day before, was now acting as a dam. This we broke down, thus letting the water pass.

We stood outside for a time in spite of the whipping showers of rain. Certainly it was a grand night, with big clouds rushing across the sky and hurling thunderbolts at each other like a charge of shadowy giants. While we were standing, there was a chorus of voices squealing high with fear and then a ruddy flare on the other side of the town. We went to see what it was all about, and we found that the lightning had struck the lodge of which Harratta, The Wolf, was the head, and where his daughter, The Quail, lived.

It was a mass of tossing flames when we got there, and we found a few bedraggled figures racing here and there for shelter. The Colonel picked up a wet buffalo robe to shield him from the leaping fires. Then he charged through the entrance into the lodge to see that everyone was out of the place.

I didn't like the business, but I was so accustomed to following where he led the way that I went after him instinctively. When I crawled through the doorway, I found a regular trap of smoke and fire inside and the body of a little seven-year-old boy lying, blackened by a lightning stroke, in the very center of the place. The Colonel scooped the body up in one arm and darted outside with it. Then he returned and began to rummage here and there. We caught the buffalo masks and the shields and medicine bags, first of all, and hurried them out of the fire. We returned to see what else could be saved before the fire turned the place into an oven. While The Colonel was fumbling about, he pulled a buffalo robe off the top of a little mound, and there we saw The Quail, sitting with her eyes closed and her hands folded in her lap. I thought that she had been stifled by the smoke or killed by a touch of lightning, but, when The Colonel shook her by the shoulder, she opened her eyes and blinked at him. She was simply paralyzed with fear, and she had given herself up for dead.

"Get up!" shouted The Colonel.

"I cannot be saved!" said the girl. "It is because I am wicked that I am to be burned."

Somehow, that impressed me more than all the fright I had seen in the males of that town. For I could not help remembering the insolent calm of this girl as Ompah, the war chief, made a fool of himself about her. I could not help remembering, too, how quietly and assuredly she had looked The Colonel over when we first met her. But even her nerves gave way in this terrible crash.

The Colonel did not wait to argue. He picked her up in his arms and carried her out, and, when I came out behind him, pulling a load of rifles and bows and shields behind me, we barely got clear before the roof beams gave way and the whole upper part of the dwelling came down with a boom and a crash. There we stood in the middle of the darkness, watching the rain boil and hiss as it fell in rivers upon the burning lodge. A flash of lightning showed The Colonel with the girl, wrapped in a robe which he had picked up. She was lying against his breast with both arms about his neck, her eyes closed, and her lips moving. I knew that she was praying as hard and as fast as her Mandan vocabulary permitted. However, there was no sign of any other human being around us. If the rain had not soaked the surrounding lodges so thoroughly, they certainly would have caught fire from the heat of the burning house. But their owners would not have raised a hand to prevent the disaster. They would simply have scuttled away for a new shelter or sat, like The Quail, letting the wrath of heaven consume them.

The first thing to do was to dispose of the girl. Then the dead boy had to be cared for, and finally there were the medicine bags, which the Indians would have valued a good deal above the girl and even the boy. The Colonel carried The Quail to the lodge of Ompah, and, when we came inside, we found a picture that I'll never forget — the complete absence of every other human being except Ompah himself. He sat by the fire, stripped to the waist, streaked terribly with war paint, with his battle club in one hand and his pipe in the other. As he smoked calmly, he raised each puff and blew the smoke slowly out toward the vent in the roof.

Even I could understand. He felt that this was an attack of the evil spirits. He would be ready for them, and he would fight them as well as he could. In the meantime this pipe was lighted in honor of the good Father who guides Indians to the Happy Hunting Grounds.

You could see what had made Ompah the leader of his nation.

Even in this catastrophe he was head and shoulders beyond every other warrior in his tribe — except one, about whom I have to speak a little later. But even Ompah had not quite had the courage to leave his lodge and go to see what the storm was doing to his lady love. He would have sat there in his war paint while the flames put out the life of The Quail! Altogether, I decided that I would never again attempt to understand an Indian, either bad or good.

When he saw The Quail, another kind of lightning glimmered across his face. He jumped up and took her from The Colonel, making no end of a fuss over her. The moment she got inside that lodge, all of her fear seemed to leave her. She sat down and put wood on the fire and chattered away as cheerful as a bird on a branch in the sun. But no matter what Ompah did to attract her attention, it was plain that The Colonel had filled her eyes for the moment at least. She kept smiling at him in a way that would have made me want to put a knife in The Colonel's back, if I had been Ompah.

The Colonel paid no more attention to her than if she had been made of wood and painted a color. He said: "There is a dead boy whose body I have just taken from that lodge. Also, there are nearly a dozen medicine bags which we have carried out of the house. You must come to see them and tell us what we should do with them."

Ompah came willingly to the door of the lodge to follow us, but, as he reached that spot, a burst of lightning hung, quivering, like a seven-branched candlestick in the heavens, and the thunder exploded like a thousand cannon volleys beneath our feet. Ompah gave a moan and staggered back to his fire, so that the last we saw of him was the way he squatted cross-legged, grabbing in haste for his pipe to send up more smoke to the Great Spirit.

The Quail gave the chief one sweeping glance of contempt, and then she turned her head with her golden smile toward The Colonel. But he had already turned away and was trudging off through the mud.

Chapter Eighteen

STONE-THAT-SHINES

Perhaps you will say that all of this was exactly as it should have been. The Colonel acted as any white man should have acted — particularly as any white man with a betrothed sweetheart in Virginia should have acted. But I admit that I was a good deal worried. I knew that The Colonel was as fine a man as ever stepped. I also knew that he was just as human as the next fellow. I thought that he should have been just a little staggered by the beauty of The Quail. As I remembered her, sitting at the fire in the lodge of the war chief, she had been like a statue of gold and fire. The Colonel was a little blind. He failed to see her so completely that you would have thought that he had no ability to see the beauty of a woman. But I happened to know that he was a painter. That reflection troubled me a good deal.

There wasn't much time to cast about in the future and worry about such things, with lightning dropping in a broken cataract on that Mandan town and the wind shrieking. First we took the boy, and The Colonel found his parents. We had to dig them out of a lodge where they were crouched under a heap of robes, and I'll never forget the scream of the young mother when she saw the dead body and began to kneel over it. There was enough grief in the father of the boy to counteract his fear of the storm to a certain extent. He was even able to raise his head and watch the flicker of the electricity in the sky beyond the smoke hole without blanching.

He said: "This is the will of the spirits. We could not have helped him. He is dead, and the medicine that Stone-That-Shines worked is the thing that has killed him. For that, I shall talk with Ompah, and we shall find out what justice is in the tribe!"

This gave me another sidelight on this storm. It enabled me to understand a bit better why it had so completely paralyzed the best braves among the Mandans. Any big wind and big rain is a very impressive thing to the Indians, the direct representation of the powers of the air and of the afterlife. But this storm was something extra. It was the very definite result of the magic of Stone-That-Shines.

The whole nation had been able to stand about and see Stone-That-Shines raking up storm clouds out of the sky where there had been no clouds at all before. They had seen him working with a dreadful medicine, so big that presently the unwilling rain came rushing in darkness out of the southeast. And now the spirits that lived in the storm, and whose breathings the storm clouds were, had become enraged, and they were trying to find the man who had forced them to come this great distance to the north and west. They were probing at the earth with their hands — and those hands, of course, were the streaks of lightning! As the idea entered my mind, everything was more or less explained, and I no longer despised the Mandans quite so thoroughly.

We turned back to the burned house, took the medicine bags into the nearest lodge, and, feeling that we had done the duties that had been before us, we started back for our own lodge.

I said that there was one man in the city of Indians who had even more courage than the war chief, Ompah. We met him as we strode along, with the wind harrying us from behind. He was staggering against the wind, head down. So it was that he did not see us, and the next moment a dreadful hand of fire reached out of the sky and threatened to tear the earth up by the roots.

The Mandan dropped to his knees in the mud with a groan of terror, and we saw that it was Stone-That-Shines himself. In the darkness that followed, we could barely see him rise again and shake his spear

97

at the sky. We heard him muttering through his chattering teeth, now and then forcing out a weak imitation of a battle shout, while he chanted: "Here I am, wicked devils! I am the man who brought you here. I am the Mandan whose medicine was so strong that you could not stay away. You would have been glad to lie in the blue sky of the southland, but you heard me calling, and you were forced to come to me. Now you are in a great rage. You reach for me out of the sky. You cannot find me, and so you break and kill in my city. But here I am. Take me then. I am not afraid! I am Stone-That-Shines! Do you hear me? Find me, if you dare. Take me, if you dare! I am Stone-That-Shines! I have the great medicine that brought you here. Now I tell you to go! Go back. You have rained enough! I do not want you here any more! In the morning, be...."

The lightning cracked the heart of the sky, and the thunder wrapped the whole world in a vast noise. Stone-That-Shines, when this vast noise flooded his ears, went staggering backward, and by that same flash of lightning he saw The Colonel, looking a good deal bigger than human, I suppose, with the buffalo robe half torn from his shoulders by the force of the wind.

Stone-That-Shines knew, in that moment, that his voice had been heard only too well, and that one of the wielders of the lightning flashes had dropped down on earth, preparing to blast him into a thousand bits of smoke and rubbish. But he was brave, and I mean just that. Staggering back until his shoulders hit the wall of the lodge, he snatched up his spear and waved it over his head. He made his shield firm, and he called out to us to come on against him, if we dared, but to leave his scalp on his head if he died, because scalps could not mean anything to spirits, whereas there was nothing quite so important to a Mandan.

It sounds pretty absurd, when I repeat it in this way, but there was nothing ridiculous about it at the time. It took my breath with a thrill. There were not many voices that could have been raised to sound above the crashing thunder. But, when the screaming challenge of

Stone-That-Shines died away, The Colonel opened his throat and cried that we were not spirits, but friends to the Mandans — the white men who had come to this city the day before.

The idea seemed to sink in on the frenzied brain of Stone-That-Shines by degrees. Finally, still with his spear poised, he made a few steps toward us, until a flash of the storm showed him The Colonel's fine smile. Then, when he was sure that we were friends indeed, I saw him reach through the darkness and clutch the hand of The Colonel.

"If you are not spirits," he said, "but only white brothers of the Mandans, how do you dare to stand out in this storm which I raised and which has already brought death to us?"

For my part, I should have laughed at him and told him to buck up, because the silly spirits, of course, did not have a thing to do with the matter. But The Colonel was ten thousand times wiser than I about such things. And he said to Stone-That-Shines: "Your medicine was so very strong that it did call up the spirits!"

"Yes," said the poor Indian, groaning. "I hear them stamping on the floor of the sky and shouting for my death."

"It seems to me," said The Colonel, "that you forget that I have not offended the spirits. And neither has this boy, who is my friend. So we are not afraid to walk out in the night."

This explanation may have made us seem a good deal less wonderful, but it gave the Mandan a key to the situation and to our mysterious courage. "Ah," said Stone-That-Shines, still gripping The Colonel's hand and almost leaning against him, "this is a sad night in my life. The son of Little Antelope is dead. The spirits who came to find me, and who could not or dared not attack me, have stolen his son away instead. He lies dead from the touch of their hands. He was burned in the lodge of his father, so that they will not even have the comfort of laying him away for the long sleep and the trip to the other world."

"That is not so," said The Colonel. "Because we carried him out from the reach of the fire with our own hands, and we know that his father and mother now have him on their knees."

Stone-That-Shines was delighted. He forgot half of his dread of the storm, at once exclaiming: "That is very good! That is very brave, too! I do not know of another brave with courage enough to stand in the same spot where the spirits have already struck down one man. Besides, now that they have his body to bury, I shall not have to pay half so much because of his death!"

Yes, there you are with the complete picture of that superstitious lot. Having raised the storm with his silly dancing and prancing, he was responsible for every drop of water that blessed the corn fields, and he was also responsible for every iota of harm that the storm accomplished. If he had goods enough, he would have to repay the Indians who had lost their lodge. There were only two things which could not be restored — a burned body which had received no burial rights and the medicine bags to which the mysterious elements in a warrior's soul were half committed. But we had rescued those things from the fire, and for everything else, even up to the life of the boy, money would pay if the young brave only could get enough of it.

Chapter Nineteen

THE STORY

I believe that poor Stone-That-Shines had about decided that life would hardly be worth living, if he tried to remain in the tribe, because he would have so many enemies who would be keen to take his life at the first opportunity. But he cheered up a great deal when he saw that his crimes could all be classed under the head of property losses. What chiefly burdened him now was a wonder how he would be able to stop this storm that threatened to overwhelm the entire town before morning, unless the violence of the wind and the rain fell away a little.

When he expressed this idea to The Colonel, the big man said: "It was the shining stone that brought up the clouds when all of your dancing and talking and medicine had failed, and so it will be the stone that will send the clouds away again. Come to the lodge where we are. Take the stone from your medicine bag and hold it up so that the spirits of the storm can see it."

This seemed to me such a transparent device that I grew a little hot with shame for The Colonel. I did not think that the Mandan would fail to see that The Colonel's idea was to get a good look at that stone at close range. But suspicion was not in the mind of Stone-That-Shines at that moment. He straightway turned around with us, and we all went back to the lodge where The Colonel and I were living. There was not a soul to mark us entering the lodge. We got a bit of dry wood that burned well by itself, when it was taken from the fire, and this we stuck up in the corner of the little skin-headed alcove that contained the bed of The Colonel. There the three of us squatted, and Stone-That-Shines lifted his head and stared at the slanting roof above him. We could just make out the fire-lit rain of the smoke vent in the center of the ceiling.

"Could the spirits hear me?" he asked The Colonel. "Should I not be standing out in the open?"

"Why, brother," said The Colonel, "the spirits have an ear sharper than the ear of a wolf, have they not? They hear better than a grizzly bear. Did they not hear you calling when they were far off in the southland?"

"It is true," said Stone-That-Shines, as naive as any little child. "But there is such a shouting of wind...."

He cringed, in spite of himself, as the thunder beat around the lodge like ten thousand great carts rolling over a bridge and dumping their loads with one united roar into the hollow of the cañon beneath.

"The spirits shout, to be sure," said The Colonel as grave as a statue. "But you observe, my friend, that they cannot help but listen to your voice, which is the voice of the magic stone, and, if they were to see that stone again, I think they would be afraid to stay here. If they saw the face of the stone, which is stronger than they, and which called them up from the south, and, if you told them to go away, you may be quite sure that they would have to hear, in spite of themselves, and that they would have to obey."

I began to think that The Colonel was almost a rascal, but, after all, I suppose that there was no really better way to have a look at the stone. It was better, at least, than knocking the Mandan down and stealing the thing from him. Stone-That-Shines listened and was half convinced. But still this matter of showing the stone again was a serious thing with him. He had brought it out in the middle of his wild ranting on the roof of the medicine lodge, when he was worked up to an hysteria of passion. And see what the production of it had brought upon the town!

"You must know, Standing Elk," he said — for that was the name

102

which the Mandans had given The Colonel because of his great size, just as they called me, half in mockery, Little Thunder, on account of my scowling face — "you must know that this medicine is so strong that, when I show the stone and ask it to send the spirits away, they may have to obey, but they may be thrown into so great an anger that they will tear me and this whole city to pieces." He shuddered and closed his eyes.

"Listen," said The Colonel, "do you think that the spirits are not using their whole strength at this moment?"

The wind gripped the heavy, low-built house and made it quake to its rain-soaked foundations.

"It is true," whispered the young warrior. "They cannot do much more to us than they are doing now."

He fell into a fit of musing once more, coming out of it to stoop and scoop up a bit of dust on the floor — for the water had not reached this far in its progress through the house. This dust he threw rapidly from one hand to the other, and then blew upon it lightly. There remained three tiny stones, hardly large enough to see, except that the torchlight glinted upon them — tiny beads of brightness no larger than the tips of needles.

"Very well," said Stone-That-Shines, throwing the little pebbles down, "the medicine that I make tells me to do what you wish."

You see, it hung upon a very little thing. If luck had placed two, or one, of those bits of stone in the dust which Stone-That-Shines had just winnowed, we would not have had another glance at his big medicine. Stone-That-Shines went slowly about the work of getting at his stone. Finally he stopped altogether in his business of opening the sacred medicine bag, saying over and over that it was bad to call out the spirit twice in a single day. I felt my hopes take wing.

The Colonel was in despair. He bit his lips, but he could think of nothing. Therefore he began to make frantic and covert gestures to me to make me try my hand. I had to do something, so I said: 'There is no medicine in all the world like this medicine which you carry,

Stone-That-Shines. Was it sent to you by the Great Spirit in the beak of some giant eagle? Or did you go out and manage to find it, traveling a great distance?"

He raised his head and smiled. I had struck on a lucky theme.

"It was a dream that took me by the hand and led me to the stone," he said.

"Ah," I said, "the thunder grows a little fainter the moment that you talk of the stone that shines!"

He listened. The thunder smashed louder than ever around the lodge, but Stone-That-Shines's mind was already wandering away with his dream, and the noise of the storm did not seem so dreadful to him. "Very well," he said. "It is true that the spirits hear me speak, and they answer me less loudly. Shall I tell you of that dream?"

"Yes," we said in one voice, and The Colonel blessed me with his eye for having hit on this theme.

"When I went away from the Mandan city, I was a boy and wished to be a brave," said Stone-That-Shines. "I had no name, except to my mother and father. Like all the other young boys, I had no name. I went to the west a great distance, and I laid down a track where the buffalo walked nearly every day. It was worn so deep that the stones had turned to dust under their hoofs. I made up my mind that I would have my dream here and see what spirits would come to me. So I lay down there and spent one day on my right side and one day on my left side. On the third day a wolf came and scented the wind above me and below me. But he was fat, and, besides, he dared not attack me because I was not meant for him. I thought at the first that this was my token, and that the wolf had come to me from the spirits, for I was so weak that my head went around and around when I tried to think. But still I decided to lie there for another night and see what might happen in my dreams. Then I did as I had decided. I lay there the whole of the next night, and finally a dream came to me.

"I was burning with thirst, for I had drunk no water and tasted no food for three whole days. It seemed to me that I waked out of my sleep, and I heard a voice like the voice of a river in front of me. I ran and found my legs very light. I ran straight before me, and in the middle of the day I came to a great white water running north, and the water said to me:'Come!'

"Out of this dream I wakened. I stood up and tried to run, but all I could do was to walk slowly forward. It was a hot day, and the sun burned me. I thought that I should die, but I kept on, and at noon, when the sun was just over my head, I came to the edge of a great river, just as in my dream, and the water was running north.

"I saw a lame rabbit by the edge of the water. And I could have killed the rabbit and eaten it, but I would not eat and drink so long as the river was roaring at me to come to it. I wondered what it meant. I did not know whether I should step in and swim, or whether I should make a raft and float down the stream until I saw the wonderful thing toward which I was surely being led.

"At last I saw that there was much dead wood along the banks, and I took the best of the logs and tied them together with green withes of vines along the bank. There were rich red berries there also, and I was hungry. Many times I found myself stooping toward the water to drink. But I knew that I was meant for some great thing, and that I must neither eat nor drink until I had seen it."

Here the lightning flashed so vividly and so close that it seemed to thrust its white hand into the very lodge where we were. Even The Colonel shrank a little, and there was a chorus of howls and groans all around us, but Stone-That-Shines was carried away in an ecstasy, and he merely lifted his head a little higher and looked around him calmly.

Chapter Twenty

MORE MAGIC

"When I had made my raft," continued Stone-That-Shines, "I launched it on the river, and that was a great work. It was not a very big raft, but I was dizzy and sick with hunger. Yet, I got it on the water at last. The current took hold on it, and I went down a great river.

"The rain fell on me. It became dark. The wind blew. I was very cold and weak, but at last the morning came again. All my body was icy, but the thirst made me like fire inside. I would not taste the water because I still hoped that I would come to a great thing in my dream.

"The sun grew hotter and hotter. I came to a white water, and the raft was overturned. But I fell in a shallow place and crawled to the shore. Then I saw a white mountain before me, and at the foot of the mountain something burned like an eye of fire. I went to it, and there I found on the ground the stone that shines. I found it and knew that this was the thing for which I was sent by my dream."

His excitement had grown as he talked, and now he snatched from his medicine bag the glittering thing which The Colonel and I had noticed the day before when he stood on the roof of the medicine lodge. Well, with the sun on it, it had been one thing. But by torchlight it was quite another, I assure you. There was only the most feeble glitter, and we saw that the strange stone was simply a bit of very clear, transparent quartz. At least, that was what it seemed to be at the first glance, but, when the hand of the Indian carried the stone nearer to the burning torch, we saw a yellow gleam mixed with the paleness of the crystal. It was very apparent to me, and it must have been to The Colonel also, for he jerked up his head and sent a significant glance at me.

"Gold," said his lips to me.

It could hardly be anything else.

"I knew by the weight of that rock," said Stone-That-Shines, "that it was different from other stones. I knew by its flame in the sun also. So I made a medicine bag and put it in. I had hardly done that when a rabbit came and sat up in my path and waited for me to shoot it with my bow and arrow. For the spirit of the stone had charmed that rabbit. Then I went down to the river, turned my raft right side up, got in it, and the river whirled me away. I fell into a sleep. When I woke up, it was early morning. My head was still dizzy, but I had some strength, and I found that I was floating slowly on a great water.

"I left the raft and wandered back to the Mandan city, but I was in a fever. I hardly knew where I was or what I did, until some Mandan hunters found me, dazed, on the prairie and brought me home. Then I was very sick for a long time, but, when I grew well again, I knew that I had the greatest medicine that was ever brought to the Mandan people. Yes, and in my very first battle that medicine gave me three scalps! And you yourselves and all of my people have seen today what it can do?"

"Yes," said The Colonel, who could hardly contain himself, "but did you never ride back to the white mountain to see if there might not be bigger and better stones there?*

The young Indian smiled. "Does the spirit throw down magic in great heaps? No, it is put in single things only. But I *did* ride back to seek for the white mountain and can you guess what I found?"

"No," said The Colonel, breathless, "I cannot guess."

He moved the torch a little nearer, and we could both see that there was a vein of yellow almost as big as a man's finger running through that piece of stone. It made me jump, and it put a fire in the eye of The Colonel.

"There was nothing," said Stone-That-Shines. "There was nothing at all. Because, you see, it was a dream mountain. I was taken to it when I thought that I was awake, but when I was really asleep. I was made sick, so that I might be taken far away and brought back again by the spirits, and not know really where I had been. Perhaps that white mountain is a thousand days of journeying away. Perhaps that mountain is in the sky. Who can tell? Not I and not you, my white brother. These are things which a man can inquire into only a little way. Just a step from the door of the lodge, but there is a great, empty night before us."

He raised the stone higher. "Listen to me, stone that shines, you have brought up the storm from the southern sky. It has wet the corn fields very much. The Mandans will be very happy when they see that the prairie is wet in the morning. But now we have no need of any more rain. The rain has come with great lightning. The thunder stone falls out of the sky and kills our people. So send the storm back into the south, for you are strong enough to do this. I, Stone-That-Shines, believe that you can do it."

There was a wild burst of mockery in answer. The wind whistled around that lodge, and the *thunder stone* flashed above the smoke vent. Stone-That-Shines dropped his medicine back into the bag and gave the two of us a black look.

"I have made the spirits angry," he said. "Do you hear them shouting?"

Of course there was nothing to answer to such a remark, except to say that it was perfectly true they were angry, but it was because they would have to run away. Stone-That-Shines listened to us sullenly, half in fear, but the thunder was louder than ever. Suddenly the smoke was beat toward us in a thick, stifling billow.

"Look," said The Colonel instantly. "The wind has changed. It is blowing from another quarter of the sky, and your medicine is very big indeed, Stone-That-Shines."

The Mandan glared about him in sudden, wild hope and rushed

out of the lodge. We followed and found him standing in front of the entrance with his arms stretched toward the sky and a wonderful smile of delight on his features. He was bathed in a shaft of pale moonshine. Looking up to the heavens, we saw that the clouds had been torn apart in the center of the sky and were being rolled rapidly back toward the horizon.

I cannot tell you what a ghostly thing it was to see. Of course, I knew that a thunderstorm is apt to be followed by a change of wind. But there was something very uncanny about all of this. As I watched the storm roll back toward the south, out of which it had come, with the lightning still flashing in its rear and the thunder peals growing more and more distant, there could hardly have been a Mandan in the whole tribe who felt any more respect for the stone that shines than I had in my breast.

Stone-That-Shines watched this with speechless delight for a moment. Then he broke out with a war whoop and began to prance and dance, regardless of the mud that he sloshed up with each footfall. He had the stone out of the bag and in his hand in a twinkling, yelling: "Clouds, you have rained enough! Go back to the south! I command you to go and take the thunder stone with you. We have had water enough. The corn has drunk. You have done damage in our city also. Therefore, I command you to go!"

This was only the beginning, as he warmed himself up. By this time his shouts had brought a few people to the doors of lodges. They heard Stone-That-Shines; they looked up and had the testimony of their own senses. In a twinkling the news had run through the entire camp. The crowd came plunging through the mud, yelling with joy at this deliverance. They immediately picked Stone-That-Shines up on their shoulders and carried him to the medicine lodge. There the medicine man welcomed the youth with a screech of pleasure, and presently Stone-That-Shines was prancing again just where he had stood when he called up the storm at the setting of the sun.

The whole Mandan people watched the storm clouds stagger away

109

to their southern home, frightened by the voice of the young medicine man and hurrying to obey him. It was a great day for Stone-That-Shines, and it was a greater night. There was only one danger that threatened him. As we stood in the crowd, we heard a stern brave muttering: "If this Stone-That-Shines could bring the clouds and send them away again, why did he let the thunder stone strike the city and burn down a lodge?"

"Listen to me," said another. "When a man works such big medicine as this, sometimes it will overflow the hands that try to hold it. Or perhaps Stone-That-Shines thought that the spirits might throw their thunder stones, but that they would not dare to strike the city. As soon as he found out that they *did* dare, he stepped out and ordered the storm to go away. And you see that it has obeyed him."

That seemed to be fairly convincing as an argument for the moment, but I had an idea that the same thought would lift its head again and not be satisfied so quickly and easily when the relations of the dead boy got into the talk.

That was The Colonel's idea also, as we walked slowly back toward the lodge through a riot of dogs and shouting Indians. This was an event of such religious importance that, of course, no self-respecting Mandan would dream of trying to sleep during the rest of the night. We were not Mandans, however — heaven be thanked!

I only sat for a moment beside The Colonel before I heard him say: "You saw the thing, Christy?"

"It looked like gold," I suggested.

"Looked like it? It was! That stone was loaded and heavy with the pure quill. I tell you, Christy, if we can find that white mountain which the boy was talking about, we'll be able to sit down and crack the rocks like nuts and take out the kernels of gold. We'll be rich, so rich, Christy, that it will be a shame. We'll be able to go back and flood Virginia with money. And think of Martha Farnsworth."

Chapter Twenty-One

BATTLE

I would have left the Mandans at once, but The Colonel wouldn't listen to that. He pointed out that the prairies were a place of considerable size, and that casting about through them for a white mountain would be a devilish job. There were two ways that we could go about it. One was to find a river running north and float down it for at least twenty-four hours. The other was to cast about among all the neighboring mountains until we located the white mountain. Both of those methods looked extremely hazardous to us, apt to draw us blanks and nothing more. The Colonel insisted that we stay with the Mandans until he had a chance to extract a little more information from Stone-That-Shines concerning his dream — if there were any more information in him.

There was no talking to him at this time. He had been translated by a single thunderstorm into the greatest man in the tribe. Everybody respected and feared old Ompah. But what they felt for him was simply nothing compared to the awe and reverence which was reflected from every face when young Stone-That-Shines walked by. The first thing that mattered was to make the earliest and best possible use of this miraculously big medicine which the young brave carried in his bag. Their reasoning was perfectly accurate and satisfactory — to them. Any man who could call up the thunder and lightning at his pleasure would be simply a howling terror on the warpath, and the best thing to do, obviously, was to launch him at the head of all the men they could get together against the most formidable foe they could think of. When it came to picking out the most formidable foe, there was only one to be really considered. They might have enemies who were as brave or braver, and individually as big or bigger than the Sioux, but, considering numbers and all, there was no tribe on the plains that could compare for an instant with the Sioux. They so much outnumbered everything else that, if there had been any real sense and direction in Indian warfare, the Sioux by this time should have owned the continent west of the Mississippi.

So it was the Sioux that this little town on the edge of the river picked out for an attack, the Sioux, with all their hard-riding thousands of trained warriors. The Colonel was aghast when he heard of it, and so was I. We did our best to try to get something out of Stone-That-Shines before he started on the warpath, but there was not a single hope for us to get near him. He fasted for three days, touching nothing except a mouthful of water once in twenty-four hours. After that he was given a steam bath so hot that it must have parboiled him. The whole nation stood about and saw him run from the bath to the icy waters of the river and dive in. The shock should have killed him. Then he waded out, was instantly rubbed down, dressed by many hands, and carried back in triumph to the city. He had been purified so that his medicine, which had been so strong before, was now sure to have a doubly keen edge. After that there was a vast deal of medicine-making on all hands and particularly by Stone-That-Shines, who was now considered a prophet of the very first water.

Thus was all being made ready. On the one hand, the smoke of the medicine fires went up night and day. On the other hand, everyone was tremendously busy, burnishing up the few firearms that the city possessed, greasing and reworking their war bows, and preparing hosts of arrows. In the midst of this equipment, by a queer trick of fate, the very enemy for whom they were preparing themselves came and knocked at their gates. The Sioux, for whom they were getting ready with such thoroughness, came and offered their heads to the lions. It was only an obscure band of one of the divisions of the Sioux; nevertheless, it was a division which contained more warriors on the trail than the Mandans could possibly muster. I was sitting with The Colonel at the entrance to the lodge when the news first came to the town. A pair of boys came scooting in, yelling so fast that we could not make out what was said, but, from the confusion that started around us and by the comments of the women, we learned everything. The cunning and daring Sioux had crept up close through the hills, and, making a hurried charge, they had swept away about half of the total horse herd of the Mandans, a blow to the prosperity and the pride of the river people from which they would find it difficult to recover.

I saw the van of the tried warriors shoot off on horses and on foot to get to the big palisade which covered the city from all land attacks. The Colonel and I went with them, and we saw the Sioux sweeping back and forth across the plain, using their little, fleet ponies with a wonderful skill, because nothing on the plains was any better than the Sioux at horsemanship with the possible exception of the southern Comanches. In the distance we could see the band of captured horses, and we were thankful that Sir Turpin and Kitty had been kept within the palisade. Only the pack horse had been lost to us, though that was severe enough. The Colonel was in a fine rage, declaring that he would have that animal back or else its weight translated into terms of dead Sioux, so we got our rifles ready. There was a good deal of firing of bows and arrows, and I had my first chance to see Indian warfare. The Sioux were constantly in motion. Apparently what they wanted was to induce the Mandans to charge out and fight them in the open. For that purpose they would come swooping up aslant, deliver a long-distance volley of arrows and a few bullets mixed in, and then suddenly twitch their horses about at some signal and race off as though in fear. They were losing no men in executing these maneuvers. They kept pretty well out of arrow shot, and as for the rifles the Mandans had nothing but old-fashioned guns. There were very few of these, and they were atrocious marksmen. They did most of their fighting by yelling and screeching — particularly the women when they saw the Sioux cavalry trampling over the fine corn fields. However, the tune changed suddenly. The Colonel and I got our guns ready and thrust them through the palisade. At the next Sioux charge he said that he would cover a big chap with a host of feathers in his hair, while I was to take another important man on a dappled gray horse. When that charge rolled in, our guns banged. The big man of the feathers was slung out of his saddle and rolled ten paces, head over heels, a very dead Indian. I missed my man but got his horse, and they went down in another cloud of dust.

How the Sioux yelled with rage, and how the Mandans screeched with joy! I could hardly reload my rifle, my fingers were stumbling so with excitement, though I could hear The Colonel beside me saying: "A very bad miss, Christy. Now, nail that fellow!"

Two others of the Sioux had swooped down on the dead chief of many feathers, and, without dismounting, they stooped from the backs of their horses, lifting the bulk of him between them. Then they started off, dragging him, because it was a tremendous calamity for a warrior to be left on the battlefield, where his scalp could be taken by the enemy and his body left with no burial ceremony. Another pair drove for the place where my target was untangling himself from his fallen horse, and I was so excited that I didn't know where or how to aim. I simply covered the whole three, but, when I pulled the trigger, luck sent the bullet home, and my fallen man pitched down from the saddle of the friend who was helping him back to safety. In the meantime The Colonel had fired again, emptying one of the saddles of the men who were carrying the dead chief from the field. Here we were then with three dead men in front of the palisades, and the Mandans screeching and yelling with excitement. They were calling for Stone-That-Shines to come and lead them in a counterattack while the Sioux were still striving to carry their fallen man away.

Stone-That-Shines wasn't backward, either. He came with the cream of the Mandans mounted around him. In his hand he carried a lance, and at the head of that lance there was the glittering bit of quartz with the sun reaching through the transparent stone and flaming on the gold. It threw the Mandans into ecstasy. This symbol of power meant that they could not fail to conquer in the battle. I saw a big brave, whose horses had been stolen by the Sioux, start leaping up and down, screeching a prayer to the Great Spirit for a horse to ride in the coming charge. Then he saw that useless dandy, Bending Feathers, seated on his beautiful little pinto not far away, looking as calm and as handsome as ever. The brave gave a snarl of mingled eagerness and disgust before he dumped Bending Feathers onto the ground, jumped into the saddle, and got up in time to make the rearmost part of the charge as it poured out through the opened gate of the palisade.

Those Mandans went for the Sioux as though they were going to eat them alive, but they were striking at a feather. The Sioux curled away from the charge, and, as the Mandans slowed up to wheel, the Sioux charged in their turn. The Mandans curled off in their own turn, and here was the typical Indian battle under way without much advantage on one side or the other. I could not see that the presence of Stone-That-Shines and his magic stone had transformed the Mandans into particularly efficient fighting men.

Chapter Twenty-Two

THE HEROES

There was apt to have been no great amount of damage done in this screeching mass of red men, but there was a kernel around which the fight had to center. That kernel consisted of the three dead men whom The Colonel and I had put on the ground. The Sioux had managed to drag them off out of our effective rifle fire. But the Mandans had made them drop them, and so things got pretty hot around the dead men.

There was only one big factor that seemed big enough to decide which party should carry off the dead, and that was a formidable Sioux warrior who wasted little breath in shouting but who made a lot of trouble for the Mandans who came too near to him. He had a long lance, and he didn't bother with gun or bow and arrows. He was a hand-to-hand fighter of the first rank, and, when the Mandans came driving up, full of courage, he met them with the long, keen head of that spear and took most of the energy out of them immediately. He had what you might have called white-man courage, and in a hand-to-hand fight that sort of courage is always sure to come out on top. Since this broad-shouldered chief was running matters around the three dead men, it looked as though he would finally manage to get away with them, in spite of all that the Mandans could do. The Colonel got on Sir Turpin and said that he would have to get out and try his hand with that hero.

There was an odd interruption here, which astonished The Colonel and me and seemed to paralyze the Indians on both sides also. I have said that Bending Feathers, the Mandan dandy, had allowed himself to be dispossessed of his horse without making much trouble. He simply got up, brushed off the dust, and made himself as fine as possible. Then he stood among the women, looking through the palisade at the fight which was going on outside and cooling himself with his perpetual fan. But just at this moment the Mandan who had borrowed the pinto from Bending Feathers decided to distinguish himself by attacking the Sioux who wielded the long spear. It was the resolve of a hero, and he met a hero's end on account of it. The shower of arrows which he discharged either missed the other altogether, or else they were turned by the hardened buffalo hide of the shield. As the Mandan rushed closer, the Sioux drove the long spear through his heart. The pinto galloped beneath, until its reins were caught by another Sioux. The hero of the spear, catching the falling body of the Mandan, held him in mid-air with one hand and took his scalp. Altogether it was a dreadfully neat bit of butchery, and the Mandans howled with rage while the Sioux screeched with delight.

That seemed to be the turning point of the fight. The Mandans began to drift back toward the town, and the Sioux began to press more closely upon their heels. But here Bending Feathers made his first appearance as a warrior. He had seen his pinto captured by the enemy; no one, save Bending Feathers himself, could understand what that meant. I suppose that the pink and white of the gay little pony was just what he needed to set off his costume and make himself beautiful in his own eyes and contemptible in the eyes of the others. He gave a scream of pain, then he bounded through the gate. There a formidable old brave was just in the act of putting his foot in the stirrup when the thunderstorm struck him. He was sent reeling away. Springing into the saddle of the new horse, Bending Feathers started, like a streak, straight for the center of the fight. In ten jumps he was through the Mandan line. He went on, waving a war club which he had lifted from the saddle bow of his stolen horse. A perfect cloud of arrows whirred at him, but he went on. I saw two or three Sioux charge him, but he dodged them, working that little trained pony like a circus performer. He dashed straight on into the knot which had gathered around the Sioux hero of the spear who was about to cart the three dead bodies of his comrades away from the field. When he saw the rushing Mandan, he jumped his horse out to meet the new danger.

I haven't any doubt that Bending Feathers never intended to undertake such a job. All that he saw was his pinto in the near distance. But, since there arose before him an obstacle which could not be dodged, he went for it with a whoop. The long spear was thrust at him with terrible speed, but he ducked under it, swinging far down on the side of his horse like the most practiced warrior on the plains. He went by the spearman at full gallop, and, as he went, he clipped his enemy across the face with his war club. It flicked that strong fighter out of his seat as though he had been a cardboard imitation of a man and not the real thing at all. He tumbled head over heels, and, when they dragged him to his feet, he was more dead than living. That wasn't enough for Bending Feathers, however. He went straight on, streaking for the bright little pinto, and, as he went, he whistled. The little horse whirled at its master's voice and tried to come back to him. The Sioux who led him didn't want his hand encumbered when he had to face an enemy of the proved caliber of this flashing fellow. He threw the reins away and jerked out his bow. However, when he had his arrow on the string, Bending Feathers threw his war club. The knobby end of it struck the Sioux full on the body, knocking him to the ground where he lay, twisting and groaning, with more broken ribs than I would like to guess at.

The rest was easy for Bending Feathers. He had only to turn his borrowed horse around, and the pretty pinto came racing to his side, tossing its head, as glad as could be to have come back to him. Bending Feathers cantered for the town, and the Sioux gave him enough ground for ten men to have ridden through. They had tasted

118

his medicine and found it exceedingly bitter. I don't blame them.

That single-handed charge of Bending Feathers, no matter how it might be interpreted, was a very dashing and flashing thing to see. It stopped the backward movement of the Mandans, and it took a great deal of the starch out of the Sioux just at the moment that The Colonel played his card. He did it as one would have expected — perfectly. He went in with Sir Turpin snorting with eagerness, and, as he rode, he shouted in a bull's voice to the Mandans. Stone-That-Shines evidently thought that the time had come to put his medicine to the acid test. He swung into that charge beside us, and we three made the point of a flying wedge that caught the Sioux just as they were hesitating.

It was a very neat charge. The Colonel's rifle, at the head, brought down a man as we went in, and we carved the Sioux into two divisions. They had enough for one day. Each man forgot about bringing off his dead and wounded and remembered that he had a life which would serve for fighting on another day. As they turned their backs and fled, the Mandans closed on them, shrieking like fiends and turning loose a cloud of arrows. As usual in Indian fighting it was during the flight that the slaughter occurred. Twenty-two Sioux went down in the battle altogether, and I think that fifteen of these must have dropped during the flight. When we came back, the Mandan scalping was being accomplished with much thoroughness. The women and children were coming out to look on the results of their heroes' fighting, and the rest were busy doing war dances and praising themselves and the rest.

The Colonel came in for a big share which he deserved, but the chief credit, as you might have expected, was divided into two portions. The biggest one went to Stone-That-Shines. It was considered that his medicine had eventually given the victory to our people. Almost an equal lot of praise went to the man who had made the single-handed charge right through the center of the Sioux array — Bending Feathers. No one seemed to think that it had been simply

119

the maddened vanity of a dandy, seeing his chief possession about to slip from his hands. It was considered that this burst of daring was the direct result of the inspiration of the Great Spirit, and therefore Bending Feathers was all the more honored. He became *medicine* on the spot. It was quite amusing to see how he took the thing.

When we got into the town, he was the center of a group of excited women and children with a good many warriors, too, who were chanting his praises. Bending Feathers was occupied in going over his pinto inch by inch and learning whether it had sustained the least harm during the fight. When Stone-That-Shines stopped with two brand-new scalps to congratulate his companion in victory, Bending Feathers turned his back on the tokens of battle with a grunt and a shudder and went on with his inspection of the pinto.

When it came to the scalp dance, where each brave stepped into the circle and vaunted about what he had done, Bending Feathers refused to take any part whatever. He merely remained on the sidelines and stood in a cluster of the admiring and delighted women, as cool as a bit of fresh ice in all that excitement.

The Colonel made capital out of what he had done in the fight, however. He had brought down so many Sioux that every man in the Mandan nation was glad to call him brother, and he took advantage of this position to get in a little conversation with Stone-That-Shines. That talk, you may be sure, centered chiefly on the direction in which Stone-That-Shines had ridden when he went out to follow his dream. The Colonel learned everything that the new chief himself could remember, and afterward he and I talked it over, charting the positions in our minds. Now we were ready for the search.

Chapter Twenty-Three

A MARRIAGE TRANSACTION

We were all ready to start traveling on the big journey when Harratta, The Wolf, the father of The Quail, came in from the warpath, having lifted the scalp of a Crow who was wandering a good distance away from his home hunting grounds. Harratta was very happy with this tuft of hair, which had rewarded him for all his long labors on the march he had made, and he did a dance all by himself in the center of the city with plenty of admiration on all sides.

After that, the sensations came so fast that they fairly lifted the hair of the Mandans. The Colonel and I got excited, too, watching it all. In the first place, as soon as Harratta appeared and got his scalp dance out of his system, Ompah, the great war chief, came to call on the warrior and smoked a long pipe with him, mixing a few grunts into the puffs of smoke. After that Ompah returned to his house and ordered ten of his selected best horses to be got together. The whole ten equipped with some article of harness — whether a saddle or a bridle or some other prized possession — were led up to the lodge in which Harratta lived and were tethered close to the entrance.

It was the marriage price for The Quail, and the whole Mandan population turned out to stare at this nine-day wonder. From one to three horses was the usual price; perhaps four would go for the pick of the girls of a whole tribe. If she happened to be the daughter of a great chief, and therefore brought a slice of political influence to her husband, she might bring a top figure of five horses, but this was very rare and something to be talked about everywhere and for many

121

days to come. You could travel a long distance among the tribes before you got to a five-horse woman. But here was a staggering price of ten horses, paid down without preliminary dickering by the head chief of a tribe to a mere warrior in the ranks of his followers. Such a man as Ompah could have had a bride for the asking, and welcome, from any lodge in the city. But out he stepped with a truly kingly generosity and tied ten ponies at the lodge of Harratta. More than that he put some article of riding furniture on the back of each — three saddles, among other things. In the eyes of the Mandans it was divine, because generosity was always considered to raise a brave to the level of the superhuman.

The Colonel and I went among the rest to see the show. Then we stood about to see the sight of The Quail led in procession by her father to the lodge of the war chief. There were very few absent from the Mandans gathering around for the same purpose. But Harratta did not appear with The Quail. We heard a great deal of unfavorable comment. The Mandans thought Harratta, a shrewd trader, was trying to boost his daughter even above this unprecedented figure of ten horses, and there were murmured exclamations of disgust.

"You must know," said Sanja to us, "that Harratta is not a true Mandan." He went on to tell us that Harratta was a stray who had been picked up with his family on the prairie by a Mandan war party. They took them in and entertained them liberally, and Harratta was finally invited to come to their city, since it was obvious that he was an outcast. This had happened four or five years ago, and he had been with them ever since. Sanja did not know the real tribe of Harratta. The language which Harratta spoke when he was brought to the Mandans had not been recognized by any of them, and he had soon melted himself into the ways of his adopted tribe. Such adoptions, in fact, were very common on the plains. However, there was some excuse for a bit of sharp practice on the part of Harratta, for it was pointed out that he had lost many valuable possessions during the fire which the lightning had started in his lodge.

122

All these conjectures proved wrong. After a time there was a distinct murmuring from the Indians who stood nearest to the new lodge in which Harratta was with his daughter. Presently the word came humming to us that Harratta was flogging his girl unmercifully. A dead hush fell over the crowd, and we could hear the strokes of the whip. The Colonel was thrown into an agony. He wanted to go into that lodge and wring the neck of Harratta and throw his head to the crows. I hung onto his arm, talking as fast as I could, trying to persuade him that we knew nothing about the right and wrong of this thing from the Mandan viewpoint. Besides, perhaps The Quail deserved a little disciplining. She had always seemed a pretty high-headed sort to me.

"Red, black, or white," said The Colonel, "a woman is a woman, and a brute is a brute. How can the rest of these fellows stand around and let this thing happen?"

I had my way, and The Colonel did not interfere, though it cost him a lot of pain to hold his hand. In the meantime the Mandans began to whisper. Such a thing as a girl refusing to marry the head war chief of the tribe had never been heard of before. Besides, she would be the first wife and had a good chance of being the only one which the chief would take — which made her conduct all the more mysterious.

After that, out burst Harratta, with his feathers in disarray and his face covered with perspiration. He dragged The Quail behind him and took her straight to the lodge where Ompah was sitting in the sun, smoking his long pipe, apparently oblivious to the commotion he had raised. Harratta threw the girl down at the feet of the chief and made a brief speech at the top of his lungs. He said that he accepted the price which the chief paid. He was glad to make this honorable alliance with man as great as Ompah. As for the girl, she was a little refractory, but that did not matter. Ompah knew how to rule a whole tribe, and therefore he would know how to handle one woman. Then Harratta turned on his heel and strode off, patently washing his hands of the whole matter. He was much applauded as having played the part of a good father and a wise Indian who knew a good bargain when he came to it. In white society he would have been considered an unspeakable scoundrel. But standards were a bit different on the prairies.

Ompah stood up and raised the girl to her feet. She shook the dust out of her dress of deerskin and brushed back her long, dusky hair. She was the calmest person in that whole tribe. We could see Ompah, inviting her into his lodge with a gesture. If she stepped across his threshold, by that act she became his wife. Furthermore, he had the right to pick her up and carry her, since the ceremony was now left in his hands. Apparently he didn't choose to do that. He merely stood there, trying the force of words, and words weren't able to budge this stubborn girl. She merely smiled at him and past him, seeming hardly to know that he was speaking to her.

He had a big string of blue and red beads around his neck. This he took off at last and draped it around her throat. Then he made a gesture which gave her leave to go where she pleased, and there was a terrible groan of astonishment from the Mandans. I asked Sanja if Ompah would not go and lead back the ten horses, but Sanja said . that he wouldn't unless Harratta took the girl back to his lodge as a member of his family. The price had been paid, and Harratta had done all that could be expected from him to make good the price of the ten horses so far as the girl was concerned.

Now there was a new center of interest, of course, and we saw the girl go back to her father's lodge, walking through mutterings of disgust and contempt and surprise on the part of the braves. The women weren't so soft spoken. They didn't hesitate for words. The strongest language was the best on an occasion like this, and they used talk that would have made tramps blush like girls. Among their politest remarks they told her that she was a disgrace to her mother and to her father, that she was fit to be flogged from the town and turned loose on the prairie, and that it would be wise to tie her to a stake and set a fire under her. She marched on through them as if they didn't exist, and her calmness infuriated them all the more, until one long-armed hag grabbed her by the long hair and jerked her backward. It was nearly the last act of that hag on this earth, I assure you. I have seen lots of fast handwork, but nothing with a snakier speed than the manner in which The Quail drew a knife and made a pass at the other woman. There was a scream and a backward tumble. The Quail walked on serenely until she came to us. Here she paused and gave The Colonel a smile that was as plain as a three-inch headline printed in red. It said: "If you approve of what I've done, I don't give a rap for the opinions of the rest of this gang." Then she went on, leaving The Colonel fairly done up and leaning on my shoulder, gasping: "What the devil does it mean, Christy?"

"It means murder," I said, "unless we get ourselves out of this town double quick. I happened to see the face of Ompah when he saw the girl pause here by us. And Ompah is thinking up a worse storm than Stone-That-Shines ever dreamed of."

The Quail finally reached the entrance to her father's new lodge, but old Harratta stood at the entrance with his pipe in his hand, drawing long puffs and blowing them at the blue of the sunny sky. There wasn't any doubt as to where The Quail got her stony facial expression. There was her exemplar, standing in front of her. For a moment they just stared at each other. Finally Harratta said: "Squaw, where is your work? There is none for you in this house. All the room in it is filled."

Chapter Twenty-Four

GIFTS

There the thing was, tied in a knot that couldn't be solved so far as I could see. The Quail no longer belonged to her father. She would not go to the man who had the legal right upon her. There was no teepee in the village that was open to her. What would happen now?

I looked at The Colonel. He had closed his eyes like a man in intense pain, and his forehead was wrinkled with suffering. Then he said to me: "What is she doing, Christy? I can't watch her. Confound her, I can't make myself see what she's doing."

"She's not coming back here," I told him. "She's going off through the town as calm as you please."

"And where will she go?" The Colonel groaned.

I gave him a quick glance and a mighty anxious one. "Where she goes doesn't matter to us," I told him. "I hope that *we* don't have to take the burden of responsibility for her."

"Oh, Christy," he said, "you have a heart of stone. A heart of stone."

"I hope that it's no stonier than yours," I told him. "Because, if yours should be too soft, now, it would just about mean the finish of the pair of us. Be hard hearted, Colonel, if you want to wear your scalp back to good old Virginia."

"Right," he said. "As usual, you are right, and I'm a blithering idiot. Besides, I have someone else to think about...someone else to think about!"

I was glad that he had not made up his mind to be foolish, but I

126

didn't like the way that he had to argue with himself. I would have been gladder to see him come to the same conclusion by instinct. I tried to drop the thing out of my head and cross no bridges whatever until I came to them. I hurried about the preparations for our departure as fast as I could.

"We have to give things," said The Colonel to me. "That leather coat of mine, and your old one...we could give those away. And then...I think that we might part with one of our guns, eh? Besides..."

"Colonel, you leave it all to me."

I was frightened to death, hearing him carry on like this. Why, he would have had to have a whole cartful of stuff, if he started out making presents on a scale like this. I had another plan. We had a few beads, which I had stuffed into the packs before we left Virginia. In addition, we had some other knickknacks which I had dropped into a junk bag from time to time — broken buttons, needles, bits of thread, and a pocket knife with one of the blades snapped off short — in brief, everything which The Colonel would have thrown away. I thought these things would do very nicely for the Mandans, if only I could persuade The Colonel to give them.

Suddenly inspired, I took some bits of paper and made a flat envelope for each of those little gifts. Then I laid them all out for The Colonel, with the name of each man written on the upper right-hand corner, all very regular and fine. I said: "You don't have to worry. I've got an appropriate gift for every one of those red beggars. All that you have to do is to make a speech with every gift that you give, so as to have those fellows think that you are extremely fond of them and that nothing but your great love for them could make you part with such valuable things."

I didn't tell him what the items were, and he didn't ask me. He only wondered what I could have got together that was so small.

"I didn't miss a single one, Christy?" he asked.

"I've given them more than they're worth. Besides, haven't we fought for those scoundrels?"

"Here's the packet for Four Buck Elk," said The Colonel. "It seems a bit slim for such an important fellow as he is."

It was a bit of broken brass button. But what difference did that make? It could be sewed on a coat, or, since it was bright and shiny, it would do to make the centerpiece of a necklace. There was no end to the possibilities of that button for an Indian. I explained that the gift was just what would take Four Buck Elk's eye, and, while I was about it, The Colonel took his pencil and knocked off a free-hand rapid sketch of that warrior. He got the main features — the long ears with the earrings that pulled them down, the low, flat forehead, and bulging jaws. He went on to the other envelopes and did the same for each. He put them in profile, catching the resemblances with a few sweeping cuts of his pencil. He said that it would keep him from making any mistakes when he handed out my gifts. Once he got down the list to Sanjakakokah, he hesitated, saying that he could hardly let old Sanja off with only a little, light thing such as this envelope, and so he laid out a single-barreled pistol for that brave.

When we were all ready, we started making our tour of the camp, and the first place that we went in was to the head chief, Ompah. He was very gracious, and he said that he couldn't take anything from our hands, because we had done a great deal for the Mandans and helped them in their battle "with the guns that do not miss, even when very young warriors use them." Ompah waved his hand at me without smiling.

Smiles or not, I had done more execution in that fight than *he* had, and he knew it. He listened to what The Colonel had to say. When the paper was handed to him, he took it, and his jaw dropped half a foot.

"Good heavens," whispered The Colonel to me. "See what you've let us in for! This stuff won't do for him. He's insulted! Confound you, Christy, and all of your ideas."

Here the chief woke up out of his trance and let out a yell that brought his neighbors piling around him on the double-quick.

I thought that The Colonel was right. He just had time to say to me: "Watch my back, Christy. We're in for it. I'll take care of them from the front, if trouble starts. I'll keep backing up, and, when we get a chance to break for the horses...."

Here he was interrupted by a howl from half a dozen throats. As many braves as could were crowding about Ompah and craning their necks over his shoulder to gape at the paper. And then Hying Dust screeched: "It is Ompah's shadow! And yet the sun does not throw the shadow that way. It is Ompah. Is not that Ompah's nose?"

There was a good deal of nose on Ompah's face, as a matter of fact, and The Colonel had done full justice to it. The rest of the braves could hardly talk enough about this thing. They didn't even think about opening that paper, which contained a needle that would be a godsend to the chief when he was having his next suit of deerskins made. That was altogether forgotten. All the hubbub was raised by the little sketch which The Colonel had made. Who could have thought of that?

Flying Dust asked in a voice full of awe if it would be dangerous for anyone other than Ompah to touch that picture. The Colonel was dumb and couldn't speak a word, but I cut in with: "It is not safe. That thing on the paper is Ompah. The Standing Elk" — you remember that that was The Colonel's Indian name — "has stolen one of Ompah's shadows and put the rim of it on the paper, and it will not come off. But if any other brave should touch that paper. ..." I stopped there, thinking that they might touch the paper on purpose to see what would happen. But, bless their simple souls, it never occurred to them to use such an experiment. That whole crowd simply bulged back and left a six-foot space around Ompah, and Ompah himself was a little too stunned to make conversation. Presently he walked into his tent, carrying that precious drawing — which was about as good as a fourth-rate cartoon — in both hands.

129

He came out again on the run, pretty soon. For there was a general shout of wonder as The Colonel handed out the next slip of paper containing the sketch of Fly ing Dust himself. That husky young brave nearly fainted when he saw his ugly, smashed-in face looking back to him from the slip of paper. Then he clutched it to his heart. He was the happiest man in the world. He told The Colonel that he was his father and that this medicine would keep him, Flying Dust, safe in battle, so long as the spears of the enemy could not come at this image of him.

Yes, sir, that was the sort of medicine that was tied by the Mandans onto this poor free-hand drawing. As soon as the idea was suggested, it never occurred to anyone to doubt its efficacy. From that instant on this was believed to be the gospel truth. The Colonel started to explain, but I stomped on his foot with my heel. Even that was hardly enough to keep him quiet. Honesty is a vice with some men, and The Colonel was one of those who were generously endowed with it.

We made one heart sad. When Sanja came to his turn and got nothing but a pistol — which was better than any other in the tribe's possession and worth at least four or five good horses, or a couple of hard-working Mandan wives — he couldn't contain his disappointment. I whispered to The Colonel, and to make things right he spent half an hour with a pot of red paint and a brush making a life-sized picture of Sanja in full war regalia. It had a profile that looked like Sanja, or Sanja's cousin perhaps. It was big; it was red; and it was *medicine*. When the sun set that day, Sanja was the happiest and the most envied man on the prairies — or in the world, for all that I know.

Chapter Twenty-Five

ON THE WAY

You may gather from this that, when we departed from the Mandans, we were fairly popular. I mean, The Colonel was popular, and, since I went along with him, I was not hated. Only, as we rode out of the town, leading our pack horses along with us, I passed Two Big Buffalo. He laid his hand covertly and significantly upon the handle of his knife, as much as to say that some time he would get at me and have our little argument out. I didn't worry about such a small thing as that — for the moment.

The Colonel had dodged a whole avalanche of return gifts by swearing that we intended to return to the Mandan town and that then we would be delighted to take whatever the kindness of the Indians suggested. He made me go along with him, even though I begged him at least to accept two or three of the best-looking horses — because horses were always handy on the prairies, and you couldn't have too many of them. He wouldn't listen to reason. As soon as we got out of earshot of the Mandans, who escorted us the first few miles out of the city and heaped our horses with meat, raw and dried, I told The Colonel what was on my mind.

He was very bland. "Why, Christy, should we take the possessions of those poor people?"

"Sir, there are twenty men in that town who could sell their goods ...white man's money...for twenty times as much as you could get for yours."

He bit his lip. "Damn it, Christy, don't bear down on me so hard,

131

will you? Let up a bit, old man. We were the guests of these people. You can't spend a weekend at a house and then let the host give you the brass knocker off his front door as you go away, and his pet riding horse as well."

"Sir, you've filled that town with medicine so big that they'll never stop blessing you!"

"Those sketches? Not bad things, in their own way," admitted The Colonel. "Very odd, Christy, how savages like that have an eye for art. Sort of an instinct for it. They recognized the merit in those sketches. There seemed to be something in my pencil when I was working. Inspiration, I'd call it. That thing of Sanja...not bad, I'd say. Good thing, of its kind...."

That was The Colonel's weak point, you understand. He was the most modest man in the world, until he got to talking about his art. Then he was apt to be a bit foolish.

"Yes," I agreed, "it's good as Indian paintings go. Compared with the rest of the paintings in that town, yours are first rate. Even the Mandans could see that."

The Colonel looked at me in a wistful way. "I have a suspicion that you ought to be whipped for saying that."

"At any rate, there's no reason why you should have turned down a thousand dollars' worth of horses, besides the trimmings."

"Well," he said, defending himself, "what could we have done with all that live stock in the first place?"

"Need them to carry the gold that we're going to bring back from the prairies," I said.

"True," said The Colonel. He checked himself and glared at me. "Is that intended as a joke?"

"Certainly not."

"I don't trust you, Christy. There's a wicked strain in that Scotch-Irish blood of yours. I can understand that you're swallowing a smile now and then, when I talk to you."

"We're getting a bit off the subject, sir."

132

"Curse the subject!"

"The Mandans?" I said. "After being their guest all this time, would you curse them?"

"Confound you, Christy! You know that that is not what I meant."

"I'd rather take a man's money and gifts than curse him," I snapped.

"All right," said The Colonel. "I won't go on arguing with you. You're like a woman, Christy. You talk too fast for me. I can't keep up with you. You and Martha would be a match for one another. Devil a bit of peace I'll ever have, unless I'm able to play the pair of you off, one against the other. Now let the Mandans go. As for their infernal gifts, perhaps I did wrong in not taking some of them. But, curse it, Christy, it's a pleasant thing to leave with the balance on my side and not on theirs, eh?"

"After painting their pictures?" I said.

"Well," he said, "no artist puts too high a price on his art."

"And fighting their battles?"

I closed my eyes and remembered those grinning, hideously painted faces, that swirl of dust, the screeching, the whirring of the bowstrings, and the trampling of the horses — the wounded and the. ...The Colonel and I were simply people of different sorts. What pleased him didn't please me, and he couldn't breathe in air that was plenty good enough for me. That was all there was to it.

We made a good long march on that first day, cutting off to the west in the direction which, as nearly as we could make out, had been taken by young Stone-That-Shines. Remembering that he had made his marches on foot, and even taking it for granted that a young Indian covers much ground, we felt that he could not have kept pace with our horses. We were guided by that, trying to figure out our marches according to the scale of an Indian in rapid-traveling trim. So we felt that about three days out we should come to the vicinity of the great river of which Stone-That-Shines had spoken.

We were worried. Even The Colonel's optimism began to fade a bit as we put league after league of the journey behind us. But, as he put it, Stone-That-Shines could not be wrong. He had floated north on a great river, and he had found a white mountain. There wasn't any doubt about that. The only thing that was to worry us was that we could not be quite sure about the warrior's estimates of time.

Time is only a comparative thing to an Indian. He will usually tell you that it is a long time when he is unhappy, and a short time when he is gay, though there may be more years in the happy time than days in the sad one. Who could tell exactly what had gone on in the starved and fever-burned brain of that youngster when he was scouting across the prairie according to the dictates of a dream? He himself had returned to the ground and striven to find that same river and, in spite of his memory of the place, had failed utterly to find a great river floating to the northward. That didn't hold out very brilliant hopes for us, and, of course, it had convinced Stone-That-Shines that the whole affair had been the product of a dream — that the stone had been placed in his hands by the blessed spirits. That was all very well for him, but we were whites, and we couldn't give quite so great leeway to the ghostly things on the prairie. We felt that there must be facts, and we were on the trail of a vein of gold of solid metal as big as a man's finger is wide.

We crossed two or three creeks before we were more than thirty miles away from the camp, but that was all the sign of water flowing north that we had during the first two days of our march. For another day we plunged vainly ahead and found nothing whatever in the shape of northward-flowing water. We knew that we would have to change our tactics, and so we sat down for a war council.

Chapter Twenty-Six

AN UNWELCOME VISITOR

We couldn't be really downhearted on this night. There was too fine an air stirring, and the sky was as clear as polished glass. Whether you wanted to look east toward the purple heavens, or west toward the red skies as they died, everything was beautiful, and, when the lower world turned black, the heavens whitened with stars.

"We must go on," said The Colonel dreamily, as he smoked his pipe and watched the little, twisted wreaths rise above his head where they were knocked to nothingness by the wind. "We must go on, my lad. Obviously we haven't passed the right river, as yet. Stone-That-Shines may have gone three times as far as he thought he went. Days mean nothing to those young scamps of Indians. We'll go on until we really hit a white mountain, eh?"

"I don't know."

"You don't know what?"

"I don't know about going on."

"Find the answer by *reductio ad absurdum,*" said The Colonel. "We have covered the ground that is behind us. The river is not there. Accordingly, we must go on."

I shook my head.

"Look here, Christy," said The Colonel, "you're disagreeing with me simply on principle."

"On principle, sir?"

"Just because you think that I'm generally wrong."

As a matter of fact, that was about it. The Colonel had a talent for making up his mind the wrong way. Still, it was hard for me to see anything wrong in what he had said this evening.

He went on: "Water flowing north. That's what we want. Haven't seen a sign of that, you know."

"We passed a creek that was running northeast," I recalled.

"Stuff!" he said. "A mere trickle of water. Not enough to float a raft such as Stone-That-Shines spoke of."

"It wouldn't have taken a big raft to float him."

"Now, Christy," said The Colonel, "you know that you're talking through your hat. If *I* had suggested that, you would have laughed and laughed. Be brave and confess."

It was true. If he had suggested it, I would have thought it a pretty silly idea. However, there was a difference now that the thing had been forced in my own mind.

He went on: "We crossed that creek before we were a day out."

I argued: "You can't tell how his days were spent. An Indian boy starting on the trail of a lucky dream wouldn't be apt to travel straight. Any rabbit that jumped up would be enough to make him run a few miles after it. Might have taken him all his time to find the creek."

"He had his sleep first," said The Colonel. "And he had that sleep in a big buffalo trail. Did we cross any deep trails?"

"We weren't looking for buffalo sign," I countered. "Besides, this all happened several years ago, and the buffalo may have changed their habits in these parts of the prairie."

The Colonel merely grunted, and I felt that I had been talking rather foolishly. The more I thought about the thing, the more I believed that we had overreached ourselves by coming so far. I suggested that we turn straight back and take a look at that creek.

"Waste of time," said The Colonel.

"We can't hurry this thing," I told him. "If we start trying to save time, we'll lose our chances at the gold. That's my feeling."

"What mountains lie yonder?"

"There might be a hill, though," I suggested.

"Mountain is what he called it."

"Medicine is what he calls the stone, too," I said.

"Christy, you don't have your heart in what you're saying. Admit it."

I wouldn't argue any more. I knew when to stop. If a person tried to comer The Colonel with an argument, he was sure to fortify himself against it. But, if you just threw in a strong suggestion and gave it time to work on him, he was more than likely to swing around to your way of thinking before the next morning. Besides, just at this time I heard the tramping of the hoofs of a horse, and I told The Colonel. We slipped away into the blackness, and, lying down in a patch of woods, we peered out and discovered the silhouette of a rider against the stars.

The horseman came straight in for our fire, dismounted with a careless swing from the back of the Indian pony — and there was the last person in the world that I wanted to see, aside from the Sioux. There was The Quail herself!

"Look what you've done," I said to The Colonel.

He groaned. "What I've done? Christy, Christy, I swear that I'm as innocent as a child. Never gave her the slightest encouragement to follow us."

I knew he was right, but I was too cut up not to want to take it out on somebody, and he was the only person handy.

"Watch her make herself at home," gasped The Colonel. "Stop her, Christy. Go send her away. Do something, will you?"

What could I do? She was calmly stripping the saddle from her horse, which she then hobbled and turned out to graze. Opening her pack, she took out some food and began to cook it over the fire. She had shot or trapped a rabbit, and now she was roasting the flesh on the ramrod of a rifle. The smell of that cooking was mighty good to us. All this time she made not the slightest effort to find us or to call to us. You would have thought that she hardly guessed we were within many miles of her.

"Oh, Christy," said The Colonel, "I'm a ruined man. No matter if I act a good bit better than a winged angel, when the news of this gets back home, the devil will be to pay."

"No," I said, "Miss Farnsworth has sense. But you've got to give The Quail marching orders. I'll wait here and stay till you've finished with her."

"Man," he said, "would you want me to do that? Go in there and face her all alone? You wouldn't ask me to do that, Christy. But we'll go together, eh? Show her a united regimental front and oust her, eh? What do you say to that?"

I knew that I'd have to go. Besides, if he went alone, he'd be too apt to weaken. That girl was too infernally pretty to keep from making a grown man a bit giddy. But I was a boy — and I wanted to keep my scalp where it was, growing safely on the top of my head and not blossoming at the belt of Ompah, where it was pretty sure to land if this girl stayed with us any length of time.

As we stood up, I said to The Colonel: "When Ompah and the rest of them get wind of this, they'll come hopping with their best braves behind them."

The Colonel merely stiffened. "Don't put it on that footing," he said. "We're not to be driven to do our duty, I hope. I trust that we can do what is right without being whipped along by fear."

I saw that I had started off on the wrong foot, and so I said no more except to mutter: "It's for her own sake, chiefly. What would become of her, tagging along with us? What would become of the rest of her life?"

"Yes," said The Colonel, "that's very true. Yes, what would become of her, poor girl. A lot better to turn her off onto the plains in the middle of this dark night. Seems hard, seems cruel to treat a poor girl like that. But what else is there for us to do?"

He was getting up his courage and making himself a little more like steel. I only hoped that there would be plenty of it in him. But I doubted. I was afraid of that Indian. She was too smart and too pretty to be trusted. Besides, there was about as much firmness and cruelty in The Colonel as there is in a great calf.

When we came up to the fire, that girl looked up to us and nodded as calmly as though we had left her there not a minute before. She went on turning the spit above the coals of the fire. I stepped on The Colonel's foot.

"My dear," he said to The Quail, giving me an ugly look, "we're surprised to see you out here."

She looked up at him, scanning him in detail, the way your eye moves when it goes carefully over an important page. Then she looked back to her cooking. Any other woman in the world would have had something to say, but she knew all that silence can do — which is a great deal more than words can ever manage.

I nudged The Colonel, and he growled back at me: "How can I talk when she doesn't even look at us?"

"You've got to."

"Look here," said The Colonel heavily, "you know that this won't do. The Mandans would not be happy if they knew that their young women were going around with white men."

"Oh," said The Quail. She turned her head and looked at me curiously, hearing me included as a man in this speech. That look upset me a good deal and made me hope that The Colonel would find some stronger language before he got through.

"Besides," said The Colonel, "Ompah is a great friend of mine."

The silence began to weigh on us.

"Will you answer me?" asked The Colonel.

At that, she looked up at him more curiously than ever. "Are you angry?'

"I'm surprised...and...."

"You *are* hungry," said The Quail. "This will be good for you, and after that you will talk more happily." She handed him the ramrod, loaded with fragrantly roasted rabbit.

139

Chapter Twenty-Seven

AN INDIAN MAID

She was a clever one. I never had doubted that there was a great deal behind her silences, and now I was surer of it than ever. I now had the proof. Of course, this would have been nothing if The Colonel hadn't taken the rod and its load of meat, but he couldn't think quite fast enough to see that he should avoid doing this. I suppose he thought that it would have been too impolite to refuse anything that a lady offered to him. He took the spit and tasted a bit of the meat — automatically.

"Don't touch the stuff," I said.

But I was too late. It was already in his mouth, though he handed the ramrod back to her at once.

"The Quail," she said, "is not a child or a fool. She does not taste food until the chief has eaten his fill. Besides, I have more meat here. There is enough for both, unless the chief is very hungry."

She got up and fetched another rabbit, cleaned and ready for roasting.

The Colonel shook his head. "I have eaten," he explained. "I do not wish to eat."

The Quail took back the rod with a smile of gratitude — the minx! "It is well, then, if the chief has eaten."

"Hospitable little thing, eh, Christy?" said The Colonel to me.

I only grunted: "Don't stop here to talk, Colonel, or the game is lost. Get her away."

"What?" he stated. "While she's still hungry, send her away like this?"

"She's able to take care of herself," I told him.

He turned back to her, much in doubt, and he found her sitting with the rod still in her hand. "Why don't you eat, child?"

"Standing Elk," she said, "I am not a child. I am a woman. See." She stood up and gave her coiled-up hair a pull. It showered in a thick shadow down past her shoulders, down past her hips, down and down in a great mass of brown-black to her heels. "Children do not have such hair as this," said The Quail, and she turned around slowly, so that he could see it.

I saw his hand go out in an instinctive gesture to touch the silky mass of it. Horsehair seems to grow on the heads of most Indians, but this was soft as down. Then she faced him again, and smiled. She fixed the rod in the ground and, taking the masses of that hair, she wove it together slowly, still looking at The Colonel and smiling and smiling. I never saw another Indian woman who dressed her hair in that way.

"Did you see, Christy," said The Colonel to me, "did you see it?"

"It's long hair," I acknowledged. "It would make a good scalp for a Sioux to get his hands on...as a Sioux will, one of these days, I suppose."

He did not seem to hear me. "There was a touch of gold in it, I thought. Like the gold of her skin, Christy. It couldn't have been just the reflection of the firelight, you know. There is gold in that brown. Well...who ever heard of an Indian with golden-brown hair, Christy?"

I didn't like this a bit, but I hardly knew just what to say.

The Colonel asked The Quail: "Why don't you eat now?"

"May I eat before the face of Standing Elk?" asked the girl, making a little gesture of apology with both hands.

"Of course...of course," said The Colonel. "Sit down and eat."

"The chief is standing."

The *chief sat* down with a bump at that, and, when he was settled and pulled out his pipe and jabbed it full of tobacco absent-mindedly, she waited until he was ready and then scooped a red-hot coal out of the fire and brought it to him. It's a trick, of course. You have to move your hand so fast into the fire and out again that the flames don't have a chance to bite into the flesh. And then, as you carry it, you shift it rapidly from hand to hand. But that coal was so big and so bright, and it glowed so in the darkness of the night, that it looked as though the girl were carrying a handful of living flame in her fingers. She dropped the coal carefully on the bowl of The Colonel's pipe, and, when the tobacco was lighted, she took it off and stood by, watching the glow of the tobacco with a critical eye before she threw the coal back into the fire.

The Colonel was staggered, and so was I. It was a very neat trick, and more pretty and graceful than I've been able to describe. "Let me see your hands," The Colonel said.

She held them out to him, and he leaned over them, studying them.

"Christy," he called to me, "there's not a sign of a blister! How do you make this out?'

"Medicine!" I said more gloomy than ever. "Big medicine, sir. A regular thunderstorm."

"Stop talking through your hat," he said. "Confound it, Christy, this is wonderful! And the skin is as soft and thin as a baby's."

He touched the palm of her hand, and her fingers furled over his like a flower closing. I saw that The Colonel was going into a trance, so I jumped up and threw an armful of wood and brush on the fire. The flames jumped up with a huge crackling and sent showers of sparks a hundred feet into the air. That broke the spell for the moment at least, and The Quail gave me an ugly glance as I stepped back. The Colonel looked a bit sheepish, too, partly recovered from his foolishness. He told The Quail to go ahead with her dinner. A mighty odd thing it was to consider how much she had made of the little affair of that ramrod loaded with roasted meat. But she had gained a pretty strong grip on things. I was only wondering how I could break up her position a little.

The fire, which I had built up, had done one good thing. It had snapped The Colonel out of his walking sleep. Now I saw that it had done a bit of harm, too, because it threw a great glare of rosy light over the girl lighting up that wonderful golden skin of hers, making her big, almond-shaped eyes more dark and shifting than ever.

There was a lot to see in her, and, take it all in all, I would have preferred to have her in darkness again. But there she sat, partaking of the bits of meat, one by one, daintily as you please, eating them without any of that show of greed most Indian women exhibit when they dine after their lords and masters are finished. You could see that she was enjoying this dinner a great deal. Yet it was not the meat that was feeding her alone.

I rooted around for something to do, and finally I picked up the body of the second rabbit. "Look here," I said to The Colonel. "There's a rifle bullet been through the head of this rabbit."

Even The Colonel got enough wits together to be surprised. "How did this happen?" he asked her. "Where did you get this rabbit?"

"It was running on the prairie," said the girl. "It stopped to look at me, from a great distance. And then I fired. So you see."

"Amazing," said The Colonel. "Where did you learn to shoot like that?"

He had missed the point altogether. I brought him back to it on the jump. "The main thing, sir," I said, "is where did she get the rifle that she used for the shooting?"

"Why, it belongs to her, of course," said The Colonel, wondering at me.

I groaned. "Did you ever hear of Indians giving rifles away to their womenfolk?"

That jarred him back on the right track, and he began to show a bit of concern in the correct direction. "Now, child," he said, "tell me where you laid hands on the rifle that killed this rabbit."

The Quail stuck the end of the spit in the ground and stood up with a laugh. "I shall show you," she said. She ran to her pack and scooped a rifle out of it. Then she came running back, laid it on the knees of The Colonel, and stood back with shining eyes.

I thought that The Colonel's eyes would pop out. "Isn't this the very rifle that belonged to the brave warrior, Flying Dust?"

"He paid eight good horses for it," said The Quail, trembling with happiness, "and he thought that it was cheap at such a price. It cannot miss. Even Flying Dust could strike the mark with it, though his eyes are dull. The Quail kills rabbits far off with it. And in the hands of Standing Elk it will be like the thunder stone!"

"But how did you get it?" The Colonel groaned.

"While Flying Dust stared at the medicine shadow of himself which Standing Elk made, The Quail slipped in from behind and carried the rifle away. Did you think that I would come to you with empty hands?"

Chapter Twenty-Eight

A HINT

To see her standing there, with her head thrown back and her eyes flashing and her breast rising and falling fast with her joy and her pride, she was a picture — the brightest picture of coming trouble that I ever saw in my life. I only gave myself time for one glance at her. Then I fell to work, stamping out the fire.

"What the devil is up, Christy?" queried The Colonel.

"Don't ask!" I said, "but help me get this fire out."

"Christy, Christy, what's in your mind?"

"Murder," I said. "Mandan murder is what is in my mind. Oh, the flames of this fire may be showing them the way to us right at this minute."

"What do you mean?" gasped The Colonel.

"Why, sir," I shouted at him, "when they find out that she's stolen that rifle, don't you suppose that they'll come hot-footed after her? They will, and they'll come raging mad. And when they arrive... they'll say that she stole the rifle for you, and therefore you're to blame for it. And after they've killed you and her, they'll carve me up and feed me to the dogs. But the main thing is to get this fire out and then to shift camp as fast as we can jump...after you've sent that girl on her way and her rifle along with her."

It was quite a hot speech, but not nearly as fiery as I could have made it. But, because I was cracking the whip to hurry him up, The Colonel decided to take everything slow and easy. That was his way — just contrary.

"You have a great deal to say, Christy," he said. "In the meantime you might leave the rest of that fire, because I don't want to catch a chill. Let us have a bit of light and warmth to think by."

I couldn't dare to argue with him after he took a tone such as this. So I just stood by and waited, wondering what would happen next. The Colonel looked that rifle over, and then he handed it back to her. Her face fell.

"You are not glad?" asked The Quail.

"Child," he said, "you are wonderful! I have never heard of a girl as wise and clever as you are, and as brave."

Why, it was like pouring wine into her. Her face lighted in a regular flame, and she panted: "Yes, I am wise, and I am brave. If he had turned and seen me with the rifle in my hand, he would have dashed out my brains, but he did not turn. I carried away the rifle for Standing Elk, and I have brought it to him."

Like a warrior boasting of a scalp — that's what she reminded me of, as she stood there by the flare of the fire. What amazed me was The Colonel's repeating—"You are a wonderful girl, and the bravest in the world!" — as if he didn't realize what all of this was apt to bring on us.

"That is not all!" said The Quail. "When the Mandans slept, and the dogs howled in the night, The Quail went back among the lodges. She went here, and she went there, and everywhere she found something that was good. She took it away, because she would not come to Standing Elk with empty hands. No...she brought to him such riches as these."

She hauled her heavy pack over and spread it out — and there was a collection of everything that a Mandan brave would value — a good new hatchet with a razor edge, never intended for cutting wood, I'm afraid. There was a pair of fine knives with closely decorated handles, beaded shirts, moccasins, and a lot of other loot, more than I can hardly name, winding up with a regular, man-size medicine pipe that must have broken some Mandan's heart when he missed it.

146

"There," said the girl. "It is all for Standing Elk. The Quail wants to see Standing Elk very happy. She has seen the greatest warriors of the Mandans kneeling in front of her. Ompah is strong in battle. He has killed many. He has counted many coups. But he could not enter the heart of The Quail. Then she saw Standing Elk, and her heart went out and lay in the very dust...right here...before his feet."

Yes, sir, she slipped down to the ground and smiled up at him, as much as to say, "You are the king of the world!" It made even me a bit giddy. The Colonel simply turned white. He picked her up and put her on her feet. Then he mumbled something and started off into the night. The Quail gave one frightened look after him and started to follow, but I said: "Come back here. Standing Elk wants to be alone."

She came back and sat down beside me, where I was squatted with my chin on my fist, thinking very black thoughts and wishing above everything else that we'd never seen the golden face of this girl. I was seeing, too, the white, fine features of Martha Farnsworth watching us out of the shadow. Ah, there was a lady for The Colonel. The Quail sat there for a minute, looking at me. After a time I had to fight to keep from looking back at her. Finally I had to turn my head.

She wasn't smiling but watching me very seriously. There was a drawing power in those eyes of hers, merry or sober, I can tell you. She took my hard paw in one of her hands, and a tingle went up my arm, spreading somewhere around my heart at the finish. I lifted her hand off mine and scowled at the fire again.

"You are not my friend, Little Thunder?"

"I'm your friend," I said.

"You are not," she said. "You do not want me to be the squaw of Standing Elk. Is that true?"

I wouldn't answer her.

"Well," she said with a sigh, "I must make you like me also.

Because, when Standing Elk thinks, he uses the brain of Little Thunder."

"No, no," I said. "A great chief like Standing Elk does not need to."

She only smiled at me. "I understand," she finally said. "He is a friend and a father to you. And you are a friend to him. Little Thunder is not old, but he is not very kind to The Quail. How have I made you angry?"

I couldn't stand it. The touch of her hand I had removed, but I couldn't remove the touch of her eyes or the velvet of her voice. "Look here," I said, "if I started to explain things to you, you wouldn't want to understand, and, even if you did understand, it wouldn't make any difference to you. But I'll give you some good advice right out of my heart. Will you listen to it?"

"The Quail sits in the shadow of the wise man and hears him speak and wonders at him," she said.

I gave her a side look, but she didn't seem to be smiling. I went on: "Very well, I'll tell you what I think you ought to do. Make up that pack of stuff that you brought to Standing Elk. Put the saddle back on the horse that you stole along with the other things and cart them off to the Mandans as fast as you can. They may be cross at you for carrying away so much loot from them. But they'll admire you and praise you when you show that you had the nerve to steal it…and then the generosity to bring it back. You take all of that stuff away from this camp and snake it along to the Mandans, and, when you get there, you leave the memory of Standing Elk farther behind you than you've left this fire. Let him go out of your head. Marry Ompah…he's a great chief. Or marry anybody else that you have a mind to. But leave Standing Elk alone, because you can't mix up the white chief and the Indian girl. It won't do. You understand me?"

She wasn't pleased. I could see that my words hadn't won anything from her.

148

"Very well," she said, and she stood up and snapped her fingers in my face.

"What do you mean by that?" I asked her.

"You are very strong with Standing Elk," said this girl to me. "You speak and you draw him this way, and you speak and you draw him that way. However, I shall be strong also. We will see who is the stronger, since you will not be my friend with him."

That was it. The clever little tiger had played her cards and hoped to win. She had lost, and so she threw up the bluff right away and let me see her as she was — dangerous, mighty dangerous! I knew then, as I looked at her, that my throat would never be safe from her knife, so long as she was with us.

"That's the way it should be, then," I said. "I like you very well because you're brave, and I like you because you're fond of my friend, Standing Elk...but you're a thief and a slippery bad one from my way of thinking. I wish you bad luck. I'm going to give you all of the bad luck that I can manage to bring your way!"

So I turned *my* back on the camp fire and walked off into the blackness, hoping that she'd fall into the fire and turn into a cinder by the time that I got back to it. I went on until I saw the looming bulk of The Colonel before me. He was striding up and down, up and down, just beyond the light of the fire, and with every step that he took he was cursing.

"All right, sir," I said to him, "I've come to report. She won't take the hint. She won't leave us, even after you walked away from the fire."

"What hint? What are you talking about?"

"I mean," I explained, "that you'll have to go back and tell her in so many words, out and out, that she has to pack up and leave."

Chapter Twenty-Nine

CHASE

It looked awkward to The Colonel, but he was about to give in and start back, I know, when a gun boomed across the silence of the prairie, and a bullet divided the distance between his head and mine as neatly as you please. We dropped to the ground, The Colonel grunting: "Give me your gun, Christy."

I shoved the butt of my revolver into his hand. At the same instant the glow of the fire behind us went out as suddenly as a winking eye, and The Colonel, as he poised the gun and looked around him, growled: "Thank heavens for that! They won't have the light to see us by. How did the girl get the fire out so quickly?"

It *was* a good deal of a miracle to greenhorns like us. Of course, she had simply thrown a buffalo robe over the flame. That stifled the fire, though it ruined a good robe. Yet, even if there was no candle being held now by which they could see to murder us, we were not in very good shape. How many Indians might be out yonder in the dark we could not guess. But there were probably quite a few. Here we were, cut off from the fire, where our guns were. And even if nothing else were accomplished, we could be turned adrift on the plains with nothing but a single Colt and its six shots between us and a wretched death.

A shadow moved dimly in the distance, and The Colonel tried a pot shot at it, getting a half-stifled yelp of pain for his answer. That, if we knew anything about Indians, would make them pretty careful. The Colonel was big medicine, too, and that would count in his favor and make them more slow and cautious. In fact, if he *hadn't* had such a repute, they would undoubtedly have rushed us at once and swept us out at the first charge.

There was a murmur behind us — a voice just barely loud enough to come to our ears, and here was The Quail, with her arms full of guns. She had slipped along from the fire the minute that she hooded it, and now matters were changed a good deal. From having one revolver between us, we now had a rifle and a revolver apiece, together with a reserve gun in the hands of The Quail. After what had been before us for a moment, this was like absolute safety and release from that danger.

The Colonel blessed The Quail in his own language and then in hers. But she didn't seem to hear him. She merely said: "Standing Elk waits here for the rest of the party to come. He wishes to make a great slaughter of the Mandans?"

"Are they Mandans?" asked The Colonel.

"Did you not hear the voice?" said The Quail. "Yes, it is a Mandan who tried to kill you. Now, of course, he has gone back to bring up all the others."

That explained everything with perfect satisfaction. One Mandan, of the band which had been sent out, had scouted along and come across the fire. Instead of going back secretly and at once to warn the rest of the band of the thing he had found, he had tried to get himself glory and a great scalp by murdering The Colonel. Instead, he had collected a bullet for his pains. But now he was off, riding as fast as his horse could run.

"Child," said The Colonel, "you have more wit in your little finger than we have in our whole stupid bodies. Of course, you're right. Christy, start moving."

We *did* start moving, and we went at a clip that would have amazed you. We should have made up our packs and got away as clean as a whistle had it not been for a most wonderful piece of honest fool-ishness on the part of The Colonel. He stopped by the dead fire and insisted to The Quail that she must leave him and cut off through the night and straight back for the Mandan village.

What did she do? Just the opposite of what any man might have expected. She simply wrapped a robe around her body and head and sat down there, like a mummy.

"They'll murder you when they come up!" cried The Colonel to her. "Murder...or worse. You know that their blood will be up. Get up and run for it!"

She wouldn't stir, and she wouldn't make so much as a whisper in answer. So The Colonel, with a groan, threw open her pack and sorted it as well as he could by the starlight. I had things ready and begged him to come along. But he remained there, sorting, declaring that he would have to sort out of the girl's pack everything that she had stolen from the Mandans.

Knowing that arguing would simply make matters worse, I slipped off Kitty and ran to help in that sorting, and so we got down to the handful of stuff that might reasonably belong to The Quail. The rest we put in a heap and left behind us the pony, too, which The Quail had brought along. Then he fetched her up and put her on the lead horse.

She didn't ask any questions; she didn't protest that she would just as soon remain behind there and let the Indians murder her when they came. In fact, she did *nothing* that a sulky white girl might have done. Instead, she gave one wild, little choked cry of happiness, and then she scudded off across the prairies behind us.

There was still no sign of the Mandans. The Colonel was for heading straight, but, since that was the direction that they would reasonably expect us to take, I begged him to drive straight back toward the site of their city on the river. He consented, though he said that we were simply running our heads into the lion's mouth.

We had half an hour of steady plugging, without a sign of Indians riding up behind us. Then we stopped to rearrange the packs, which had worked loose during our hasty gallop. The horses needed breathing, too. Owing to The Colonel's confounded sense of what was right and just, we now had a hundred and fifty extra pounds to distribute over our three horses that already had all they wanted to carry.

We kept forging away all through the night. I knew that these Indians, even the children, have a wonderful instinct for direction, and to keep us from riding in a circle I got The Colonel to let The Quail establish our line of march. She rode a length or so ahead of us, and that was a good thing in another way, because The Colonel and I were frightened enough to hurry those horses beyond their strength. The Quail had enough Indian instinct to make haste slowly. She kept the marching down to a jog trot most of the time, and, when we came to a rare hill, now and then, she let the horse walk. It made us nervous, of course, but we had to admit that it was probably wise to keep some strength for running in our mounts.

As soon as dawn came, The Quail halted. She started unsaddling the tired horse that she was on, and then we saw a little trickling stream of water close ahead of us. With the saddle off The Quail led her horse into the water and began to slosh double handfuls over it. Then she took it out and rubbed it fairly dry. After that, she wrapped herself in a blanket and lay down, tying the horse to the saddle which was under her head. It could graze in this fashion. If the tired girl fell asleep, the first snort or jerk of the horse would surely awaken her.

We did not wait to see all of this before we started to follow her example. After the long march of the day before, this night business had about finished our mounts. They were too tired even to look at the grass, but the cold bath cooled and refreshed them a wonderful lot, and, when we lay down, the trio was munching fodder and laying up the strength which we were pretty sure to need in our service that day.

That halt was two hours. The Colonel told The Quail and me to sleep, that he would watch, but, when I was wakened, it was by The Quail, and her tired eyes showed that she had done the double duty.

The Colonel lay on his side with his head pillowed on his arm, snoring soundly. The Quail already had a saddle on her mount.

When she pointed to the sun, I didn't need to be told that it was time to march. In five minutes we were on our way again, and it was a ridiculous thing to watch The Colonel apologizing for having fallen asleep at his post — and he a soldier. It was stranger still to see the way in which The Quail took this apologizing. She said: "Why should not the squaw watch when the chief sleeps? It is her happiness."

The Colonel was silenced. He cast a wretched glance at me, and I glowered back at him. The more I saw of The Quail, the more clearly I could tell that she was a rare one indeed — a jewel of her kind, if ever there was such a thing among Indians. She was as brave as steel, as true as a sword, and prettier, in her own way, than Martha Farnsworth would ever be — even when a painter tried to idealize her.

Still, the thing couldn't be. And the more I realized that The Quail was a queen, the more miserable the whole affair made me. I blamed The Colonel a lot, too. Not that he did anything absolutely wrong, but he certainly should never have let her settle herself beside our fire. If he wanted to leave her there, he should have carted himself and me away and forbade her to follow. That was the only way out of the bad corner that we were in about The Quail. Yet, here we were, riding for our lives, and the girl showing us most of the ways in which those lives could be saved. Nothing could have been worse.

We went on at a steady march all that morning, only making three short pauses, and these were all at the suggestion of The Quail. For, when we came to big stretches of rock three times in a row, she made us slow up and follow her, while she rode in circles through the rocks and laid down a trail problem which might make some Mandan brains ache a bit before the nightfall. Perhaps it was nothing but these that delayed the band so long, but the sun was hanging deeply in the west before the dust cloud which we had been dreading showed on the edge of the sky.

154

Chapter Thirty

IMPENDING BATTLE

The cloud of dust began to grow very fast. I saw The Quail throw one desperate glance at The Colonel, and, by the expression in her eyes rather than by anything that I could find in my own knowledge of the situation, I knew just how badly off we were. We gave the reins to the horses and raised them to a gallop, but ten minutes of that work brought the sweat streaming off them, without holding off the enemy to any appreciable extent. They still gained with a wonderful rapidity. This was our first practical experience of what those uncouth, shaggy-sided Indian ponies could accomplish, when they were put to it. Tired as our horses were, with their long legs and their fine blood, one would have expected them to hold off the little Indian midgets much better than they did.

They had hard work behind them, but so did the Indian ponies, and yet that cloud of dust kept growing and growing behind us, until we could make out the shadowy shapes which were raising the white mist that rolled toward the sky. And then the Indians came into full sight. It was much worse than we had expected — a great deal worse.

Ompah was the head war chief and that made a difference, but at the most we never expected him to bring out more than half a dozen men to corral the woman who had run away from the tribe. But you could gain some idea of the importance that the big chief attached to the girl by the fact that he had at least thirty men riding yonder with him — thirty picked men, too, by the way they rode and the quality of the ponies that were working to bring them up to us.

One of the reasons for their rapid advance was clear to us now. Behind the advance party of the Indians, well behind their heels as they flew along, was another rolling dust cloud. As they swung nearer to us, we could see that this was an ample body of reserve horses, herded along by several light-riding boys who could perform this duty better than the braves themselves. For every warrior in the gang there must have been at least three ponies. The result was that they could change every hour in the day, and constantly rested ponies could take up the burden of the hunt. That was the reason that they had been able to take a handicap of several hours of travel, in the morning, and then catch up with us at the close of the day.

The Colonel said with some bitterness, looking down to the head of Sir Turpin, which was nodding with exhaustion: "When in Rome, do as the Romans do, Christy. We might have saved all our trouble and expense of time in bringing such horses as these out West. Half a dozen of those cheap little rats would have served us better... much better, Christy, and lived without yearning for oats, either."

Other men have made the same discovery in the history of the Western migration. For the sort of work that was required on the prairies, the long marches frequently without much water, heat and dust in the summer, cold and wind and snow in the winter, for these hardships, supported on a diet of grass, the Indian pony was better than the Thoroughbred ever dreamed of being. A Thoroughbred, reared in the same environment might have done just as well, though I doubt it. But he never *was* handled as the Indians handled their stock, for no white man could afford to gamble with horseflesh as precious as, for example, the saddle stock of Kentucky. Out there on the plains, if a man had to make his choice for a thousand-mile march between a common Indian nag, with its thick furry legs and squat body and cartoon of a head on the one hand, and the finest Thoroughbred in the world, on the other, the wise fellow took the cartoon and let the picture horse go.

I should not have broken in here to talk about the comparative value of horses, except that our hearts were torn when we saw our big animals falter, while those ratty ponies carried their masters up to us, hand over hand. The girl watched them draw closer and closer with many backward glances. Then she would look anxiously to The Colonel, and finally she said: "Shall we stop our horses, Standing Elk, and lie down behind their bodies until the night comes?"

That was the old dodge which usually worked against Indians in time of need. The cornered men stopped their horses, made them lie down, and then lay down, using the horses as breastworks as they held off the redskins with leveled rifles, the important point being that Indians won't charge home on a loaded gun. A hundred of them will split and run at the last second before a rifleman who dares to hold his fire until the crisis. The difficulty is to hold it long enough. Once the rifles are emptied, the Indians will swoop in to deliver their blow before the guns are reloaded. That was what the girl wanted to do. It seemed to be high time, for the Mandans were already in long range and coming closer at every jump. We would hardly have time to get arranged before they would be at us with their first charge, which was always their most fierce and most apt to be pushed home regardless of loss. I hoped that The Colonel would listen to the advice of The Quail. In her life she must have seen these affairs before, or at least she must have heard all about the fine points of them a thousand times, whereas he and I were tenderfeet. But I didn't dare to say too much in a time like this, because I knew that The Colonel was a rare fighting man, whatever his other limitations might be. He seemed to pay not the slightest attention to the glances which the girl and I threw at him from time to time. Neither did he pay any regard to the Indians who were boiling up from our rear. At last he turned a little in the saddle and said to me cheerfully: "Christy, I want you to ride straight ahead with The Quail."

He pulled Sir Turpin up short. When The Quail saw that, she gave a little wail. "He is going to make his death charge," she said, and started pulling up her horse. I saw that there would be a mess here

157

in no time. Just what The Colonel intended to do, I didn't know, but I understood that in a time like this the main thing was for me and The Quail to follow orders quickly and without too much talk. I scooped in her bridle reins and forced her horse on at a gallop once more.

The Colonel made no long halt; neither did he deliver any death charge. He paused just long enough to get his rifle to his shoulder and draw a bead on a leader among the Mandans. Then he pulled the trigger, and I saw one of the distant figures throw up his arms and dive sidewise from the saddle to the ground. The whole gang of the Mandans in the front rank — and Ompah with the rest of them — scattered right and left, ducking back to get out of range of this deadly marksman.

It *was* fine marksmanship, and The Colonel was a great hand with guns of all kinds, but just the same that was a lucky shot. He was grinning and laughing when he came back to us. "Did you see me raise the dust, Christy?" he cried. "That'll keep the beggars at a little distance for a time, I hope!"

It gave us some priceless moments in the meantime, during which the Mandans gathered around their wounded or dead warrior. Those moments meant a mile or so of clear gain to us. However, here came the Mandans again, and they came fast. But they were very bothered. They wanted our scalps badly, and they had numbers enough to swamp us, but they hung back. We could see them brandishing their arms and yelling to one another, yet they wouldn't close on us. When a white general enters a battle, he plans on enduring a certain loss and perhaps a fat loss at that. He is willing to endure the loss, if he can win the fight. But an Indian does not think along the same channels. Every loss is bad. Of two chiefs, the one who brings back fifteen scalps and pays for them with five deaths in his party gets a great deal less credit than the leader who sneaks in with two scalps and has not a single casualty to show for his work. Any chief who rides his men at a sure death is a bad leader, the Indian thinks, and he will not follow. That was the instinct that held them back now. The first long-distance shot of The Colonel's had killed a man, and they couldn't take another chance with his marksmanship. They wanted to have some sure advantage in the first place.

The sun was drooping toward the west very fast when we came up to a sharp-edged gorge in the bottom of which there was a dry bed. It was one of those gulches that run high and white in the season of the heavy rains but that are dead throughout the rest of the year. We scrambled down into the bottom of this gorge, but, when we would have ridden straight up the farther bank, The Quail waved us to follow as she rode down the ravine. It seemed a rather silly artifice. However, we were desperate enough to take the very smallest chances. When we got around the next sharp bend of the gorge, we pulled our horses down to a walk, so that the noise of their going would not get to the ears of the Mandans. Presently we heard the rush and whoop of the war party as it stormed across that gully and went smashing on into the rolling ground straight beyond to hunt for us there. They were crashing out of earshot, and we rode our horses into a pool of standing water to refresh them.

Chapter Thirty-One

THE EXPEDIENT

They were very far spent, these horses of ours. Their heads were down, their ears flagged back, and their nostrils gaped tremblingly open. We loosened their girths for a moment, sloshed the water over them, gave them a few swallows, and they started slowly down the ravine ahead of us. Still the noise of the Mandans did not come back at us.

It was only after we had covered a considerable distance that we heard the booming of their voices making thunder behind us. Through the ruddy air of the sunset we listened to that thunder rolling away from us — they had followed the wrong course, missing the sign of our horses altogether. We knew they would soon discover their error and come rushing back toward us on their tireless horses. But we had another feature worth noting.

The ravine, which we had entered, still ran due north, but the walls on either side were now higher and higher, and a horse could not possibly have climbed them. If the Mandans charged down into that same pocket, we would be able to hold them back far more easily than on the open prairie. However, if some of them kept to the upper bank on either side, we were hopelessly in their hands. All three of us saw this at the same moment, and we looked at each other in despair and raised many an anxious glance to the upper edges of the banks above us.

Presently we came to a forking of the ravine, where an eastern-flowing stream tumbled into our cañon and filled it with white water.

The Quail wanted to take the way up this gorge, but The Colonel would not listen to that good advice. He insisted on keeping straight ahead.

We now had narrow footing at the side of a stream which ran as fast as though it were down a flume. That current was even more powerful when the time of the rains came. Along the bank we could see where the big trees had been carried down and lodged among the rocks.

Another idea came to The Colonel. He called to me to halt, and the two of us dismounted, while The Quail rode slowly ahead with the horses. Then we started to work, rolling logs down into the water and binding them together with the strands of the green climbing vines which grew along the shores. It did not take many minutes, but we were still at the business when the yelling of the Mandans came piercing down the heart of the gorge. That was not what interested us. We kept scanning the upper banks, to see whether horsemen might not appear there.

"Christy," said The Colonel, "I think that a kind God has sent all those Indians crashing into the same pocket that has caught and is now holding us. If they're here...why, I think that we'll be able to last long enough to see the day come."

We launched our raft by this time, and, the moment it took the water, the current sent it shooting down the stream. At the next bend we caught up with the girl and the horses, and she screamed with joy at the sight of our device. There was no time for congratulations. We could hear the roar of the war party as it strung out along the ravine, rushing the horses. So we fell to work in a frenzy. We tore the saddles and the packs off the packhorse and Kitty, leaving the saddle on Sir Turpin because he was the strongest after the day's march. All the luggage and the two saddles we piled onto our raft and heaped the stuff aft, where it would serve as a sort of breastwork. Then we pushed off with difficulty to the center of the stream, just in time to have a view of the leaders of the Indians as they came streaking around the next bend.

The foremost man lived. The Colonel's bullet missed him and knocked the life out of Indian number two. As that brave rolled on the rocks and then slid down into the water, the Mandans recoiled with yells of wonder and rage and fear. It looked like a miracle to them at first, I suppose. They could not see the details. In the late dusk of the day and at that distance, as we swung around the next bend, it must have looked rather like a real boat than a mere raft. The white man's medicine had snatched him from the back of wearied horses and placed him on a boat to use the speed of the waters.

In the meantime we commanded the pass from its center, swinging along on the current, and from behind our piled luggage we could lie at ease, one of us with a rifle ready for the Mandans, while the other worked with the improvised paddle that guided us straight. And there were the horses, freed from their packs, resting as they jogged down the easy slope of the canon.

Here the water quickened, and we saw a white streak ahead of us. We put in to the bank and took The Quail on board. Then she held the three bridles, while the horses swam behind us. The Colonel and I worked with poles to direct the course of the raft as it came around the bend into the rapids. They were not real rapids, but here the creek joined the other river, and the meeting of the swift currents at right angles caused a boiling turmoil that looked more dangerous than it really was. Straight ahead we were swept through a passage where for half a mile there was hardly footing for man or horse on either bank — the walls of that ravine climbed straight and high toward the sky. All three of us thought of the thing which The Quail put into words: "How will my brothers, the Mandans, follow here? Have they wings like a bird? Or have they medicine as strong as this?"

She struck the big logs of the raft and laughed like a child. It *was* medicine to her. She had seen us start the business with the work of our hands, and she must have known that it was completed in the same fashion. Yet that did not matter to her. The main item was that we had been snatched from the horses and placed here in comparative safety. That was a miracle; that was "medicine," and all the explanations in the world did not make it any less important. As a matter of fact, I felt that The Colonel was about the greatest man in the world for this contrivance and the courage he had had in stopping to construct the float with the Mandans tearing after us. Nothing was too good to think or say of him. As for the horses, they had simply to let themselves drift with the stream, with their heads held high out of the water by the pull on the bridles.

It was a good, steady current now. We heard nothing of the Mandans behind us. Also we were making excellent mileage. With nothing but starlight to shoot by, even if they managed to get their horses out of the ravine and ride around on the upper level to head us off, they would be shooting at a small, flat target which would probably be missed by their clumsy weapons and inaccurate eyes.

When we got to a point where the footing on the shore permitted it, The Quail and I went with the horses and rode them down the canon steadily. In the meantime that blessed river was steadily driving the raft along and carting it precious miles away from the Mandans.

What would they do? How far would they have to ride back before they managed to get to the surface of the upper prairie? And, after they reached it, how would they ford the two big, foaming streams which came down from either side to join the original creek? In fact, it looked now as though we had a good deal more than a better chance to get away from them.

"They'll lose heart," said The Colonel. "They'll give up this wild-goose chase."

But The Quail answered slowly: "They will never stop. Never while Ompah lives, Standing Elk. When he rides, he brings back scalps."

This took away a bit of our enthusiasm, I admit, but still our heads

163

were fairly high. By the time that the dawn came, the horses were too exhausted to go forward even without saddles or packs. We were now on a much broader stream, and The Colonel planned a still more ambitious scheme. We moored the raft at the edge, where a bit of deep water extended across the front of a flat rock. Then we dragged down more and bigger logs and bound them to the others, as well as we could. We had a craft twice as big as the original, now. Upon this we put the horses, making them lie down and hobbling their legs so that they could not get up. It was a risky business, getting them onto the raft, and, when Sir Turpin came aboard, I thought that it would be the finish of our raft and the things stacked on it. We weathered a bad tip, and with those three big animals aboard, and the rest of the luggage and ourselves stowed to counterbalance their weight as well as possible, we headed down the stream again.

This was a different matter. The little raft had floated true and straight, but the bigger one with the bigger load had a ridiculous way of wanting to turn end for end — and, when it had turned once, it would want to turn again. Where we were in more shallow waters, we managed very well with the continual use of our long poles to keep the course straight enough, but, where the water ran deeper, we lost control of it repeatedly. Three times we lodged against the banks at rapid bends, and we had to work nearly half an hour at one of them before we managed to float away again.

Every mile that we made on the river counted for more than two. For the horses were resting while we were still making vital progress away from Ompah. If only we could keep clear of them until nightfall, we felt that we could then gallop away on perfectly refreshed horses up any one of a hundred gullies that opened on either side of the river, and we would have fresh horseflesh and the dark to favor our escape. Matters changed when in the late afternoon we saw *real* white water ahead of us.

Chapter Thirty-Two

GREED

The white riffles which we had seen ahead of us the last time, and which had seemed dangerous enough in the distance, were nothing compared with the boiling spray that we saw out in front now. This was the real thing, and we knew it at once. The Colonel stood up straight and stiff for a moment, and then he picked me up and held me above his shoulder.

"Can we make it, Christy?" he asked, because I could see things better from such a height.

"I don't think so, sir. But if we bear over to the right bank...the water seems calmer in there. We've got to try that if we want to get through. Otherwise, we'd better go ashore here."

As a matter of fact, I was for landing and told The Colonel so. But he wouldn't hear of it. So we set about poling the raft toward the right bank, doing very well until we hit a stretch where our poles would not find bottom. Then the current took hold of us like a great hand, swerving us irresistibly to the left. We fought hard, but in another moment The Colonel's pole lodged in the bottom and was torn out of his hands. I handed him mine, but it was too late, for the raft had begun to spin, and I saw The Quail looping up her hair into a hard knot and getting ready for swimming without a word of whining. Ah, but she was a game one.

We had lost all control of the raft, and now we could see the water boiling up among the rocks, and the rocks themselves reaching like shark's teeth at us. It was very bad. Even The Colonel set his teeth

165

and breathed hard, and it looked to me as though there was nothing for it except one chance in ten of swimming to the shore.

The Quail had more sense in that pinch than both of us combined. She had the wits to take her knife and cut the ropes that tied the feet of the horses. Otherwise I'm sure that we two would have let them go in the crash that was sure to come. We were too busy thinking about ourselves to pay any heed to them. She cut their ropes and roused them up. They dived off the raft, one after another, and Sir Turpin, going in last, nearly capsized us. The raft righted itself a little, and, as we spun down the river, swinging end for end, we could see the three horses striking out bravely for the shore.

The Colonel waved to The Quail to go after them, but she shook her head, a perfect little mule for obstinacy, and so we let her stay with us, because there was nothing better to do. It was a fine picture to see her standing there so slim and pretty and calm, with her eyes glistening as she noted the dangers ahead, and her smile always turning toward The Colonel.

I only had half a moment to note these things, and then the raft struck. The forward end smashed against a rock with a force that knocked us all flat, and there the raft stuck for a moment, held straight by the force of the stream. My heart was in my mouth. When the raft began to swing off the rock, it turned not toward the center of the stream — that would have been the end of us all! — but toward the shore. We had a fighting chance again. It was better than a fighting chance we could see almost at once, for the stream was setting harder toward the left bank than we had guessed, and the raft was driven in for the land. We shaved a reaching rock on our right hand. An inch more would have wrecked us and sent our bodies hurtling down the stream. When we crashed again, we were very close to the bank.

That last shock cut our raft in two as cleanly as a knife could have turned the trick. What had been a perfectly good float one minute was a disordered mass of logs the next. Saddles and packs dropped out of sight, and here we were, heading out for the bank as hard as we could swim. Luck was with us again. We had shallow water here, and in a moment our feet hit good, hard sand. We could stand up and fall to salvaging the wreckage as it drove by us.

Though a good deal of stuff was lost, nothing of importance was missing except all our stock of dried meat. That was a very great loss, but it was still more important to see to our powder and lead, and The Colonel had made sure that these were always kept wrapped water-tight. He was too good a soldier to let such a thing as a heavy rain spoil his ammunition.

In another few minutes we were all laughing on the shore and busy spreading out our things to dry in the sun and the wind, and shouting to the horses, as they came galloping toward us like three dogs, and smiling at one another, and gaping at the flash and roar of the river as it went on in thunder down the ravine. It was a grand thing to have solid ground beneath us. We were so happy at that moment that I think we should hardly have cared if we heard the whooping of the Mandans coming streaming down from the heights to us.

Our things were dry enough in an hour or so to start the repacking. Above all, we wanted to get away from this river, now that we could no longer use it to carry us along. For unless we left it, sooner or later the war party of Ompah was sure to find us.

We were busy at this work when The Colonel stumbled over a stone and hopped about, holding his injured foot and cursing in grand style, until something that he saw made him stop. He forgot all of his pain and his anger. He stood gaping at the ground and then staring wildly about him.

"Christy!" he gasped at last, pointing with a stiff arm.

I ran to him at once.

"The white mountain!" cried The Colonel.

I stared and thought that he had gone mad. It was only a dumpy little hill, set back from the river a little more than its neighbors, with a dirty streak of white rock across its forehead. "The white mountain?" I repeated.

He pointed to the stone which he had just kicked over. Half of it — the upper half — was a dull gray stuff. But the part which he had turned up glistened and winked in the sun — a pure, crystal quartz! I could then see how his mind worked out the thing. The same hope leaped into my mind, too.

"But how could it be, Christy, when we traveled on no northern river?"

"The dry ravine!" I shouted, as the whole thing became clear to me at a stroke. "The season that Stone-That-Shines rode out in was the rainy season, and therefore that dry ravine was full of water when he found it...water running north, though it carried him at last into the streams running in this direction."

"By heaven, that's true. And here's the white water that tumbled him just as it tumbled us later on. Bless me, Christy...I tell you that I can feel the weight of pure gold in my pockets at this minute."

So could I, for that matter. I had never thought of this thing seriously before, and that was all the more reason for it to strike my mind with a crash when it *did* come home to me. But to find that thick gold vein — ah, well, I can't tell you all that came rioting in me.

We forgot the packing. We forgot the horses. We forgot The Quail, who went on patiently completing our work without a murmur. The two of us ran for the white mountain. Yes, we found that what seemed a broad white streak at the distance was really composed of the same beautifully transparent quartz, and in five minutes I found the actual vein. It was big enough and bright enough for any child to have found it. It shone there, yellow and clear, just at the edge of the crystal rock and the dirty gray where the two different kinds of stone seemed to be shouldering each other. There was not a long patch of it, but no doubt the vein opened out tremendously under the surface of the ground.

168

I dropped on my knees and tried to tear at the stuff with my bare fingers. The Colonel swung up a massive boulder and splintered it against the quartz. In that way he broke off a five-pound chunk of the stone with the vein bedded in it. Then he fell to work, breaking up the main chunk and chipping it away until there was left of the fragment only a thin flat strip — and the weight of it was heavier than lead. Gold, gold, gold!

The Quail came up, leading the horses with her. We did not speak to her. She came with a pleasant little cry of surprise and looked at the shining stuff. Her simple mind did not connect it with the medicine of Stone-That-Shines. As far as she was concerned, there was no relation between the two.

In the meantime we got out the pick and the hammer and drill, and in an hour we had planted our first charge of powder. The explosion ripped out a huge section of the stone. Then we worked in a savage frenzy, clearing the crystal quartz away and leaving the gold itself only thinly sheathed with rock. It was a freak — a thing not to be believed. I knew that most mines are rich if there is a mere color in them, or at the most perhaps the dim glitter of the thin wire gold. But here was a surface vein of the precious stuff.

"It may go a mile deep," I gasped.

The Colonel rolled eyes at me that were savage with the gold greed. We toiled on. We kept at it until we were exhausted and trembling. And here was The Quail, calmly cooking at the fire — cooking venison, at that. She had not wasted her time while we were so busy. Oh, how sweet that meat was and how ravenously we fell upon it, with never a word to one another. After we had eaten, and The Colonel was smoking his pipe and examining the blisters on his hands, he said: "Christy, what a pair of beasts we have been since we first saw the trace of this gold. What good can come out of such a thing as this?"

Chapter Thirty-Three

DREAMS

There was no doubt but that we were a good deal changed, and, if we hadn't fallen quite as low as The Colonel's words, at least we were not what we had been before. I can remember now how The Quail used to wander about, doing work for us, cooking, washing, mending, tending like the mother of a family, with never a word of complaint, never a word of curiosity. She simply worked and worked, always watching us with a tremendous curiosity and fear. I understood finally that she had no comprehension of what we were doing. We felt secure for the time being; our pursuers would take a long time to find us here.

One day, when my arms were aching and trembling with the fatigue of the great labor, and when The Colonel had gone away on a brief hunting trip — because as a rule The Quail did the hunting for us, as well as the cooking — I decided that I would try to explain everything. I showed her some of the yellow metal and asked her if she wanted to know what it was. Her eyes shone with eagerness, and she was nodding, but suddenly she answered me that she would not ask because she understood that the medicine which made Standing Elk work so hard and so cruelly would be too big and hard a medicine for a mere squaw to understand. I told her that there was no medicine here at all, but I said that this was money. There had been enough trading done up and down the river for the Mandans to have heard what money was, but it was still very dimly in their minds. Of course, they never *saw* any of it, except when it was changing hands among the whites, and no trader dreamed of taking cash with him to buy stuff from the Indians. They were paid in beads, hatchets, whiskey, rum, sugar, tea, coffee, buttons, wire, nails, feathers, blankets, and above all in rolls and rolls of the brightly colored cloth which the poor people seemed to value above everything else that was offered to them. A few yards of a rich yellow or crimson cotton stuff worth a matter of pennies at the factory were enough to separate a great chief from his best horses and even from his wives.

I had a good deal of trouble in telling the girl what money was, but I tried to make her see that money was what the whites used for trading among themselves, and that gold was the very stuff out of which money itself was made. She nodded, but her face was a little blank, so I decided on a more concrete representation. I said: "You see this little lump? You see how small it is in the palm of my hand? But what would you say that it is worth?"

"It is very pretty and bright" said The Quail. She picked the bit out of my hand and pounded it on a rock. The hard edges of the quartz sank readily into the malleable gold. The Quail said, handing it back to me: "It is bright and pretty, but it is not much good, except to shoot out of a rifle. Yes, it should be very good for that."

It staggered me a bit to think of using gold for bullets, though, I suppose, that would have been about all its use to Plains Indians. I explained: "Let me tell you that with this little bit of gold a white man could buy many rifles in his own country, and he could buy horses, too. Three rifles, and three horses, and ammunition to shoot out of the guns. I could buy all of that with this bit of gold I can chuck up into the air and catch again."

The Quail raised her dusky eyes and her golden hands to the sky. "Is there such medicine in it?" she asked.

"No medicine at all. Simply money, you see."

She shook her head. "You call it money...and the Indians call it medicine. That is the same thing, it seems to me."

It struck me that she might be right. At any rate, I saw that I should

171

not have any great amount of luck in trying to persuade her to a new view of things. She then asked me if it could really be true that three rifles and three horses could be locked up in that morsel of yellow metal. I told her on my honor that I had understated it, and that one could have also paid the price of three suits of the finest clothes, from boots to hats — and for enough ammunition to keep the three riders for months upon the plains.

"Then," said The Quail, "the white chiefs will try to get this yellow medicine instead of braves because, if they have this, they can buy the braves to follow them."

I admitted that this was correct, and I told her that some of the white men had so much of this same yellow metal that they could have bought more braves than there were in the whole Mandan nation. This was a good deal for her to swallow, and she asked me, if there were such men among the whites, why didn't they do as I said that they could? Then I told her that most of the whites put their attention on each other, in trying to get richer and richer, in building bigger and bigger houses, in putting finer clothes on their women, and in buying and riding finer horses.

Finally she asked: "What is the biggest lodge in the whole world, if there are no scalps hanging near the fire to make the hearts of the young men proud and the hearts of the squaws warm?"

This was a stumbling block. I had started to explain to her, as to a child, why The Colonel and I were working so furiously to get this yellow stuff out of the rock. I had to wind up by letting her think that it was simply a medicine stone, and that with it as medicine The Colonel could surround himself with warriors, arm them with fine guns, and build himself a lodge big enough to house the entire Mandan tribe. When I finished with this argument, The Quail didn't say that I was a liar, being much too polite for that. But she covered her mouth with her hand and sat looking at me for a long time — the universal method among Indians to express wonder. Before she moved that hand, I could see by her eyes that she was also covering a smile and not merely wonder. I gave up trying to make her understand.

Immediately after that we had something to think about other than the opinions of The Quail. For, as our weary arms and tired hands sank the hole in the rock deeper and deeper, and widened our narrow trench so that we could work with the greater ease in the bottom of it, we found that the vein was pinching in at either end. I can't tell you with what a savage despair we considered this thing. Our heads had been in the highest clouds. My own dreams were big enough. I would go back to Virginia and buy a plantation, and there I would have a hundred slaves working for me. I would hire teachers who would make me as clever and polite as any of the gentry of the land, and I would have my own ships sailing up the river to my own wharves. I would build me a house that would stand on a hill and overlook the shining blue and the dusky green of the river and the richness of the fields beyond.

Those were my dreams, but The Colonel used such stuff for a mere starting point when he leaped away into the air. I cannot remember all of the wild aspirations which he had. But I know that among the rest he had decided that he would accumulate his money until it was invested securely and well, and that then he would gather some trusted men, and that he and I would start off for Central America where, he had inside information, a bit of money well invested would start a revolution that would topple one of the native governments right out of its seat.

"You and I and the rest will set up a model government down there, Christy," he said to me, "start a government and show the world how things can be done on a big scale and yet with clean hands, too! I could handle the military end of things...we'd reasonably have to expect a bit of a fuss, now and then, with our crooked neighbors. You, Christy...why, in a few years, you'd be old enough to handle the political end of things. You have sharp wits. The sort that would make it easy for you to run a country, eh, Christy?

173

And on the side, I'll tell you what we'd do. We'd just quietly work up a little navy. A big job, you say? No, sir. What would we do? We'd hunt around until we found one of the first-rate powers about to junk one of their big battleships, because the craft would be too old-fashioned to be of service in a clash of the major powers. But never mind that, Christy. We would never have any trouble with the first-class powers. We would simply need a few ships with heavy guns to protect our ports from Latin-American raiders and to smash the fiddlings out of any seaport of our neighbors, when the rascals grew too nasty, eh?"

"It looks to me, Colonel," I broke in, "that you're going to have a pretty rough time with your quiet little model government down yonder."

"Nonsense, Christy," said The Colonel. "I simply mean that in time of peace we would always be prepared for war, as Washington told us to be. And having prepared for it, why, we'd be pretty sure of having our hands full of trouble. They always have it down there in Central America and such places, Christy. Pick up any newspaper. It must be a great thing to live in a place like that...with a war always just around the corner...why, that's the place for sport, eh, Christy?"

"Maybe, but not for model governments, I shouldn't think."

He scratched his chin. "Don't be so damned absolute, Christy!"

"No, sir," I agreed.

He was back in his dreams straightway. But you can trust me that there was no more dreaming when we found that our vein showed signs of pinching out. Because a definite limit and boundary were drawn around our imaginings right there on the spot.

Chapter Thirty-Four

THE END OF THE VEIN

The whole thing had been much too good to be true, as any other than The Colonel should certainly have guessed from the beginning. You couldn't expect a streak of solid gold to last very long. It was only a miracle that there should have been anything like it and that we should have had the luck to find it in that wilderness. I have talked to a great many miners — men who have had their experience in the California and Montana mines — and, though they could all tell of richer streaks than the one that we found, not a one of them could say that they had ever heard of a more concentrated bit of wealth.

That streak narrowed in from either end gradually and steadily, day after day, from the first day onward. Still, The Colonel and I used to promise ourselves that we would be able to open out the vein in the next day's digging. We ripped out hundredweight after hundredweight of the pure quill, as though it were no more than dirt, we were so hot and eager to see the golden vein expanding again. But it didn't expand. It scooped in more and more quickly. Right at the bottom, as it pinched to a point, we had our greatest hope of all and our best find, for there we found several precious pockets, and The Colonel was in heaven: He told me that the other part of the vein had simply been the door, and that now we were opening that door and getting into the heart of the rich stuff. But the very next day we cleaned out the last of the pockets and found not a sign of a streak of color in the rock beneath. We weren't content there when we should have been up and away from the spot as soon as we found that the gold had petered out.

That was on the ninth day after we had started to work at the mine. We were narrow of face from the famine of long labor because we hadn't spared ourselves. And we were hollow-eyed and silent. However, we wouldn't pause at that. I watched The Colonel still grinding away, sinking that trench deeper and deeper in the hope that we would be able to come on the vein again. So we kept at it with one of us working in the trench and one of us scouting about through the hills, trying to find any more fragments of the rock or, best of all, another vein of the same stuff.

We got a few fragments, such as the one which had rolled down with other stones and been found by Stone-That-Shines on the shore beneath us, but there was never any token of another vein. We kept at this useless grind for two whole days, and finally we admitted one night that we were finished — The Colonel with a groan, and I with a fallen head. We dropped off to sleep, too weary to eat the dinner which The Quail had ready for us.

In the morning we decided that it would be necessary to remain still another day on this spot, resting, and then we would begin our trip. That day The Colonel and I did nothing but gather the metal together and begin to estimate what we had taken out of the rock. That wasn't hard to do as The Colonel knew the weight of his rifle to an ounce, and we pitched on a system of balance scales which gave us pretty accurate results, we thought. It seemed incredible that the little heap of metal, heavy as it was, could figure up to as many dollars as it did. We began to feel better and better, the more we reckoned on the actual results of our labors. But I had a shock, and a great one, coming to me.

"I want you to understand that when we get this stuff back East, Christy, you and I split it half and half," said The Colonel.

I was simply amazed. "Why, sir, I'm simply on this job, taking pay from you, the same as I took back in Virginia. I've no right to anything at all...except a bonus, if you think that I've been worth it."

He shook his head. "Of course I don't like to give up that much to you. It seems like a lot...for a boy, at least. But, when I think the thing over, I see that my conscience would never rest easy unless I gave you a full half of it. Why, Christy, we would never have got here at all if it hadn't been for you...never in the world. So that's the way that we'll have to divide things, whether you want it that way or not."

I can tell you that it filled me right up to the top of the throat with gratitude to him and admiration of him. Anyway, that was the way that the matter had to stand. And we spent the rest of the day estimating how we would handle the fortune. The Colonel said that he knew of ways in which a man could get a ten or twelve percent return for his capital with the greatest ease in the world, but I pointed out to him that I would be perfectly well satisfied with a six percent turnover, and that I knew that a man could get that much with a *safe* investment. Safety was what I should want. At any rate, I didn't wish to be founding new governments in Central America or in any other place. It really strained my imagination to look forward to a sum like that and think how it would be invested and handled.

We were interrupted here by The Quail, coming back from the look-out and suggesting that, if we were not intending to dig any more medicine out of the rock, it would be a good idea to start traveling before Ompah got to us. I tell you that we had entirely forgotten that an Indian of that name ever lived. The Colonel insisted that Ompah must have given up the trail long before this, no matter how patient an Indian he might be. We would not start before the next morning.

So we turned in and slept that night, and, when the morning came, while we sat around eating our breakfast, The Quail jumped up and pointed straight to the west. We turned our heads in the same direction, and there we saw the worst sight that has ever greeted my eyes — an Indian warrior mounted on a horse with his war lance balanced across the pommel of his saddle — all very clearly against the rose of the sky, for his horse stood on the crest of a hill higher than ours. He saw us, too, at that instant and twitched his horse away in a moment and was out of sight.

"It's not a Mandan!" exclaimed The Colonel to The Quail. "Not a Mandan! No, don't tell me that!"

She nodded, very grave. "It *is* a Mandan. I think that it is the band of Ompah which has come upon us at the last."

We got ready for a flying start, but by the time that we had caught our horses and brought them in, before we had so much as begun to load them, we saw that the game was up as far as flight was concerned. The Mandans came screeching out from behind the hills and scattered in a loose semi-circle all around us. Rifles began to spout smoke from twenty different points of advantage. We were besieged on the top of a hill, with the river behind us, and the Mandans on the three other sides — two of us against some thirty. It was a pretty bad hole, and I don't think there was ever a sadder or a more foolish-feeling man than The Colonel for having turned back the suggestion The Quail had made the preceding afternoon.

I think that it would have been too late, even then. Certainly we would never had left our gold behind us in our haste to retreat, and in order to transport it there was only one way of proceeding — to carry that bulk of stuff below the long reach of the rapids, there to build another raft, and then drift as before slowly down the stream. But this would have taken quite a long time, and the Mandans would surely have got to us before we ended our preparations. I pointed this out to The Colonel, and he felt a little brighter, although we were now so busy that we had little time even for regrets. In ten minutes there was a steady shower of lead spattering on the rocks around us, and we were busy filling up the chinks in our natural fortification. We had a little citadel of rocks on the crest of the hill, and all that we had to do was to fill up the interstices between the big, solid boulders with the smaller rocks and the rubbish which we had broken out of the quartz in freeing the gold. This did not take us long, and, after that, we had enough room to shelter us and the horses from anything that the Mandans could do.

What happened in the day was one thing, and what happened in the night was quite another. The worst of it was that all the sides and the crests of the surrounding hills were covered with dense forests and close-growing shrubbery, which would allow the Mandans to creep up almost in touching distance of us. The Colonel showed us a way of remedying that evil. There was a strong wind cutting across our position from the east, and so he took some embers from our fire and pitched them down the face of the hill into a dead shrub. The shrub smoked; the smoke died, and a tiny head of flame showed itself. In another moment there was a tall hand of flame. It jutted out on either side. Other shrubs caught, and presently through the sun-baked foliage the flames were running like active red snakes. Down the hollow swept a wall of flames and rushed up the farther side. How those Mandans scattered and yelled with fear and with rage as the fire marched toward them! By the time it had burned down, there was no longer a sweep of brush through which they could stalk to our very gates.

Chapter Thirty-Five

THE STORY OF OMPAH

It was a comforting thing to hear those Indians howl. I don't mean to suggest that any of them was actually made a casualty by the wall of flame. They could dodge through the fire or get shelter along the rocks. But a lot of them were badly singed, and, as the fires topped the rise of ground on which they were posted, we heard an explosion and then a scream of pain that ended in mid-breath. We knew that no powers of self-control could have enabled the sufferer to check his outcry as briefly as that. It was death that had clapped a hand over his mouth, and it was a dreadful thing to hear and to know. Some Mandan had dropped his gun, and the thing had exploded and put an end to him, or to one of his comrades, and that was good news to us. It did not seriously diminish their numbers, but the more misfortunes an Indian war party had, the more apt it was to consider the business as bad medicine and give it over. Irritate a white man with such pin pricks and he simply turns into a bulldog and decides to hang on. But an Indian is different.

On the whole, we were fairly cheerful — more so than you would have suspected, considering what we had before us. But, as a matter of fact, with that river to keep our backs from attack and with the hilltop and the rocks that fortified it and with the stock of dried meat which The Quail had laid up for us while we were working at our mine, we were a great deal better off than we had been when the Mandans were pursuing us across the plains with fresh horses against our fagged ones. In the place where we now stood, we had more than a good chance of standing them off for a decent while, and there was always the possibility that their patience would leave them.

The Colonel asked The Quail what she thought of this. She had not uttered a sound during the fighting and the starting of the fire that had swept her kinsmen back. Now she was busily at work, building for herself a new fireplace of matched stones, set in a circle, with drafts arranged from beneath. She could make one of these things so that an open fire would burn in the face of a perfect gale. But she looked up from her work very seriously.

"I don't think that Ompah will leave," she said, "until I am dead ...or he has me."

Very short and neat, that answer, saying all that a man could ask. It took my breath, and The Colonel made a face.

"He'll be tired of this business," said The Colonel with a good deal of decision — just as a man will usually speak when he's not at all sure of what he has to say. "The Mandans are no more patient than other Indians."

The girl nodded at him and smiled. "Wolves are not patient in the summer when they are fat," she said. "But in the winter, when the ground is crusted with hard snow and when there is no food, then the wolves get much courage, and they are very patient, too, Standing Elk. They will sit in the snow and wait for the cow moose to fall with weakness. Ompah is like that now. Be sure that he will not be made to go away easily, Standing Elk. He will stay."

"His war party will leave him then," I said.

She shook her head again. She was infernally sure of herself. "They would leave other chiefs," she said. "But Ompah never fails. He has a big medicine. He will never fail on the warpath, and so, no matter how long it takes, the others will stay with him. Once he went to hunt the Crows. That took a long time, and he had forty warriors with him. But at the end of eight months they came back with many scalps."

You can understand how much this stuff interested The Colonel and me. The Colonel said: "Now, tell us all about that, will you, my child?"

Tears came up in her eyes. "Am I still a child?" she said.

"Woman, then," said The Colonel heartily. "Queen...best of cooks and queen of huntresses. You are all of that, and more. Tell us the story about Ompah. Christy, look sharp through this chink. I think that I see the outline of a man's shoulder behind the skeleton of that burned bush yonder. Look and see what you make out."

I put my eye to the cleft through which The Colonel had been peering, and I reported that it was only an outline of a rock. The Mandans were not showing themselves so early in the game. That trick of the fire attack had taken some of the ginger out of them.

"I am telling you of a time when Ompah was very young," said the girl. "He was very young, and I was not yet born. But I have heard about this very often, every year of my life."

"Have you?" said The Colonel. "Well, let's have the whole story, just as you last heard it." He added to me: "I wonder how many bones of fact there will be under the fat and flesh of this bird that we are about to eat, Christy?"

She raised a finger at him and smiled a little sadly, as I thought at the time. She was never very gay, and lately there had been a settled gloom that fell over her more and more deeply. It was as though she were afraid of the future and what it held for her — and well she might have been. I used to tell myself that it was because she made so little headway with The Colonel. He might not call her "child" so often as he had at first, but he still treated her like one. He was like a father to her, and never for an instant did he allow himself a single look or word or gesture that might have been construed as affectionate.

It seemed only the right and proper thing to me, at that time, but I was only a youngster then. When I look back to it and to the beauty of The Quail and to the way that she worshipped The Colonel, I can see that what he managed to do with himself was little short of a miracle. After all, was it right? Poor girl, it broke her heart. I am sure of that.

The Colonel was saying: "I shall believe every word that you say. You may talk forever about Ompah, and I shall still believe you."

She began: "He had made a great tight against three Rickarees the year before, and he had killed them all in that fight, so that he had a big name with the young men among the Mandans, and they were willing to follow him and fight for him. Forty and more of them went out with him, and they journeyed a long way up the river until they came to the land of the Crows, who are the tallest men in the world …as tall as Standing Elk, even the smallest of them.*' She said this gravely, measuring The Colonel, and loving him with her glance. "This war band traveled a while in the land of the Crows, until they came on a sight, among the mountains, of a big war band of the Crows putting away a great cache of dried meat and such food into the mouth of a cave. When the big war party went away, Ompah and his men went into that cave and moved away the great rocks which the Crows had piled up before their provisions, and they saw what had been done.

"Then Ompah said: "These people have put all this food here, and they have not put it here for the sake of letting it be a sacrifice. They have put it here, so that they may be able to come back to it in the time of their need. So they will surely come back, for every year the Indians are hungry, are they not? And, when these people return, we will all be waiting for them, my friends. Ompah said this to the warriors, and they remembered how he had killed the three Rickarees and believed that he was great medicine and could not be wrong. So they decided that he might be right again and that they would wait there with him. So they lived quietly and never went out from the big cave except in the night, and they had the big store of the dried meat to live on. So they spent months and months, and they worked on the making of war arrows, and they painted all their clothes, and they decorated themselves with beadwork, like working women.

They did everything else that they could think of doing, but the months went slowly by them, and still the Crows did not come back to that place.

"The young men wanted to be away. They said that half a year was gone from their lives, and that it could never be taken back again. The older warriors wanted to return to see their wives and their children and their friends. Ompah would not listen to them. He told them that they would be shamed if they went away and left him there. He said that he would remain and never stir from the place and that, when the Crows came, he would find a way to take more scalps than any other Mandan had ever taken before him. Every week he made medicine, and every week, after he had made it, he showed them that the medicine said that he was sure to win a great victory if he could only keep his warriors here.

"In this way he managed to keep most of his men with him. One of the young men started to leave the cave. But he was killed by a grizzly bear in the sight of all of the others, and then the other braves knew that the bear was a spirit in disguise, who had been sent down to give them a lesson and make them obedient to Ompah. So they stayed until eight months were almost over. Then, one day, the Crows came.

"They were not just the warriors. There were women also, and there were children. The hearts of the Mandans were glad when they saw these people coming...."

"The women and the children, too?" asked The Colonel.

"Does not a woman's scalp make a fine thing to dry by the fire?" replied The Quail simply, and she touched the coiled masses of her hair. She went on: "They fell on those Crows, who were all weak with winter and who besides expected no danger here in their own country. It was the greatest victory that the Mandans ever had. They did not lose a single life, except that of the man who was killed by the bear. Every man in the party brought back at least one scalp. Ompah had five!"

Chapter Thirty-Six

CATASTROPHE

You may write down this speech as small as you please. Still, there was enough in it to make us see that Ompah was the man among a hundred thousand, so far as the Indians were concerned. Perhaps the eight months was only the total amount of time that his war party was out on the trail. And perhaps not more than half of that time, or even much less than this, had been spent in the cave. What was most wonderful to us was that Ompah even as a young man had been able to keep his warriors together so beautifully. Certainly he would be able to do as he pleased now. Here was The Quail, a most open-minded and sensible girl for an Indian, who declared that Ompah could not fail. And what must be the faith in him which existed among the rest of his followers? The longer that she talked, the more my face fell, and even the poor Colonel began to look a bit frosty before she had finished her story.

"So you see," said The Quail cheerfully as she made an end of that yarn, "there is not much chance for us, unless Standing Elk will make another big medicine and carry us away from Ompah and down the river, or unless he makes a still bigger medicine and carries us away through the air."

She bent back her head and looked down at the rolling form of a big white cloud that the wind was trundling gently and slowly across the face of the sky. Yes, her faith in Ompah was great, but her faith in Standing Elk was nothing short of superhuman. The only doubts that she seemed to have were whether or not he would think that it was worthwhile for him to bother to make his big medicine. As for his ability, that was as boundless as the sky through which she half expected that he would make us sail.

The Colonel looked at me, and I looked at The Colonel, and we knew that our fortunes were at a considerably lower ebb than we had been thinking a few minutes before. "We go on rations, all the three of us," said The Colonel at last.

And on rations we went. We cut down our allowance of dried meat to the vanishing point, and we ate according to The Colonel's directions — three times a day, but only a scanty mouthful on each occasion. It worked wonderfully well. We grew a little thinner, but, after all, we could stand that. We had nothing to do but sit about and nurse our provisions, so that the wonderful way in which that supply of dried meat held out was a game to us — a game to me, I mean. To the girl, it was simply medicine. As a matter of fact, it *was* rather miraculous to see the way in which she held out. If The Colonel and I grew thinner, she did not seem to change at all. Yet she would hardly eat the amount that was due to her as her share.

The Colonel caught her on two occasions smuggling the share that had been given her back into the main supply. He gave her a terrible lecture, and, after that, he made her eat her portion along with us. But still it was medicine to The Quail to see how the bit of meat held out and hardly seemed to be diminished at the end of five days.

We had other things to amuse us, too. For one thing, one of the three of us constantly had to be on the look-out, watching for the Mandans to sneak up on us. The rascals tried a scheme of getting down their hill behind big boulders which they rolled slowly in front of them. It seemed a very good scheme, too, and they got one big stone down to the foot of the slope and even began to work it up toward us, while the rest of the Mandans screamed like madmen with their joy, they were so certain that they were about to have our scalps.

But that big boulder — at which it was perfectly useless for us to shoot — had no sooner started its journey up the slope toward us, a

186

revolution at a time, worked out with infinite labor — than The Colonel and I started to work, loosening the base of a big stone that stood on one side from our little citadel. The foolish Mandans might have guessed that such a thing would happen to them. But I confess that for my part I did not think of it at all, and it looked to me as though there would be no way of stopping the advance of that infernal stone until The Colonel made his suggestion.

We got the boulder undermined pretty far. Then, with The Colonel giving it the final thrust which would direct its rolling down the hill, we turned it loose. It went with a rumble, then with a bound like a running horse, and the Mandans who were watching from the farther hilltop screamed with excitement and with fear. Their warning made two of the Mandans leap out from behind their shelter. When they showed themselves, the rifle cracked in the ready hands of The Quail, and one of those braves fell and slid, sidling down the slope, it was so steep.

The other scrambled for cover, and, when I would have shot in my turn, The Colonel knocked up the gun. "Give them a chance, the poor rats," he said.

Very foolish, as you will have to admit. You may admire such generosity at a distance, but not when your life may depend upon the greatest amount of execution that you can work in the ranks of an enemy.

In the meantime we were watching the course of our own rolling boulder. It went down the slope like a runaway horse, and it covered in half a dozen leaps the distance between it and the boulder with the Mandans behind it. One of those Indians who remained behind the stone heard the approaching thunder and ran out to take his chances with bullets rather than with such a mystery as this. I shall never forget how he threw up his arms above his head, and how he screamed with terror and wonder when he saw the big stone that we had turned loose — bounding into the air like a frightened colt. Then he turned and scrambled, too, and after him ran his companion, the last of the four who had undertaken the silly labor of working that boulder down the slope and up toward our fort.

I think that all would have come off scot-free, except for the fellow that The Quail had downed with her steady hand. But that boulder, which we had put in motion, had a devilish will of its own. It did not strike the Indians' stone. Instead, it bounded over the top of that boulder, and, angling sharply and most unexpectedly to the right, the huge rock struck the fourth of the Mandans as he fled and crushed him.

There was not a sound from him. He must have died instantly. And that huge rock struck terror in the Mandans who were watching at a distance. It was not so much the actual death that seemed so monstrous to them, but the means by which it was accomplished was dreadful in their eyes — and even in mine it had looked as though that stone of ours was actuated by a fiendish will of its own. This made the fourth one of the Mandans who had died since they began to chase us, enough to have given pause to the whole party—enough to shake even the reputation of Ompah — and certainly enough to remove from this particular war trail the least semblance of glory, even if Ompah returned with the girl and both of the scalps of the white men.

We did not have much time and chance to think about that, for now, as we came back from watching the effects of the stone, we saw The Quail standing beside a tall rock, looking through the cleft before her at the destruction in the valley. I suppose that another Indian girl might well have been doing a war dance on her own account, after having killed a brave with her own pull on the trigger, but all that The Quail was doing was standing there with a smile of the most exquisite satisfaction on her lovely face.

She looked aside at us, and one flash of the disgust and horror in The Colonel's face was enough to show her that this latest triumph of hers was no sensation with him. She wiped that smile of hers out completely, but she really didn't know what was wrong, and she followed The Colonel with her eyes like a beaten animal. It was a horrible thing to see. I pitied her with all my heart, but I knew that The Colonel could not help the look that she had seen in his face. It was more than a mere exchange of glances between them; it carried the beginning, the crisis, and the catastrophe of as vital a tragedy as was ever put on the stage in five acts and an epilogue. Something smashed in The Quail. Up to that time she had had a bit of a hope. Now she knew that there was no chance. I suppose that she expected to be heartily congratulated for the thing she had done with this rifle. Instead, she found that she had been put down in the list of the destroying pestilences. It was very hard on her, and after that she never looked on The Colonel with a real glimmer of possibility in her eyes.

We were wondering what would be done about the burial of the two bodies in the valley beneath us. The Mandans would not risk coming for them during the light of the day, and, as for making the try at night, there would be a full moon in the sky, and the moon that shone from those clear and cloudless skies gave almost as good shooting light as could be asked for.

The Colonel thought this matter over and asked The Quail what she made of this thing. She said that she did not know. She admitted that it was a dreadful thing for a Mandan warrior to remain unburied, for then his soul could never get to the Happy Hunting Grounds. She was sure that this would be a blow that would topple the prestige of even Ompah. If he had to allow two bodies of his warriors to lie unburied in the sight of his men, it was liable to break down their discipline altogether. The Colonel listened to this optative speech with a curling lip, and then he crisply directed me to put a white rag on a stick and wave it to the Mandans.

Chapter Thirty-Seven

THE CRISIS

There had been enough association between whites and reds by this time for them to understand that there was some pacific meaning in the waving of a white flag. Pretty soon there was a similar flag waved from their own line and then out rode our old friend, Sanjakakokah, waving the white flag like a madman. It was tremendously good to see Sanja again. It was reassuring. I could only wonder why it was that he hadn't let us hear from him before this? He rode very slowly down the slope, and, when he came to the hollow where the two Mandan warriors lay dead, he hesitated and stopped his horse for a moment.

Plainly he had his doubts of this business, but The Colonel shouted in a voice of thunder that no harm in the least would come to him and that he should march up as cheerfully as possible. Sanja apparently put his doubts in his pocket at that. He rode up, still waving the flag, although he seemed to think that, the minute it fell from his hands, he would be a gone goose. The Colonel stepped right up and shook hands with him — apparently certain that the Mandans would not dare to risk shooting at such a distance when one of their own chiefs was in such danger of their own bullets. And they did not shoot.

"Sanja," said The Colonel, "this is a nasty business. I like it as little as you can possibly like it."

Sanja smiled. "The medicine of Standing Elk is a very great medicine. It struck my brother, The Badger, and there he lies."

"Was that poor fellow a friend of yours?" asked The Colonel earnestly.

"He was my brother," repeated Sanja.

"Your real brother?" cried The Colonel. "By heavens, Sanja, I'm dreadfully sorry to hear about this. It was an ugly business, though. You understand we had to stop the rolling of that stone, don't you?"

Sanjakakokah nodded his head. "It is not for that the heart of Sanjakakokah is sad," he said. "It is because he now lies and looks at the sun with his open eyes, and he can never ride into the Happy Hunting Grounds after his death."

"Do you think, man," cried The Colonel, "that we would keep you from burying him and the other poor unlucky fellow also?"

I tell you that Sanja nearly dropped from his horse. "That is good," he said. "Standing Elk gave life to Sanjakakokah. He gives more than life to my brother. And what shall Ompah be asked for in exchange for this?"

"Asked for in exchange?" said The Colonel. "Not a thing in the world, Sanja. This is mere friendship. I couldn't let those poor fellows lie out there unburied."

The eyes of Sanja positively flashed fire. The generosity of The Colonel had granted him his life once before this. But this second instance seemed a hundred times more forcible to the chief. He said nothing. Perhaps he was afraid to put too much emphasis on his feelings and let The Colonel see what a great thing he had done — from the viewpoint of the Mandans, at least. He said finally: "We are sorry to close up Standing Elk like wolves around a bull moose in the snow."

"That is war," said The Colonel in his simple way. "We are getting along very well, and my serious advice to you fellows is to get out of here, Sanja, before you have any more bad luck. You can tell a trail's luck by its beginning, you know, and this beginning has been bad for all of your party."

'The rivers work for Standing Elk," said Sanja. "By what medicine did you bring the horses down the water?"

"The same medicine that brought Christy and The Quail and me. But the medicine is not what counts here. The thing for you and Ompah to consider is that this has been forced on us."

"The Mandans," said Sanja, with his nostrils quivering a little, "looked on Standing Elk as a brother. But he took a horse and many rich things, and one of their women who was already bought and paid for by Ompah."

"I took nothing," said The Colonel. "She followed us of her own free will...and I left behind us all of the things that she brought with her. I would not take the stolen things, Sanja. You found them on the plains."

Sanja nodded. It was plain that that restitution had bothered him a great deal. "We wanted her to go back to Ompah," said The Colonel, "but, when she would not do that, we gave her one of our horses to ride. You understand, my friend, that was a heavy burden and a weight that slowed our horses so that we were in great danger of being taken?"

Sanja nodded again. "Ompah," he declared, "says this thing. Give us the girl, and then Ompah and his men will ride away."

"Could I trust in that?" asked The Colonel. "What would force Ompah to keep his word?"

"One of our braves will be given to you in exchange for The Quail. I, Sanjakakokah, will offer myself to you, if none of the younger men are willing."

That was business, and good business, and I cried out to The Colonel to strike the bargain at once. But he shook his head. The stubbornness of that man was a thing to tell but hardly to believe.

He said: "She doesn't wish to go back to Ompah. She left him once, and she would leave him again, and I can't force her to go. A white man can't do such a thing, Sanja."

The Mandan puckered his brow while he tried to understand this viewpoint, but it was a good deal too hard for him. Finally he said:

"This is the last thing that Ompah says: Will you let him come to talk freely with The Quail, between the two camps, where the rifles of the Mandans and the rifle of Standing Elk that never misses look down on them?"

This seemed fair enough. There was not much to be gained by it, because we could tell beforehand that The Quail would not let herself be persuaded. But The Colonel asked her if she was willing to see the chief, and she declared that it lay in the hands of Standing Elk. She would do whatever he decided might be best for her.

So The Colonel gave his answer that Ompah could come without danger, when he chose to come, and The Quail would walk out and talk with him on the neutral ground between the two parties.

It was arranged. Sanjakakokah, pressing a little closer to The Colonel, turned one of his saddle bags upside down, so that a great chunk of fried meat fell out on the ground. Then, without a word, he turned his horse and rode slowly back down the slope, still waving the white flag every step of the way. For this flag medicine was a great matter with him, and he would not trust his life in the open without its magic protection.

The Colonel in the meantime picked up the fallen meat and stepped back inside our little fortress. That meat, carefully rationed, gave us a full five days perhaps, in addition to what was left of our stock, and therefore it was a most important matter. The Quail, when the meat was brought in, instantly cut off a corner of it and put it into her mouth. She acted so quickly and decisively that I hardly knew what she was about, but The Colonel cried to her not to eat it, since it might be poisoned for all that we knew. Sanja seemed a very good fellow and our friend, but he might not be above trying to put an end to this weary battle in a quiet way of his own.

That same thought had been in the mind of The Quail, and she'd been brave enough to make the test on herself rather than submit The Colonel to any danger hereafter. She had courage. I never saw any woman with so much of it. It was all the more touching, because, as you have been able to see for yourselves, she was fighting for a lost cause.

Ompah did not appear at once, and I went down to get a supply of water. That was another of the ways that kept us amused while we were in our fort. There were two Indians from Ompah's party stationed all the time on an edge of the bluff that overlooked, from a distance, the water's *edge*. On a dark night we could get down to the water and back again with perfect ease. During the day or during a time of bright moonshine, every approach to the water was sure to bring the fire of that pair — and they shot uncomfortably well, too. However, we felt that while these negotiations were going on, they might let up their vigilance, and so I went down.

We didn't know the Indians and their ways. The moment that I showed myself near the shore, two guns cracked, and one bullet hissed past my face, while the second chipped a little corner from my ear. That wound hurt a good deal more than lots of much bigger ones. Before the pair could load again, I jumped out to the river's edge, filled my canteen, and leaped back among the rocks, just in time to escape a second volley. If an Indian can do nothing else with a gun, he knows how to load with rapidity.

When I worked my way back to The Colonel and The Quail, I found them in a towering passion, The Colonel striding up and down with his rifle in his hand and anxious to make a killing. There was no Mandan in sight for that pleasant purpose, and then presently the white flag began to wave again from the Mandan rocks, and here was Ompah riding down into the hollow to begin the negotiations.

The crisis of our game had come. I did not know what loophole of escape there might be, as long as The Colonel insisted on treating The Quail in the grand manner, but I knew, if we *did* fail here, we might as well resign ourselves and fold our hands, because we would never get out of this corner alive.

Chapter Thirty-Eight

THE MEETING

It was not the most reassuring sight in the world to see Ompah come prancing down the hill on his war pony. These horses of Ompah's were hardly to be matched among Indians north of the Comanches. He had a grand eye for horseflesh, and, in all of his raids and his campaigning, he had never paid any heed to gathering anything for himself other than horses. His whole property, therefore, consisted in horseflesh except for a very few trappings. He hardly had enough regalia to make himself fit to be seen among men as a chief.

The Colonel said to The Quail: "Ompah does not ride out like a rich man. He comes more like a young warrior who has never taken a scalp or brought spoil to the lodge after the battle."

I expected that The Quail would come out with some nasty answer, knowing as she did that all of her misfortunes sprang from this war chief of her tribe. But she had a good many surprises up her sleeve. She simply said: "Ompah is not dressed in many feathers, but in his own great name, which is enough."

It was enough to make The Colonel look a bit silly, and so should I, if I had been in his boots, but he declared that he had meant no insult to the chief. He went on: "Now, when you get out there and talk with him, child, what will you have to say?"

She answered: "I shall say whatever you bid me to say."

"Will you really do that?" he asked.

"What should a squaw do?" said the girl. "Standing Elk can think for himself and for his woman also."

The Colonel bit his lip and threw a wild look at me, but I only grinned at him. It rather pleased me to see her torment him in this fashion. If she had been the queen of England, he could not have kept at a more polite distance from her than he had done during her stay in our camp. But that seemed to make no difference to The Quail. She looked upon herself as his wife, and that ended the matter so far as she was concerned. Some day it might please her lord to take her into his wigwam. It was not for her to try to understand the strange workings of such a great medicine chief as The Colonel. I admired The Colonel a good deal in this role — but he was also more than a little ridiculous.

Now big Ompah worked his war pony into a smart gallop and brought it to a plunging halt just outside of our little fortress. "The Quail will come out to you," said The Colonel.

"I wish to speak to a man first," said the chief.

I should like to say that he had a grand and dignified look, but I have to confess that Ompah's face had a very lopsided effect. He had painted himself up with a great deal of care, but he had laid on the red with a little more largesse on the one side than on the other. If his face didn't appear well proportioned, at least he looked terrific as a thunderstorm — with all of the lightning effects thrown in.

"Very well," said The Colonel. "What have you to say to me, Ompah?"

"Standing Elk," said the chief, "I have talked with Sanjakakokah, who is your friend and mine. He speaks a very loud word for you, and he declares that the woman was not stolen by you, but that she came after you to your camp."

"It is true," said The Colonel.

"Then," said the chief, "I shall make my young men forget the warriors who have fallen before the rifle of Standing Elk. I shall let you have your life and the life of Little Thunder. Only give me the girl."

"You may have the girl and welcome," said The Colonel, "if she is willing to go with you."

The chief shook his head. "If one of my horses wanders into your herd, and I come for it, will you say I may have the horse, if it is willing to go along with me?"

The Colonel could not find an answer very readily, and I hardly blamed him. This was a new viewpoint for both of us. To us, a woman was a human being, with the rights of a human being, but to the Indians a woman was simply an article of property, to be possessed or lost — like a horse — and of very little more importance than a horse.

"Every nation has different ways," said The Colonel, "and to the Mandans a woman is a thing that can be bought and sold. But the whites do not buy and sell women. If one of your warriors goes to a different chief and says that he will follow the new leader, you do not force him to come back to you. It is the same with white women. They go where they please, and they follow the man who pleases them and not the man who buys them. There is no buying and selling of women among us. I know that Ompah is a great warrior and an honest man and that he has paid a high price for this girl. But, according to the way in which we white people see things, she cannot really be bought. That is why I cannot force her to leave and go back to you unless she wishes to do so."

"Good," said Ompah, though his nostrils flared a bit. "That is very good, and I see the heart of Standing Elk speaking truly and with one tongue. You must tell me whether The Quail is a white woman or a Mandan?"

There had seemed to me no good answer to The Colonel's argument, but I had to admit that this little retort of Ompah's pricked the bubble pretty effectively. There was not much left of The Colonel's logic — at least from the Indian viewpoint.

The Colonel mulled this matter over in his mind for a long moment. "What you say has a great deal of truth in it," he agreed reluctantly. "Perhaps The Quail did wrong in leaving her tribe and coming after me. In this matter I wish to do what is just. But I cannot find in myself enough strength to drive her away, unless she wishes to go. Neither would you be happy to have her, Ompah. She would not make for contentment in your lodge. There would be much displeasure there. If you think of this, you will see that I have told you the truth. Because no matter what other women may be like, The Quail is not like a horse. You may pay down much property for her, but still she cannot be bought and sold. There is something in her spirit that cannot be exchanged for horses."

The chief nodded at once. He was surprisingly reasonable, I thought, considering the immense loss that he had sustained in reputation and property on account of this girl. For the first time in his life he had been unlucky on the warpath — so unlucky that both our scalps and the recapture of The Quail could not have redeemed the expedition and made it a success. However, he listened to everything that The Colonel had to say, and one could see that he was making a great effort to put himself in the shoes of the white man. Finally he said: "I think that Standing Elk is an honest man. So thinks Sanjakakokah also. We have talked about you very often. We know that you have a powerful medicine. We have seen it working, and we know that it is very powerful. We have seen you fight for our nation, and the Sioux were grass…they dropped before Standing Elk like dead grass crushed under foot that does not rise again. But, when we talk about these things and about The Quail, it is clear that what Standing Elk thinks is right is not what I and Sanjakakokah have been taught to consider right."

That was about the finest speech, for sheer reasonableness, that I have ever heard an Indian utter, and I could see that, if this chief had had half a chance to form relations with the whites on an extensive scale, he might have become a grand intermediary between the two peoples and the two diverse ways of thinking.

"That is all very true," said The Colonel. "I have wanted to tell Ompah how much I respect him, and how much I wish to be his friend. If we can forget this girl, we could be friends, Ompah. What a bitter pity if that cannot be."

Here there was a little interruption. The most important thing had seemed to be the meeting between these two big fighting men, one red and one white. But now a third voice cut in and made the pair of them seem a little lighter in the scale of the situation. It was The Quail: "Tell me, Standing Elk, that you wish me to go back to Ompah?" The Colonel was staggered by this direct putting of the question to him. Again the girl said: "If you wish me to go back to Ompah and become his squaw, I shall leave you, and I shall leave you now." She kept her voice as level as you please, but even I could feel the agony that was behind it.

The good Colonel said, making a little gesture of despair: "Child, there's only one thing that I want out of this, and that is justice for Ompah and for you. You claim that you are free. He claims that he has bought and paid for you, and that therefore he has a right to keep you."

"Why did he not take me then, by force, on the day my father sold me?" cried the girl.

"No," put in Ompah, "I would not take her by force. Then or now! But I would keep my woman from going to another man."

It was rather a twisted viewpoint, I suppose. But then the chief was too much in love to be exactly logical.

Finally The Quail said: "I shall do what Standing Elk bids me do."

"Do what you think is right," said The Colonel. "I'll never force you a step of the way back to him. I'd rather die a thousand times over than force you a step back to Ompah, unless you think it is right that you should go. And Christy would rather die for you, too."

Chapter Thirty-Nine

THE QUAIL'S PROPHECY

I didn't need to tell her that The Colonel could talk freely enough for himself, but that I preferred to be left out of the thing. She turned those dusky eyes of hers on me, and I thought that the shadow of a smile came on her lips. She walked past The Colonel, and, hesitating there for an instant, she stared up into his eyes. When she had passed, he murmured to me: "Why did she look at me like that, Christy? What's in the head of that strange girl?"

I couldn't guess, but my opinion now is that, the moment she left us, she had fully determined on what she would do. She went out in cold blood to end everything, and she took a characteristic way of doing it.

Ompah dismounted at once, and he led the girl off a little distance. He stood, talking to her in a low monotone of which only a steady rumble came to us, and she listened until he had finished the whole, long speech. I suppose that he was justifying himself for the manner in which he had pursued her, and I think that he was inviting her to come back and live as freely as ever among the Mandans — so long as she gave up the thought of any husband other than the chief himself.

The Colonel was much impressed by the dignity of the chief. He kept murmuring to me: "Look at him, Christy. You'll never see another Indian like him, if you live to be a thousand. Paid ten horses for her, without bargaining. And he would have paid ten thousand, if he had had them, and never thought anything about it. He has a brain that's as generous as the wind, I can tell you. Oh, there's a soul in that Ompah, Christy. If we have a chance, I'm going to make that fellow my friend. Would like nothing better than to ride on one of his war trails with him. He'd show you leadership...and sport, too."

That was an odd speech, considering everything.

The Quail listened to all the chief had to say, but then she drew a little away from him and tilted her head back and laughed. Yes, she laughed right in his face, and we could see the wonder and the rage spread over his features.

"The little fool," said The Colonel. "Doesn't she know enough not to beard a tiger like that?"

"She knows what she's about," I suggested. "She's known Ompah a lot longer than you and I have known him."

"I'd rather make faces at a free tiger than talk to Ompah like that. Let's see how he takes it."

Ompah took it with a scowl, and he began to talk a little louder — a regular rolling thunder came to us, though we couldn't make out the words. When he finished, she snapped her fingers in his face. From her gesture it could be seen that she was saying she valued him no more than a pinch of wind. What she said, I don't know, but it was enough to bring a snarl of rage from Ompah. Perhaps her courage deserted her then. She whirled about and tried to run back to us, but Ompah leaped after her with the gleam of his knife in his hand.

The Colonel shouted and snatched for his pistol, but it was too late for that. The Quail seemed to feel the shadow of the reaching hand of the chief. She whirled about toward him and took the knife thrust in her breast, dropping dead at his feet.

My heart stops even now, when I write of it. It wasn't only the horrible fact, but it was because I could see she had intended this when she left us. Things were in a villainous snarl for her. There seemed no good way out, and so she had taken this way of doing it.

The knife of Ompah ended the tangle for her.

Ompah gave one glance at her, and then, with a war cry that split my ears, he leaped over her fallen body and sprang straight at The Colonel. He had gone berserk. Now that The Quail was dead, he did not want to live himself. At any rate, he had seen The Colonel fight, and he must have known what would happen if he attacked with his knife such a man as The Colonel, armed with a gun.

The hand of The Colonel went up as steadily as though he were at target practice, as he shouted: "Ompah, keep back from me. I want to do you no harm!"

Ompah came on like the tiger that he was. The pistol boomed, and he fell. The shriek of the Mandans came wailing at our ears. Then there was a rattling of musketry, and a whir of leaden bullets.

The Colonel strode through that storm without changing a hair. He got to the girl, lifted her, and brought her quickly back inside the rocks, running as lightly with her as though she had been a child. When he placed her on the ground and closed her eyes, her pitiful dead smile and her smooth young face made her seem like a child, though, when she had been alive, she was as much a woman as any man could ever expect to find.

"I've done this," said The Colonel to me. "I've brought about the death of both of them, and God forgive me for it."

He covered her in a buffalo robe, which had been stretched over the mound of our gold before. As he made the exchange, I couldn't help thinking that this was the price that was paid for our riches — the death of the girl and of Ompah, too. Perhaps that was fetching my ideas from a great distance.

The Mandans were yelling and whooping and wailing and firing their guns, as fast as they could reload and discharge them at us, but we were safe enough for all of that. They were no nearer to capturing us. They were, in fact, a good distance farther from winning than they had been before, and after a time good sense got the better of their rage, for here came Sanjakakokah with his waving white flag again.

He asked no questions, and The Colonel made no explanations. The Indians had been able to see everything that happened, just as well as we had been able to see it. They must have known that we were not at fault. What Sanja wanted was a chance to bury his leader. He was a big man in that war party, and it was up to him to bury his dead leader, even if he could not avenge him.

The Colonel gave him the permission that he wanted. Big Ompah was carried away, and the two dead warriors in the hollow were removed also, while The Colonel and I made the grave of The Quail on top of the bluff and put in a blast of powder that we had left from our mine work. It rolled a ten-ton crag across the grave. That was her monument.

The Colonel said: "There is one thing that troubles me more than the rest, Christy, and that is the thought that almost from the first she guessed that no good was coming out of this affair. You remember how sure she was that Ompah would never give up the trail until he had found us?"

I remembered that, but I thought it would be best not to agree with The Colonel.

We waited up there on the bluff for two whole days. Then we ventured a little reconnoitering expedition, finding that the hills opposite us were no longer occupied by the war party. They had gone, and on the crest of the next low range beyond there were three bodies buried after the Indian fashion, supported each on little oblong platforms, raised on the pales of saplings, fixed firmly in the ground. Wolves could not get at the bodies of the dead men. There they could lie, wrapped in their best clothes, with their weapons beside them, and under each warrior there was a shapeless mound, which we knew was the body of the brave's best horse that had been slaughtered there, so that the spirit of the charger could carry the soul of the dead man across the empty space of air and time to the Happy Hunting

Grounds, where all the shadowy herds of dead buffalo are ranging, and where bullets never miss, and the arrows are charmed to the mark. Up there in that kingdom of ghosts the spirit of Ompah would walk with the war paint on his face, a king among them, just as he had been a king on earth.

We went back to our own work. I think that during the next week we spoke seven words. First, we worked in a frenzy to get the gold away from that cursed hill where the body of The Quail lay under the pinnacle that looked over the river. It took us two days to carry that heavy burden of metal down from the height to the bank of the river. After that, working with a great deal more care, we took strips of rawhide and bound the logs firmly together. When we were finished, we had a light, water-tight raft.

So we started drifting down the stream. I managed the raft and the burden of treasure that was upon it. The Colonel, on the shore, kept the horses in hand. In that way we could make excellent progress. But I was a little surprised when I saw The Colonel ride at a gallop to put the first bend of the river behind him. I did not feel that way about it. I sat there on the raft with the steering oar which we had made, prying steadily at the current, and I looked back until I could see no more the lifted finger of rock pointing to the sky and marking the place forever. Then the stream carried me softly around the bend, and I saw before me a long, straight course down the waters, with hardly need to touch the steering oar once a day.

Chapter Forty

DANGER!

The logical thing was to head straight down the river and get rid of the horses at the first opportunity, because they would only impede our movements. The raft could take us all the way to the Mississippi. For that matter, we could go all the way to New Orleans on this craft. But I had a terribly hard job with The Colonel on that subject, and finally he refused altogether to listen to me when I talked about it. He had traveled with Sir Turpin and Kitty and the pack horse all the way from Virginia to the West, and he swore that he would go back the same way. When I pointed out that the safe conduct of so much gold was worth a little more than a sentimental idea such as his, he simply shrugged his shoulders and stuck to his point.

I gave up the argument, and we worked along at a wretchedly slow rate. Sometimes we had to stop the horses because there was a bad passage of water through which the raft had to be taken. We would need both hands aboard. First the horses were tethered, and then the boat was worked through, after which The Colonel would come back and bring down the three of them. More often, we had to stop the raft and give it a mooring along the banks of the stream, while the horses were taken around some hills or bluffs that came down to the water's edge.

We plugged along in this slow way for a full month. Several times we had to stop. Once we made a four-day halt, while we hunted and then sun-dried some beef. Again we had to pause to right the raft, when the load shifted — and there were other causes that ate into our days. Even when we were marching, I don't think that we averaged more than twenty or twenty-five miles a day. It was a miserable business, particularly when you consider that we had so much gold on board. Every minute we wasted seemed to me to be a criminal expense.

The Colonel was easy enough about this slow campaign. He said that it made no particular difference, and that we should be glad to have a chance to look the country over at our leisure as we went. "How many New Yorkers, Christy," he said, "and how many of those dusty businessmen in Richmond would be mighty glad to have this chance to idle through the great West?"

"Not with this much gold."

He admitted that there was something in this, but he would not change his way. We had been going on like this for a month when we came to a spot where big red cliffs walked down to the edge of the river, and The Colonel had to ride the horses around them. He told me to drift the boat on down the river and moor it at a safe distance from the shore — safe against Indians was what he meant. He would break through from the mountains at the first good wide gap that led down to the water.

I agreed to that and turned the raft loose with the current, but we floated for fifteen miles, I suppose, past a long succession of cliffs, with no real opening into the inland. When we got to the bottom of that stretch, I moored the raft just below a point where a little river came whirling into our big one. There I laid low and waited. The evening came on almost at once, and I was not surprised that The Colonel didn't show his head.

When it turned dark, I supposed that he might have got deeply inland, trying to find smoother going for the horses. Still, I was a little worried because it was the first time in all our trip that we had been separated. I did little sleeping on the raft that night.

In the morning I had nothing to do but chew dried beef — how I hated it! — and tug at our mooring stone with the wooden windlass that we had rigged up — to make sure that the stone would not lodge too deeply in the bottom ooze. But I grew pretty anxious by the time the day had worn to prime, and, when noon came with no sign of The Colonel, I was the most nervous boy in the world. The noon passed, and then the afternoon came along at a prodigious rate. Still there was no token of The Colonel. It was a dreadful time for me.

The sun was well down in the western sky before the north wind blew the sound of a rifle explosion in the far distance. The next minute had not run out before I heard another. This got me on the alert. I had my rifle loaded, and the extra gun was prepared. But I charged the revolver, and then I laid out my ammunition belt. Perhaps it might not be The Colonel at all, but something told me that it was, and that these explosions of the gun were minute signals to ask me where I was. So I fired — then I worked up a little barricade of robes and gold on the right side of the raft. After that, I had only a few seconds to wait before I saw the thing that, in my heart of hearts, I had been half expecting to see.

The Colonel was riding over the first rise of ground on Sir Turpin, and I needed only one glance at them to see that the stallion was completely beat. He rolled and hammered in his stride, and, as they went down the slope, The Colonel was leaning forward, jockeying him desperately along. The reason came right behind him — almost on his heels. I saw The Colonel swing in the saddle with his rifle at his shoulder, and right behind him came three Indians of a tribe I had never seen, riding like fiends. Strung out behind them were a dozen more, all beginning to screech as they saw the raft and me on it.

I suppose they were more or less taking their time, knowing that they were heading The Colonel toward the river. But now they saw that the river offered a chance of refuge for himself and his scalp. They whipped up their horses to full speed, paying no attention to his leveled rifle, which made me decide that he had emptied it and used up his last ammunition. He convinced me that I was right by

207

throwing it away as a useless burden and trying to drive Sir Turpin faster.

There was no more speed in Sir Turpin. The poor stallion had done his best, but it was not good enough to hold off the challenges of these wiry Indian ponies. They were gaining at every jump, and, though at that distance I knew that I had a very good chance of knocking The Colonel over instead of dropping one of his enemies, I had to fire. I took a quick aim, prayed, and pulled the trigger. I missed The Colonel, thank heaven. But I didn't drop one of the Indians. I did a bit better, for that bullet went through the shoulder of the leading brave, and he turned in his saddle with a shriek of rage and pain, while the two companions who rode on each side of him forgot their quarry for a few seconds and turned aside from the new danger. I picked up the spare rifle, and, as they came on again after that failing stallion and my best friend on earth, I tried for them again, but I was over-anxious to get a dead bead, and I must have put my bullet at their feet.

They were so keen on that scent that they paid no more heed to me. But the diversion which my first shot had made was enough to give The Colonel part of a fighting chance. He opened a fairly large gap before they straightened out after him again, and my courage was beginning to return when Sir Turpin threw up his head and went down as though he had been shot. He had worked himself until his heart broke with the strain. There was never a truer horse than that old stallion — steel all the way through.

I thought that The Colonel was a dead man instantly, but, no, there was still a fight left in him. He rolled twenty yards in front of his dead horse. Then he pitched to his feet and began to sprint toward me. He was a fast runner, too. But he seemed to be standing still and pawing the air foolishly, compared with the speed with which those Indians came swooping in at him. Ah, how they wanted that scalp of his! I tried again, as quickly as I could reload my rifle. There was no use wasting *that* ball. I got my bead on the first Indian as he rode up on The Colonel, and I held my fire until the red brute was swinging up his war club. Then I pulled the trigger. I knew that, if I missed, The Colonel was a dead man. But to tell you the truth, I felt pretty cool. I *knew* that I would not miss. I simply could not afford to.

So I drew that bead and held it steady, and, as the war club began to fall, I shot the red man through the body and pitched him off his horse. The third fellow had enough. He had seen one of his companions wounded and another dropped dead, and he had no liking for charging into the mouth of certain destruction. He dropped off his horse, in his turn, and he drew a bead on The Colonel just as that big man reached the edge of the water. Well, it was so short a distance that I knew that even an Indian could not miss. There I stood with two emptied rifles, and my fingers fumbling as I tried to jam in the fresh load on the double-quick. I screamed: "Dodge, Colonel, for heaven's sake!"

He was a good soldier, I tell you. He didn't stop to ask questions, but he leaped to the side. The next instant that Indian's rifle spoke, and The Colonel dived into the river. I didn't know whether or not he had been struck by the lead, but in another moment I saw him swimming with long, even strokes, like the fine athlete that he was.

No, that was not all the danger. There were a dozen redskins now, distributed along the shore in every promising clump of brush, or in the trees, and they could open a plunging fire right onto the raft. I cuddled in under the parapet and began to work that wooden windlass for all I was worth — because we wanted to be moving with the stream by the time that The Colonel got to us. And moving we were, with the rifle bullets slicing through the water all around us.

Chapter Forty-One

DOWNSTREAM

You might say that we were out of danger now, but really this was only the mere *beginning* of the trouble. Those Indians had lost enough men by this time to want revenge. They had seen their quarry snatched out from under their teeth, so that they were raging for a good chance to get at us. They followed us along the shore, and, as the raft drifted slowly down the stream, they took possession of the commanding points among the rocks and even climbed into the tops of the tall trees, so that they could get a better chance to view us on the raft and send their shots angling sharply down upon us.

In the meantime we lay low under the little breastwork which I had built to give us shelter from the shore. We had to stir once in a while to use the steering oar, and every time that we budged, trying to work the raft gradually out toward the center of the stream, we were pretty sure to fall under the fire of those Indians. In the midst of this trouble one of the rascals laid my shoulder open with a glancing rifle ball. The Colonel cleaned the wound and tied it up, but not before I had weakened with the loss of a good deal of blood.

Just after this a lucky arm of the current reached out to us and pulled the raft into the center of the stream. This meant that the red men had a longer distance to shoot and at a faster moving object, so that the real heart of the danger was over. However, they were not finished with us. Four days they stuck with us, and during that time they paid for their persistence. The Colonel got in two long-range shots which killed a pair of them. In the meantime he told me how the whole thing had come about. He said that he had found a long and winding valley that reached into the inland from the river, and that he had decided to follow it and then curve around and come back toward me. But after he had ridden for a time, he got a chance to trail a grizzly, and he could not resist that temptation. He lost the trail — a grizzly is always a hard brute to follow — and, since it was close to night, he camped.

The next morning he cast around, trying to get his bearings, and he had just about decided through which of the passes among the hills he should ride when he was jumped by this small party of red men, who burst at him out of the brush. By luck, he was in the saddle on Sir Turpin. Kitty and the pack horse were abandoned to the red men at once, and The Colonel thanked heaven for his fine stallion as the latter stretched away across the ground, dropping the Indians rapidly behind. The Colonel, at the end of a half hour's running, was well out of sight of the Indians, and so he halted Sir Turpin to give him a breathing spell — by way of thanking him for his speed. He had just finished triumphing in his mind at the superiority which the stallion enjoyed over the Indian ponies, when here they came, streaming again through the hills. The Colonel merely laughed. He mounted Sir Turpin and put him to a good, round pace, expecting the Indian ponies to flag and fail and die out of the race.

They did not fail. They did not flag. They did not fall out of the race. Instead, with an astonishing persistence they hung on, and The Colonel began to feel his first worry, for he recalled some of the stories which he had heard about the weight-carrying powers of these midget horses of the plains. He gave Sir Turpin a little more rein, but it was not until the stallion approached his full speed that he could shake off the Indian ponies somewhat. Even that was no decisive advantage, and so The Colonel began to try to keep the Indians back to a respectable distance with an occasional shot from his rifle. He wounded one of the foremost riders, and he was sure that he had killed a second, but these fellows would not keep off at

211

a good distance, the way the Mandans had done. They possessed a rash fearlessness which reminded The Colonel of nothing more than the spirit of a lot of young white men in the hunting field. Though here the prize was something more than the brush of a fox.

It was a stern chase, and it was a long one. Before they had been an hour under way, The Colonel knew that he was certainly riding for his life. The earlier burst in the morning had been easy enough for Sir Turpin, but, when he came to meeting the same horses in the afternoon, he had not so much power. Finally it became not a question of the speed of the stallion but rather of the marksmanship and the amount of ammunition which The Colonel could show. He rode on with his gun speaking continually, and I myself had heard the last shots as he came over the hills toward the river. He told me that nothing since the beginning of the world had ever brought so much joy to him as the sound of the guns which I had fired to direct the fugitive toward me. So he came over the hill and down the last slope to the river with a dreadful certainty that all was lost and that he would be butchered by the fast-speeding Indians on the very shore of the water.

"I know now that they could have closed on me at any time during the last five or six miles of the trip," said The Colonel. "But they were enjoying the fun. And they knew that they had me well in hand while their own little iron horses seemed to get stronger and stronger, the longer the work lasted. The more that you take out of those ugly beasts, Christy, the more remains in them. They're like something out of a fairy tale. They thought that they would hem me in against the river, toward which I was riding, so they were in no hurry to close on me. Besides, they knew that I was spending ammunition fast, and presently I would come to the end of my bullets. Then they could close in and finish me off without any danger.

"I saw you on the raft, Christy, and I'll tell you that, when I laid eyes on you, I had a strange sense of security fall around me. I knew that the odds were very, very big against me, but I felt that you would

212

find some way of making your hand felt even at that distance. And you did, old lad, bless you. When I heard that first red man screech behind me, I knew that you had put one of the dogs out of the picture. Then I had a new burst of hope, knowing that was what made me give Sir Turpin strength and lift him over the last seventy or eighty yards, when he was already a dead horse under me. Good Turpin. He fought it out to the last stride, and I thank heaven that, if he had to die, he died while his head was still in front. He wasn't mastered by those little prairie rats. But, gad, what iron must be in their legs and what lungs of brass they must have.

"So, there I came running, and I felt the shadow of my death swing up behind me. He would have bashed my head to bits. Then I saw the smoke of your gun as the ball tore through the body of that scoundrel. Ah, Christy, that was a time. And after that you know how I got into the water, though I would not have managed even that, if it hadn't been for you. For, as I jumped to the side, I heard the rascal's bullet whistle and…look at this."

He showed me where a bit of cloth had been nipped from the outside of his sleeve —just about heart high. It was plain that, if he had not dodged, and dodged wide at that, he would have been no better than a dead man. Yet here he was, alive and well and laughing, and we were a little closer to each other than we had been before. There was another shadow left behind us — Sir Turpin and Kitty and even the pack horse. We'd grown so used to them that every wrinkle in their foreheads, their voices when they neighed, and even the rhythm of their walking and galloping steps had become very familiar to us. The Colonel cursed himself and his fortune and wished that he had turned them loose on the plains, according to my advice.

"Because the next time that we come out here, Christy," he said, "we'd certainly want to take a look for them, and, nine chances out of ten, we'd find them, lad! Now we've lost them forever, because I was a fool and stuck to my own way of doing a thing. Oh Christy, hereafter when you put down your foot, I'm never going to question you…trust me for that."

He meant it, too, for the time being. But it was always hard for The Colonel to stick to a promise. He gave them with the best heart in the world, and the best intention of keeping his word most scrupulously. But no sooner had he pledged himself than the promise even, because it *was* a promise, began to be a burden to him. That was The Colonel's way.

Meanwhile the raft wound slowly down the great river, and at the end of another week we reached a trading post. We sold them some robes and such stuff. In exchange we got enough wood to make us thirty small boxes. We loaded those boxes with dead leaves and in the center, firmly tied in place with strips of rawhide, we distributed our gold. When we got through with our work, we had our treasure pretty well disguised. It did not look bulky enough to be reasonable, even considering its weight.

After that, we took to the river again and drifted clear down to the Mississippi. The Colonel had a foolish notion that he would like to drift on to New Orleans and take an ocean steamer around to Hampton Road. But I managed to dissuade him, and he listened to me. Instead, we took a steamer that carried us up the Ohio and then up the Allegheny. We left waterways, transferring our luggage to a strong wagon with four tough mules to pull it. We had two horses to ride, and we hired a Negro to do the driving and the cooking, too. So we dropped down over the mountains and into Virginia in real style.

Chapter Forty-Two

LOYAL AND TRUE

After we left the steamer, we had still a weary, long way left ahead of us, but after the distances to which we had been accustomed on the plains, we thought that the time would go quickly enough. It didn't, though. Traveling on the plains was like cruising in a ship. You just sat back and watched the horizon and the stars, marking your progress by the number of hours that you had been traveling each day. There was nothing to see; no landmarks, to speak of, that would interest anyone other than an Indian. It was like being at sea, of course, and sea voyages are pretty relaxing to the nerves. But as we came down out of the mountains and into the Virginia that we loved, I can tell you that our nerves grew tenser and tenser all the way. We got so that we could hardly talk to one another, we were so irritable and just plain mean.

Finally we came into The Colonel's own county. He was in a quandary. He wanted to get to Martha Farnsworth as quickly as possible; and yet he didn't want to be seen on the roads where he might be recognized, dressed like a tramp, as he was now. Eventually he decided upon a forced march all through the night. He gave the Negro a dram of whiskey. We tied the horses behind the wagon, deciding that we would sleep until we were fairly close to the house of the Farnsworth family. Then we would wake up, spruce ourselves up a little, and try to look respectable. All our plans went wrong. The wagon got stuck in a rut, and we had to work most of the night to get it out. Instead of being at the Farnsworth house in the middle of the morning, we were simply camped in the woods.

We spent a wretched day there, with The Colonel saying every now and then: "It's been a whole year since she's heard from me, Christy, or has it been more than a year?"

I told him again and again that we had been gone a year and a half.

When the afternoon came, The Colonel got into another agony. He said: "Christy, she's never heard from me since we left her. And that's enough to make any girl marry another man just out of the purest spite, you know. Now even Martha...."

Of course, she *was* just the sort who might do foolish things if one appealed to her pride. I knew that, and I could only assure The Colonel with about half of my heart. The other half was just as frightened as his was. Finally I suggested that I should ride on ahead. No one would know me, I had changed so much. For I looked more like a man, I had grown so much. I could get there and perhaps give her word of The Colonel and explain why he had been so silent for so long and get her ready for his coming.

The Colonel agreed that that was probably the best thing for me to do. "Go to the Farnsworth house as though it was filled with Mandans, with Ompah at the head of them, raging for my scalp. Stalk that house, Christy, and find out what's going on inside of it before you go in, because, if Martha is engaged to another man during my absence, I'll see myself doubly cursed before I'll look at her again. I'll go to Africa...or some other place, Christy. You'll go along with me, old boy, I know. And we'll forget this Virginia and the women of the state."

I did exactly as he wanted me to do, and, when I came close to the Farnsworth house, I didn't dream of going to the front door as I had done a year and a half before, when I carried The Colonel's letter and poetry to Martha Farnsworth. I went back to the kitchen door. Kitchen doors hung on well-oiled hinges in those days before the war, and a fellow could always expect plenty to eat. Old Sally, the cook, was there, cooking up a great supper and in her sharp, squawk-ing voice ordering around the half-dozen other Negroes who assisted her on great occasions in the kitchen. When I asked for something to eat, Sally flew into a rage and asked what good-for-nothing white trash meant by begging at kitchen doors on such a night as this. However, she could not help giving me something, and I didn't mind her talk. I was so glad to be back at the heart of my own country that nothing was wrong. The worst sort of abuse was sweet to my ears.

I had a plate of fried chicken in front of me before you could say Jack Robinson, and I sat down on my heels — because there were no chairs in the place on this busy night—and went after that chicken with a wedge of delicious corn pone to use for a pusher. It was a wonderful thing to see the way that chicken and pone disappeared. I had not tasted anything like it since I left Virginia. But, while I ate, I listened and I found that the name I wanted to hear was cropping up a good deal more frequently than any other. Someone of those slaves told about the dress that Miss Martha was going to wear. Another described how her silver slippers looked, and how much they had cost, and how long it had taken to make them in Richmond after the patterns of an old pair that had come straight from Paris. But everything was about Miss Martha, until I put in and asked if this were the lady's birthday.

"Hush your talk, boy," said Sally. "Birthday? This heah is a secret party, and nobody don't know the reason of it, or why there is so many asked to it. Nobody don't know!"

She began to laugh and all of the others laughed, until I thought that they were either silly or mad. Finally I got the truth out of them. This was a party at which an engagement was to be announced — the engagement of Martha to young Tucker Lampson. It turned me cold to hear that, and I forgot the chicken that remained on my plate. I stood up and slipped through the pantry toward the dining room and then turned up the side stairs until I got to Miss Martha's room

217

upstairs. I knocked at her door, and there was a rattling of voices. The door was opened a little by a maid in a white dress — a white maid in a white dress, so I knew that Martha had got herself a servant that wasn't a slave to help make her beautiful.

"Well, well?" snapped this girl, starting to close the door on me. "What do you want? What do you want?"

I could hardly understand her, her mouth was so full of pins. So I jammed my foot into the narrowing crack of the door. "Call your mistress," I said. "I won't talk to you but to her."

She was so astonished that she dropped all of the pins out of her mouth and started back with a little squeal. I heard her turn and rattle out an excited lot of nothingness. Then came a quick, steady step, and the door was opened by Martha Farnsworth herself. She looked grand, I can tell you. "Well, young man?" she said, looking me up and down.

"Send your servants away," I said, thanking heaven that I was able to talk bass, since at this time it varied from a squeak to a rumble. "I want to see you...alone!"

At the last word my voice slid right up to the top of its scale and squeaked at her like a mouse, but she didn't laugh. She caught me by the arm and dragged me in where the light of her room could fall on me. There I stood, the room all littered with laces and frills and so forth and three or four foolish-faced Negresses standing about holding things, because they hadn't sense enough to put them down, I suppose.

Miss Martha gave herself one glance at me. Her eyes widened, and her face grew white. She gave those servants one gesture, and they scattered out of that room like trained geese. It did me good to see them go. "Christy," whispered Miss Farnsworth. "And" — she glanced at my ragged clothes — "you've come back...alone?"

I felt a good deal of sorrow for her, but I couldn't help thinking, too, of the terrible dangers The Colonel had undergone, the labors he had performed for her sake on the plains, how true he had been to her in spite of more temptation than most men would ever see in their lives. A pain ripped up and down my shoulder where the bullet had cut me. I stopped pitying her and admiring her, and I said: "I've come back ahead, but not alone, Miss Famsworth."

She gave a gasp and sank into a chair, whiter than ever, but with her eyes beginning to shine.

So I nodded at her. "I went on ahead to see how things might be, and to tell The Colonel whether or not he was welcome here."

"Go back as fast as you can ride," said Martha Famsworth, "and tell him to come quickly! Heaven knows how I shall manage to explain everything...but I don't care...explanations! Nothing matters except that he's come back to me...and...and I thank God that he came back even poorer than when he started out."

She looked at my ragged clothes when she said this. I said to her: "I'd like to ask you one thing."

"Ask it, then, Christy," she said, "and then, for heaven's sake, fly back and find him and bring him here before my heart breaks."

"I'd like to ask you," I said slowly, "whether you were going to marry Tucker Lampson because it was a good match, or because your pride was hurt by The Colonel keeping away so long?"

It threw her into one of her quick furies. "How dare you speak to me like this, Christy?"

Then, seeing that I didn't drop my eyes in spite of her fury, the anger died out of her like flame killed in the wind. "I've got a right to ask, even if it's not polite," I told her. "The Colonel is my master, but he's more...he's my friend...and you're going to eat humble pie, Miss Famsworth, if you want him. Because I can ride back to him and tell him what I've heard about here, and he'll start for Africa or some other place as fast as a ship can get him to it."

"You *wouldn't* do that!" cried Martha Famsworth.

"I would, though. He's waiting, and he's told me what he'll do. If I were The Colonel, I'd never look again at a woman that couldn't remember him and wait for him in a single year."

"A year and a half, Christy," she put in. "Eighteen mortal months that I haven't heard from him, and I thought that he didn't *want* me to remember him any longer. Christy, Christy, where is my pride to talk to you like this? But I haven't any pride. I know you can twist him around your finger, and I want you to twist him my way. Oh, Christy, swear to me that you'll bring him back with you."

When I look back to it now and remember how lovely she was, besides being fine in a thousand other ways that I knew about, I cannot help wondering what was in me on that occasion, but I tell you that I hung there in doubt, staring at her. For one thing, my eyes were still a little blinded by the golden beauty of The Quail, and, if Martha Farnsworth's voice was soft, it would never have the music which was in the throat of the Indian girl. So I stared at the Farnsworth heir, and finally I said: "I don't know. I won't know until I get to him again. But if he should decide to come back here with me…I suppose that the party will be postponed?"

"Not a soul will be in the house except my family," said Martha Farnsworth. "Only…tell me, Christy, that he's coming back safe."

"He's still wearing his scalp," I told her without a smile, because I didn't care how much she worried, for a little while, about The Colonel.

Then I left her, very brutally, without another word. I hadn't ridden two miles up the road before I heard a rider coming with thunder of speed toward me, and here was The Colonel, sweeping around the next bend. He had waited as long as he could, and then his patience had given out with a crash. He saw me and stopped with a shout.

"Have you seen her, Christy?"

"Yes," I said.

"And…?"

"She still loves you."

He pulled off his hat and raised his face to the stars. "Ah, thank God, thank God," said The Colonel.

I decided that I would let him have the second bullet straight through the heart. If he couldn't stand it — then let him go to Africa, or wherever else he chose. "And tonight she was giving a party, to announce her engagement to Tucker...."

He didn't wait for me to finish. He groaned. "Don't say it. Then I'll find him and kill him...the cur!"

"Is it the man's fault?' I snapped at The Colonel. "I've come to tell you what I found. I told her that you were near, and it worked her up a good deal. She wanted to know how you...well, in short, she promised that she would break up the party and have no one but the family there when you arrived. But...."

"You mean that she...ah, Christy!...she couldn't be true to me.

"Why the devil should she?" I shouted at him. "How did you dare not to write to her for so long?"

"Can a proud man let himself be treated like this?" asked The Colonel. "Thrown away and picked up again at her pleasure?"

"How should I know?"

"Curse it, Christy," said The Colonel. "Don't be so harsh. But tell me...what would you do, if you were I?"

I looked at him and could not help smiling, he was such a great baby and such a great hero, too. I could not help nodding, too, and I said: "Well, sir, if I were you, I suppose that I would go on to that house and forgive her."

"Bless you, Christy!" shouted The Colonel. "That's the very thing that I wanted to do, but I was afraid that you would scorn me forever."

And away he went down the road again, like a madman, whipping his poor horse at every jump that it made, though he couldn't extract any more go out of it.

The Colonel and Martha Farnsworth postponed their marriage for one month, while The Colonel was looking about for a suitable place to buy. He was about to take hold of the old Cranston estate and get horribly cheated with a grand old rattletrap of a house and worn-out land, when I persuaded him to try the upper country. There the two of them hit upon the very thing for them — a great tract with a dozen sites for big houses, when they were ready to build one.

I stayed for the wedding. The next day I was to start for Boston to attend school there. I had given The Colonel my oath that I would see four years of schooling through, though it was a bitter pill to swallow. Martha cornered me in the afternoon and pointed at The Colonel, who sat dreaming at the fire, scratching on a bit of paper.

"What is he doing?" asked Martha. "Is he drawing Indian beads?"

"He's drawing an Indian head," I said.

"Someone who tried to scalp him?"

"No," said I, "not that."

THE END

OPH 11-16

Made in the USA
Charleston, SC
16 April 2014